RÉSUMÉ WITH MONSTERS

WILLIAM BROWNING SPENCER

Borealis is an imprint of White Wolf Publishing.

Cover art by Bill Koeb
Cover Design by Michelle Prahler

White Wolf Publishing
780 Park North Boulevard, Suite 100
Clarkston, Georgia
30021

PRINTED IN CANADA

PART ONE

THE ESTRANGED LOVERS

alph's One-Day Résumés was located in an industrial park that also housed insurance salesmen, auto mechanics, computer repairmen and a karate school. Philip Kenan accelerated to make the left into the parking lot, then braked hard to avoid losing his muffler on the huge speed bump that must have been a legend amid the local hordes of fire ants.

Philip parked, unbuckled the seat belt,

exhaled. *Work*. It could be worse. It had been. This was safe harbor. So far, he had seen no signs of Cthulhu or Yog-Sothoth or his dread messenger, Nyarlathotep.

Philip waved to the receptionist, a pretty blond girl who was talking on the phone. He walked quickly down the hall and into the bathroom which, while cryptlike and dank, contained no hideous, disorienting graffiti from mad Alhazred's *Necronomicon*.

It was five in the evening, time for a middle-aged, lovesick, failed-novelist and near-obsolete typesetter to get to work. He just needed a minute to collect himself, to splash some water in his face, to check for nosebleeds, see that his eyes were in their sockets, see that no lichen grew on his forehead, that sort of thing. All was in order. *Sane as rain*. He smiled at himself, a pathetic attempt at self-affirmation. *I will win Amelia back*, he thought. *We will put the bad times behind us.*

He left the bathroom and walked on down the hall and into the break room where he punched his card in the time clock. The machine's worn ribbon produced a mark so faint that it could only be read by the ancient—and perhaps psychic—Mrs. Figge in payroll. Philip had actually seen her read the time cards by pressing them fiercely against her forehead and closing her eyes.

Philip left the break room and entered the long production room where the usual frenzy prevailed. A paste-up artist was sobbing while a secretary shrieked on one of the phone lines. A new printer, hired the previous week, was complaining that he had not been given a chance. Passing employees nodded their heads in perfunctory commiseration. The hard truth was, you had to fire a printer every now and then. Anyone in the business knew that long-term employment robbed a printer of his edge, and dispatching a printer invigorated those of his trade who remained.

The boss, an extremely thin, sharp-faced man named Ralph Pederson, rushed down an aisle where graphic artists labored over light tables and typesetters hunched over drab-green terminals. "Are you almost done? Finished? How's it going? An hour? What happened here? Shouldn't this be done?" He seemed, as always, to be in great pain, tortured by the money-consuming slowness that surrounded him. He waved at Philip and moved on.

Philip sat down at the terminal next to Monica, a stout, middle-aged woman with short-cropped brown hair who was the fastest typesetter in the whole world, perhaps, and who vibrated as she worked, her small feet bouncing on the dirty linoleum floor. Like all typesetters, she talked to herself in a loud, hearty voice. "If that's Avant Garde I'm a poodle!" she would exclaim. Or, "By golly, this isn't on file. I don't care what they say!"

Monica turned to Philip. "I had to set all that stuff you left last night. I've got my own work, you know. Let's get with the program, okay. We are production here, not design. This isn't some high fashion magazine where you can lay back in a barcalounger, sip some wine, and gossip about editors. This is slap-it down, out-the-door production, like it or leave it."

Philip promised to improve.

"You just got to get that speed up," Monica said. "I know you have only been here a couple of weeks; I understand that, but you gotta be aware, you know."

Monica and the rest of the production staff left an hour after Philip's arrival. He had the room to himself.

He grabbed another handful of business card orders and began to type.

Much of what he typed was banal. For some reason, hordes of old men wished to have business cards announcing that they were retired. *No Job No Money No Worries* these cards would announce. The purpose of such a business card was unclear. It was, however, a popular item, as were cards reading: *Hi, I haven't even met you but I've fallen in love with you and I am heartbroken because I don't even know your*

Name:

Address:

The recipient of such a card was supposed to write her name and address on it.

Philip tried to imagine a woman being charmed by such a card, but the best Philip could do was conjure up a vision of a hardened hooker smiling gamely and saying, "That's funny. That's really funny."

And sometimes, amid the banality and insufferable self-advertisements, there were true and decent aspirations.

Résumés of the young, narrating honors seminars and obscure college awards and summer jobs, full of fine sentiments (*I wish to be of service to other humans and to work toward a cleaner and more healthful environment*) could bring a sudden hollow stillness to Philip's heart, as though a loved one had just fled his embrace, and Philip would hear himself whisper, "Be careful."

At ten, Philip called Amelia up from the phone in Mrs. Figge's office.

"It's me," he said.

"I know that," Amelia said. Her voice still set his heart racing. It was such a wonderful, bell-like voice, although these days it contained a certain wary edge.

She had rationed him to one call a week, and this was it. She had been unhappy when he followed her to Austin, and she had refused to talk to him at first, letting her sister, Rita, take the calls. But she had relented under his persistence.

Philip had followed her to Austin from traffic-snarled Fairfax, Virginia, a suburb of Washington, D.C. They had both worked at MicroMeg, where they had met and fallen in love, and where, finally, the ancient, implacable curse that his father had called the System or sometimes, Yog-Sothoth or simply the Great Old Ones, had torn them asunder. He was here now to win her back, and he knew he had to proceed with caution. So far he had only spoken to her on the phone, although he had seen her a number of times. He had spied on her; he had crouched low in his car in the shade of live oaks down the street from the house where she was staying with her sister.

He would watch her come out of the house

in the morning, get into her car and drive off. So far he had resisted the urge to race up to her, to enfold her in his arms. He didn't want to send her running again. He might lose her forever in the vastness of America.

Amelia, traumatized into blind denial by the doom that came to MicroMeg, refused to acknowledge that the Old Ones even existed, preferred to think that her lover had lost his reason; preferred to flee him rather than confront the truth, as though such flight could negate the dreadful, ghastly facts, the irrefutable history that she and Philip shared.

"You can't deny what happened!" he had shouted.

Oh, but she could.

She loved him, still. Philip could hear that love in her voice, beneath all the careful reserve and skirted subjects.

Philip kept the phone conversation casual, asked how her job search was going.

"Not good," Amelia said. Austin was a city with a large college population. Employers could hire from this student population. There were also a substantial number of people who had gone to the University of Texas for as long as possible, accrued as many degrees as parental funds and grants permitted, and now waited tables, clerked in government positions, or sat in the rental offices of apartment complexes—anything rather than return to, say, El Paso.

And who would want to leave? Austin was lovely, a laid-back town, the last refuge for hordes of aging hippies who drifted up and down the Drag, gray-bearded artifacts who knew all the lyrics to old Leonard Cohen songs and could talk knowledgeably about astral planes and karma.

"I can't find anything," Amelia complained.

"You will," Philip said. "It just takes a few days sometimes, and you want to be careful anyway. You want to see that there aren't any signs of—"

"Philip."

Philip stopped abruptly. *Easy.* "I just mean you don't have to grab the first job you are offered."

And you want to look in the bathrooms and see

what is written there on the walls, and take a peek in the furnace room, and perhaps, quite casually, stick a good-sized pin in a long-term employee and see if she howls.

"I don't feel right about staying here with Rita too long," Amelia said. "She doesn't complain or anything, but I know I'm in the way."

"You could come and live with me," Philip said.

Silence. Philip's heart crawled out of his chest and jumped up and down on the desk: *Boom boom boom.*

"Are you still writing that novel?" she asked.

His heart climbed back into his chest and lay down, curled on its side, defeated. Why lie? He couldn't fool her. "Yes. Sure."

"Philip, I can't live with you. Look, Rita is expecting a call. I'll talk to you next week, okay?"

"Okay," Philip said.

He went back to his computer and began typing again. The phone call hadn't been a bad one, really. She hadn't said never to call again. She had said, "I'll talk to you next week, okay?"

That was certainly positive. She seemed to have accepted his presence; she wasn't sending him away or running again.

He lay in bed that night and thought, "I'll win her back." In the meantime, of course, he would have to hang on to his own reason; he would have to be ever-vigilant. Once you have gazed on the baleful visage of Yog-Sothoth, your own thoughts are forever suspect.

He needed all his wits, and the first thing he did on arriving in Austin was to throw away all of Dr. Abrams' well-meant prescriptions. Pills might blunt the edge of his fear, but they were not the answer. A man could not spend his life splashing himself with tap water if he lived in a burning house. He had to fireproof his soul.

Books were perhaps the best antidote. Philip purchased used paperbacks. Occasionally, when he couldn't find the book elsewhere, he would check it out of the library, but he disliked returning a book once it was in his possession, so he availed himself of the library only when diligent search failed to discover the sought-after book.

He read *Crime and Punishment*, *The Enormous Room*, *Bleak House*, *Green Mansions*, *Invisible Man* (Ellison), *Tom Jones*, *Heart of Darkness*, *Eternal Fire*, *Hall of Mirrors*, *A Princess of Mars*.

He found that he did not have to read certain books, that simply keeping them near or upon his person offered protection. These books were *The Catcher in the Rye*; *Cat's Cradle*; *Little Big Man*; *Something Wicked This Way Comes*; *The Sot-Weed Factor*; *Alice in Wonderland*; *The Horse's Mouth*; *Winesburg, Ohio*; *Sense and Sensibility*; *The Way of All Flesh*; *Titus Groan*; and *War and Peace*.

And, of course, he kept the Arkham H. P. Lovecraft books close by, a reference and a warning (*The Dunwich Horror and Others*, *At the Mountains of Madness and Other Novels*, *Dagon and Other Macabre Tales*).

Philip continued to work on his own novel—oh how Amelia hated that novel; and oh how she was wrong about that—presently entitled *The Despicable Quest*. The book was completed, but he constantly altered it. In over twenty years of alterations, it had grown to four times its original length. He had been sending it to publishers and agents since the late sixties, and he had a drawer full of rejections. Most of the rejections were form letters, often badly photocopied scraps of paper, but occasionally an agent or publisher would actually write or type a brief note, notes dashed off in great haste and suggesting a life far more eventful and momentous than Philip's own grind of blighted hope and menial toil. Recently, these occasional personal missives were filled with words and phrases like "unwieldy," "diffuse," "directionless," and "muddled." The influence of Lovecraft was noted by one agent who said, "Not everyone is familiar with Lovecraft's works or his Cthulhu stories, so a two-thousand-page novel about these obscure monsters might have a limited audience."

In any event, the novel, despite its increased thickness, was beginning to fail Philip as a buffer against dark thoughts and nameless anxieties. Where once the novel had been a refuge from hostile realities it now seemed—Philip stopped, stunned by the possibility that Amelia, intuitively, was right. She had said that the novel was not good for him, was the cause of all his mental problems, and while that was patently untrue and part of her own denial system, what if the novel were, in some way, a malign influence? What if the novel had become a sort of psychic magnet for ancient beasts? What if, every time he typed a sentence, vile, star-shaped heads turned on gruesome necks and listened with outrageous, febrile antennae?

No, the novel was what *kept* him sane. Indeed, the thought that it might be otherwise was probably *planted* there by inimical Powers.

These thoughts seemed to heat his brain. He realized that he needed help, someone who could aid him in sorting the clutter of his thoughts.

The next day, Philip perused the ads in the back pages of the Austin *Chronicle*, a free weekly newspaper. As Philip scanned fine-print blandishments for massage, Tai Chi, psychic healing and self-esteem counseling, he had to battle a growing sense of hopelessness. Was there really anyone who could help him?

He paused before an ad entitled GREEN COUNSEL, *How to seek solace and wisdom from common houseplants* and he saw himself sitting in a room confiding his troubles to an indifferent cactus or a coolly aloof African violet. At that point he almost abandoned his quest. Fortunately, his eye had to travel less than an inch before arriving at a small box with a dotted border. **ISSUES ADDRESSED!** it stated (in fourteen point Optima bold). It continued in an unassuming, eight-point serif: *Experienced counseling professional can help you define and address your issues. FREE initial session to determine client-counselor compatibility. THERE IS HOPE! Call now.*

Philip called the number (twelve-point Helvetica bold).

"I can see you today," the woman said.

"Ah," Philip said. He did not know if he wanted to address an issue that very day. He was coming down with something, the flu perhaps or a bad bout of Austin's famous cedar fever.

"Don't waffle, man," the woman said. "Where do you live? Yes? Well, you are right around the corner. I'll give you directions. I can fit you in at three."

The address proved to be a residence, a small, wood-frame house in a weedy lot.

A frail, elderly woman wearing a Grateful Dead T-shirt and an ankle-length purple skirt rocked on the porch swing.

"You're Philip Kenan," she said. She looked disappointed, or perhaps even disgusted, although this may have been an expression created by the sunlight in her eyes.

Philip nodded his head.

"I'm Lily Metcalf," she said. She came forward and deftly hugged Philip around his middle, leaning forward and pressing an ear against his stomach. She smelled like baked bread, and her thin arms embraced Philip with surprising strength. Lots of gold and silver jewelry jangled on her wrists.

Philip tottered backward.

"Be still!" she shouted.

Philip froze, like a dog surprised in the act of chewing his master's slipper. Lily Metcalf's voice had an imperious quality, such as is found in certain high school shop teachers.

He was locked in her embrace for what seemed long minutes, although perhaps it was only seconds. Then she released him and squinted up at him.

"I like to listen right off," she said. "Before a client makes those interpersonal adjustments that are automatic."

"Well?" Philip said.

She shrugged. "I don't know. Sometimes I get a feeling, sometimes I don't."

They went inside. The living room was small and full of light from the gossamer-curtained windows. A breeze made wind chimes sing. Philip sat on a small couch—he'd encountered larger armchairs—while Lily Metcalf made tea.

"You can call me Lily," she said, returning with the tea. She sat down on the couch next to

Philip. "I hate it when people call me Dr. Metcalf."

Lily closed her eyes and leaned back. The sunlight showed her face to be a net of wrinkles. Her hair was a gray, spun-glass cloud.

She opened her eyes and cast a long, sideways glance at Philip. "You are what, forty, something like that?"

"I'm forty-five," Philip said.

She sighed and absent-mindedly patted Philip's thigh. "When I was forty-five, my son Homer rushed off to Vietnam full of patriotic piss and vinegar and got himself killed almost instantly. I hope you are having a better forty-five." She sipped some tea, closed her eyes. She seemed to lose track of time, drifting into a brief stupor of melancholy. Philip studied the bright walls of the room. They were covered with miniature oil paintings of a traditional nature (the ocean, some cows, or perhaps bears, on a hillside, a boat—toy, or menaced by a fifty-foot child). Philip studied the mahogany end table, the faded oriental rug, the bookcase full of paperbacks, and was surprised when Lily spoke, being himself fully occupied in his study.

"So, what's your issue?" Lily asked.

"Ah—"

"Yeah, sometimes it is hard to leap right in. Maybe I can jump start you. Mid-life crisis? Relationship problems? Wait, would you say you want to address high-level or low-level issues?"

"I'm not sure I understand," Philip said.

"Well." Lily put her teacup down and rested her hands on her knees and leaned forward. "High-level stuff would be self-actualization issues. You might feel restless. Anxiety might trouble your sleep. You might wonder if your success was fraudulent. You might be immobilized by boredom and a lack of purpose."

Philip shook his head. "No, nothing like that."

"Good. Frankly, self-actualization is not my long suit. I'm not good with people who don't have real problems. I am better with people who come here because their lives are in the shitter. I prefer crisis issues, I guess."

"I guess that describes my situation," Philip said. "I guess I am in crisis."

"All right. Good. You mind if I smoke?"

"No. Certainly not."

Lily swept a pack of cigarettes off the end table, banged one out, and lit it in what seemed a single motion. She blew smoke at the ceiling. "Some people see smoking cigarettes as a failure of character. They don't want a therapist who smokes. 'If she can't even quit a bad habit, how is she going to help me?' they ask. What do you think about that?"

"I don't know."

"Good answer, Philip. But the truth is, Jesus Christ probably smelled bad. You know what I mean? Nobody is perfect."

"That's true."

"So what is the crisis?"

"It's a long story."

"I bet. Let's have something shorter up front. How about if you tell me, in one sentence, what's going on. Maybe there are a lot of things going on, but just give me one incident. For example,

'My wife left me' or 'The bank repossessed my car.' We can get at the underlying issues later, but I want to see a problem first, an event."

"Ah—"

"You think you can do that? Just one sentence. You understand what I'm asking here?"

"Yes. Yes I guess so."

"Okay, let her rip."

"Well, I lost my job and my girlfriend left me."

"Good," Lily said, nodding her head in violent affirmation as a cloud of cigarette smoke merged with her cloudy hair. "That's just what I meant. Now we are getting somewhere."

"And hideous, cone-shaped creatures from outer space are going to leap, telepathically, across six hundred million years and destroy human civilization."

It just came out.

Philip glanced at his newfound counselor. Her eyes were closed, and she continued to blow smoke toward the ceiling. She seemed unperturbed by this revelation. Perhaps she was asleep, smoking in her sleep.

But no. She turned her head toward him and opened her eyes, blue eyes that had seen things.

"You are going to be an interesting client," she said.

2

he session was over.

"Tomorrow, same time," Lily said. "You better come every day for awhile."

Philip asked about the cost.

"A hundred dollars an hour," Lily said.

"Jesus. I can't afford that," Philip said. "I work nights at this ratty print shop. I get eight dollars an hour."

The old woman shrugged. "Okay, ten dollars an hour. Take it or leave it."

Philip took it. Walking away from Lily Metcalf and getting into his car, he felt a rush of well-being, an elevation in his self-esteem. He had just saved himself ninety dollars an hour on therapy. Not bad.

At work that evening, Philip was introduced to a new printer, a man named Al Bingham. Bingham was an older guy, sixty or so, bald except for a fuzz of fine gray hair that hovered over his baldness like steam. He possessed a long, pale face furrowed with lines that expressed weary incredulity.

"Pleased to meet ya," he said, shaking Philip's hand. "My heart goes out to you typesetting lads. You've got to read the crap. That has got to take its toll."

Ralph Pederson, Philip's boss, laughed nervously. "It is not for us to judge our customers," he said. Pederson, Philip had noted, was superstitious about such things, believing, perhaps, in an ever-listening god of customer wrath that was a jealous god and would brook no calumny. You never, not ever, said anything negative about a customer. In the restrooms were signs (72 point Helvetica extrabold) that read:

THE CUSTOMER PAYS OUR SALARIES.

"People are okay, but the public is an asshole," Bingham said.

This guy is going to last less than a week, Philip thought.

It was Tuesday, payday, and Philip got his check along with the usual motivational literature.

Philip knew that he shouldn't read the little pamphlet that came enclosed with the check. These were the mind-rending voices of the ghoul-lizards, the creatures of the System. These tiny tracts had titles like "Be a Team Player" or "Dress for Success" and were produced by some company in New Jersey and were illustrated and designed and written by someone who had not been out of his house since the early fifties and did not, apparently, have a television or other means of discovering changes in fashion or the elimination of sexist language ("office gal," for instance, was no longer synonymous with secretary in the larger world).

Philip thought of calling Lily Metcalf so that she could tell him to throw the pamphlet away without reading it, but he saw the title "Maintaining a Positive Attitude" and he was lost.

The unctuous, self-satisfied tone asserted itself with the first sentence, "Life sets some hard tasks for those who wish to succeed, and an employee who sees such tasks as burdens, who says, 'Why didn't my boss give this to Jones? I've got all I can handle without this,' could find himself out of a job when such an attitude affects his performance."

The writer of these pamphlets had been around—although Philip suspected that he was now a bedridden and bad-tempered invalid—and was inclined to illustrate his message with anecdotes. This time, the writer told the story of Sally, a waitress who was told that her uniform needed to be dry-cleaned every day. Sally, one of the malcontents who populated these moral tales and generally came to a bad end, said, "Why should I have to pay my hard-earned money to have uniforms dry-cleaned every day? I think it is a stupid rule. I'm not going to do it. I can't afford it on the tips I make."

Philip's heart went out to Sally. Why, indeed, should she have to obey such a rule—and spend her own money to do so? If her money-grubbing boss was so set on dry-cleaned-daily uniforms, why didn't he foot the bill?

Melanie, a perkier and no doubt younger waitress, said, "I think it is a good rule. I will do it. By having a bright, sharply pressed uniform every day, I will look and feel better and the customers will see this and give me bigger tips. Even though I will be spending my own money to have my uniforms dry-cleaned daily, the extra money I will make will more than compensate for that initial outlay."

Philip was always impressed by Sally's restraint upon hearing this nonsense. Sally never attempted to strike the smarmy apple polisher.

Philip put the pamphlet down and took a deep breath. A black miasma of despair clouded his mind. This was powerful motivational stuff, almost as strong as the rant on dressing for success which had urged the wearing of suits. The motivational material that Ralph purchased by the case was not tailored to print shops.

Philip got up from his terminal and walked outside. The night air was damp and full of the day's heat. A match flared, and Philip saw the gnarled features of the new printer as that man leaned into the glow of a match, lighting his cigarette.

"Hey typesetter," he said, nodding to Philip. "How is the résumé racket doing?"

"Okay, I guess," Philip said. "I'm typesetting business cards right now."

"Business cards. You reckon our boss ever wakes up in the middle of the night and wonders what the meaning of life is? You reckon he shakes his wife awake and says, 'Honey, tell me again why we are in such a godawful hurry to see that every asshole in Travis County has five hundred pieces of cardboard with his name on them.'"

Philip laughed nervously. "No, I don't think our employer worries about that sort of thing."

Bingham laughed, smoke erupting from his nostrils. "You bet he doesn't. Any capitalist worth a goddam knows there's no profit in the meaning of life."

Philip agreed that there was no profit in philosophy. All was unknowable, blessedly unknowable, and what was glimpsed of truth was a ravening beast whose corrosive breath alone could boil human flesh. Philip left Bingham and returned to his computer. *No Work No Worries No Money*, some old fart declared.

"I love her," Philip said. They were sitting in Lily's backyard, sitting in lawn chairs in the shade of twisted live oaks.

Lily was wearing a shapeless yellow dress and sunglasses. Her feet were bare. Sunlight, filtered through the leaves, wove green shadows over the both of them.

"So you followed her to Austin," Lily said.

Philip nodded his head. "Yes. And at first she wouldn't talk to me. I mean, she wanted to put it all behind her, and I was part of it. I understand that. She doesn't want to believe that the Old Ones exist, even though she was right there, even though—"

Lily interrupted. "The Old Ones are the monsters from outer space, the creatures from hundreds of millions of years in the past who controlled this corporation you worked for, this MicroMeg."

"Well, not exactly. They didn't control it, at least not originally, but it was a Doorway."

Lily waved a blue-veined hand. "If Amelia were here, how would she explain her actions?"

"She's confused. She doesn't want to look at—"

"Philip. Tell me what she would say if I asked her why she came to Austin."

Philip rubbed his hand on the back of his

neck. This therapy was hot work. "She would say she had to get away from me, that I was crazy."

"Crazy," Lily repeated. She lit a cigarette and waved the match out. "Are you crazy?"

"Of course not."

"How would Amelia describe you?"

"She would say that I had no ambition and didn't like going to jobs. She would say that I was easily bored, and so I turned everything into fantasy. She would say that the novel I was working on, which is a sort of H. P. Lovecraft type story, had gotten out of hand, had driven me crazy."

"Hmmmmmm," Lily said. "Your Amelia says quite a lot when given the opportunity."

Philip shrugged.

"How do you feel about jobs?" Lily asked.

"What do you mean?"

"Have you ever had a job that you liked?"

Philip frowned. "No, I guess not."

"Tell me about your first job," Lily said.

Philip looked up. "Well, I had chores and stuff for my allowance, but I guess my first real job was mowing our neighbor's lawn. That was Mr. Bluett. He was a very weird dude, a fat, pear-shaped guy who wore these big, oversized shorts. He was an old guy with a lot of money. He told jokes, lots of jokes, one right after another."

"So how was the job?"

"At first it was just fine."

"And later."

"Later it wasn't so good."

"Tell me about it."

he lawnmower had stalled out in a huff of blue smoke, vomiting clumps of cut grass. Philip yanked on the pull rope, and the motor coughed like a fat man choking on cigar smoke.

Great, just great.

It had to be a hundred degrees out, August, not a cloud in the sky, the sun a bright, unfocused blur. Philip itched all over, tortured by the gritty paste of grass and dust that coated his skin.

Philip pulled on the cord again, and the engine caught. The mower leapt forward, an undisciplined dog tugging on its leash.

Mr. Bluett's house was a big white mansion two streets over from the house Philip lived in with his mother and the ghost of his father and the ancient, ever-watching Elder Ones. The lawn was a long, rolling expanse, green even in the last sere days of summer.

Philip finished mowing the lawn and was emptying another bag of grass clippings into a trash can when Mr. Bluett came around the corner of the house.

"Wicked hot, isn't it, Philip?" he said.

"Yes sir," Philip said.

"You don't have to call me sir," Mr. Bluett said. "The queen didn't make me a knight." He laughed. He was a soft old guy with boiled-red flesh and thin, reddish hair that rippled tightly over his skull. He was rich, having made a fortune in real estate. He wore a shirt decorated with colored fish and big, floppy blue shorts and flip-flops.

"Thirsty?" Mr. Bluett asked.

"Yes s—Yes."

Mr. Bluett nodded. "Come on. I got iced tea."

Mr. Bluett put an arm on Philip's shoulder and led him around the house to the swimming pool in the back.

A big pitcher of iced tea rested on a white patio table.

The ice rattled as Bluett filled a large plastic tumbler and handed it to Philip.

"Looks good," Bluett said, surveying the lawn with his hands on his hips. "You do good work, Philip. How old are you?"

"Thirteen," Philip said.

"A teenager! Well, damn. I was a teenager once myself, although you might find that hard to believe. You getting any pussy?"

Philip said nothing. He was feeling uncomfortable. Adults didn't say "pussy." Kids like Ronnie Hargrave and rowdy Butch Walker said "pussy." The iced tea made Philip's stomach hurt, and Mr. Bluett was leaning forward, his face oily with suntan lotion, his breath sour and fleshy beneath a coating of minty mouthwash.

"Maybe you ain't worked up to pussy yet," Bluett said. His voice sounded different now, shifting the way a grown-up's voice will. "You might be practicing with your buddies first. You know, sucking each other's dicks."

Philip shook his head, frowning. "I have to be getting home," he said.

"Hey," Bluett said, standing up, "it ain't no big deal. Let me pay you for that lawn. You done a fine job."

Bluett pulled out his wallet and thumbed through the bills. He frowned. "Looks like I got nothing but a twenty. Well damn. Hey, you been mowing my lawn all summer, call it a bonus."

He handed the twenty to Philip.

Twenty dollars! Great!

"Thank you," Philip said.

"Hey, you're a good kid." Bluett reached forward and ruffled Philip's head. Then, suddenly, he leaned forward, cupped the back of Philip's head with his hand, shoved his face into Philip's and kissed Philip on the lips.

Philip shouted, fell backward. The plastic tumbler bounced on the flagstones and ice leapt out.

Philip got up and ran. He heard Mr. Bluett behind him, shouting.

"It ain't no big deal!" Mr. Bluett was shouting. "It ain't anything to get exercised about!"

Philip reached his bike, jumped on it, and raced down the hill.

"So that's how your first job ended," Lily said.

"No," Philip said. "I worked for him the next summer too. I got twenty dollars every time I mowed his lawn."

"And did he make any more sexual advances?"

"No, not exactly. Sometimes he would ask me to get something out of the pool. I'd have to take off my clothes to go into the pool. I forget why, but you couldn't wear clothes in the pool."

"How did you feel about that?"

"He gave me thirty dollars on pool days."

"So how did you feel about it?"

"Creepy."

That night Philip dreamed he was underwater, down in the green shadow world of old man Bluett's swimming pool. He had gone in to recover a watch. The watch was a waterproof Timex and, if Philip wasn't mistaken, Bluett had been wearing it only twenty minutes earlier.

The cold water enclosed Philip's nakedness, cut out the hot, drumming day as death itself might, and plunged him into this dappled, chill world. The chlorine stung his eyes.

What if his mother were to march briskly, that very instant, through the Odells' yard, across the street, down the little path between the Clarks and the Wardens, across another street and, moving faster now, down the new-mown hill to the swimming pool?

Philip would jump, dripping from the pool

and his mother, her gray eyes flashing, would turn to old Bluett and demand an explanation and Bluett would mumble that it was no big deal, but he would not be able to meet her eyes and shame would descend on Philip like hard rain on a tin roof.

Philip concentrated on the thirty dollars. His eyes sought the watch.

He saw, for the first time, that the bottom of the pool was not concrete but a twisting lattice of pipe, pale white tubes that intertwined elaborately. As Philip drew closer, the pipes began to move, flowing like the bodies of thick serpents although never was a head revealed, nor a tail, and perhaps they did not crawl between and around each other but merely gave the illusion of doing so through a wavelike rippling of their flesh.

Philip knew it for what it was, this loathsome, monstrous knot of serpents: Cthulhu, bathed in eldritch green light, sprung from watery R'lyeh.

Philip, numb with revulsion and terror, swam

closer yet, powered by the perverse will of the dream.

A hand reached out from between two tuber-like trunks, a white hand, gnarled, its nails bitten. Philip saw the truncated ring finger—cut long ago on a lathe—and tried to turn before he saw any more, but it was too late. His father's face, white and glistening, bloomed like a poisonous mushroom. His father's mouth opened in a scream, and Philip spied a ragged tongue, spotted with barnacles, and the mouth shaped words that were lost in the sound of vast machines laboring.

Philip fled to the surface, fighting the gravity of his fear.

The words his father had spoken followed Philip to the surface, and they broke in oily bubbles as Philip blinked at the sky.

His father's words burst upon Philip in a strangely dispassionate staccato: *It's. A. Rigged. Game.*

Bingham was staring up at the stars when Philip walked outside on break. Way off in the distance, stuttering light inflated the clouds.

"You ever been struck by lightning?" Bingham asked.

"No."

"Me neither," the older man said. "But I knew this guy, guy named Merl Botts. He was from upstate New York, used to drink with my uncle Hark. Anyway, Botts said he had been struck by lightning seventeen times. I figure he was telling the truth. And he had this theory, this idea that God was trying to communicate with him, was trying to get his attention.

"I was just a kid when he told me that, but it made an impression. I mean, think about it. What if God just don't know his own strength, like that cartoon character, what's his name, Baby Huey? 'Look out!' God hollers and a tidal wave destroys a seaport. 'Heads up, Merl!' God roars, and a lightning bolt sends old Merl tumbling down a hillside, the soles of his shoes smoking."

It was, Philip agreed, food for thought.

"I thought about it a lot when I was a kid," Bingham said, "but you lose interest in some of the big mysteries. Yesterday, my son, James, up in Newark calls and says, 'Hey Dad, old Mrs. Grady died; I thought you would want to know.'

"'That's a shame,' I say. Old Mrs. Grady. Course, I don't think of her that way; I see her eighteen years old with her blouse unbuttoned and her mouth half open. There's only two women I ever loved, and I married the other one. Old Mrs. Grady's true name was Helen, Helen Oakley, and I think, 'Helen's dead,' but nothing happens. She's still glowing like neon in my mind and dead or alive that's where I keep her. I haven't seen her in thirty years, and it's when I'm dead that it will leak out, all go in a rush like dishwater down a drain.

"Think about it. We are a lot of containers for each other. We should be careful."

"I know that," Philip said, but by the time he said it, the old printer had gone back inside.

Philip went back in, greatly shaken. The concept of humans as containers was not one he cared to contemplate. He felt hollowed out, decided a candy bar might ease the distress, and walked down the hall. A strange, dank reek of salt and decaying fish filled the corridor, as though some lumbering monster had risen from the ocean floor—Dagon perhaps—and slithered through the building. Philip could almost hear its clotted vocal cries and the ghastly noise it made as it forced its quivering bulk through a narrow doorway. But this was just his imagination.

The vending machine was ancient. Behind its glass window, a wobbly Ferris wheel of candy bars and stale pastries awaited the consumer. You put in change, you pushed a button, and, with a limping, mechanical clunk, the wheel turned. When the object of your desire appeared in the window, you opened the window and retrieved it.

Philip imagined some third-world denizens regarding this machine with awe, uttering a chorus of delighted exclamations each time the wheel lurched forward.

Philip pushed the window open on a Milky Way. As he reached in, the window snapped shut on his hand and the wheel turned. Philip reacted quickly, jerking his hand away before his wrist could be broken.

Nursing his scraped hand, he retreated to his

computer. He fished in the pile of résumés, and pulled one up that contained the following instructions:

"Please make this resumes most excellent as I am desirous extremely of a good job."

5

" couldn't write a novel," Lily said. "I don't have the imagination and even if I did, I lack the concentration. I know my limitations. I don't have the detachment either. I wouldn't let anything bad happen to the people I made up. If one of them got sick, I'd stick her right in bed and fill her up with chicken soup and have her back on her feet in no time.

If someone had cancer, I'd find a cure. I wouldn't let anyone be unhappy or in danger or unloved. Marriages would never end. I wouldn't let a dog get run over by a car, and I wouldn't let misunderstandings lead to tragedy. I just couldn't do that. The way I see it, if I am going to make a thing up, why make it up bad?"

"Sometimes it just is bad," Philip said. "There's no way around it."

"Spoken like a pathological party pooper," Lily said. She got up and shuffled into the kitchen. She was wearing a ratty yellow bathrobe and floppy, blue slippers. She looked older than usual. When Philip had come to the door that day she had said, "I believe I am dying. You'll have to get another therapist. Just as well. You're one of those heartbreaker clients, I can tell." But she let him in. She drank some tea, and appeared to rally, launching into her speech about novel writing.

Now she shouted from the kitchen, "Tell me about Amelia."

"Amelia's beautiful," Philip said. "She's sort

of hard to describe, because she likes to experiment with cosmetics, and she can look different on different days, but she has got this really wonderful heart. I mean—"

Lily came back into the room and lay full length on the couch. She interrupted with a wave of her hand. "Tell me about your father."

"What's to tell?" Philip said, suddenly wary and listening for the footfalls of some monstrous beast. "He killed himself."

Lily sat up. Her sharp, blue eyes studied Philip. "That's something to tell," she said.

Philip felt queasy. His insides had turned to hot, prickly flannel.

"Excuse me," he said. He got up and walked down the tiny hall to the bathroom. He ran cold water and splashed it on his face. His image in the mirror looked a little like his father, if only in the fatalism written there, the way the brown eyes held caution and disbelief, the way the mouth turned ruefully upward.

"Philip, are you okay?" Lily shouted through the door.

"I'm okay," Philip shouted back. The bathroom was as full of sunlight as the rest of the house, with more old-fashioned prints on the walls and a shelf full of organic shampoos and soaps and a peeling Happy Face sticker on the mirror. A copy of *Prevention* magazine lay on the sink. The magazine had fallen into water—the tub, no doubt—and was now swollen and curled. Philip absently turned its pages, encountered an article about the health benefits of zinc and read it while standing up.

"Philip?"

Philip finished the article and came out. "I was feeling sort of sick," he said. "I'm okay now. Gosh. Look at the time. I've got to run."

He canceled his next appointment with Lily. He said he would get back with her to schedule a new one. He didn't call back. When she called, he let the answering machine catch her no-nonsense voice, although he was in the room on the bed, feverish from reading the long sentences of Henry James.

She called twice more that week. Both times Philip was there, and the second time he almost answered the phone when she said, "I know you are there," but he was still reading James, and so he moved in a twilight lethargy, hobbled by fine delineations of thought. By the time he reached the phone, she had uttered the last of her message, "What if I really am dying. How would you feel if I died and you hadn't said good-bye?"

Pretty cheap for a therapist, Philip thought.

Ralph's One-Day Résumés was a circus—worse than usual. Typesetter Monica was wearing a soft collar, one of those bulky, neck-brace things that whiplash victims wear prior to litigation. A paste-up artist named Helga had attempted to throttle Monica over a disagreement on the kerning of a typeface.

Helga, a silent, gloomy employee with no

friends and uncertain mental health, had been fired immediately, but she was still an ominous presence. She would drive into the parking lot where Philip could see her through the lobby's plate-glass window. She would rev the engine of her old Ford pickup and glower at the building. She would stare for half an hour or so and then abruptly accelerate in a scream of tortured rubber and race, heedless of traffic, back onto the highway. Her behavior was unpleasantly similar to accounts Philip read in those follow-up articles to tragedies (*TWELVE GUNNED DOWN BY IRATE POSTAL EMPLOYEE*, for instance). These articles would always begin with a survivor saying something like, "I guess we should have seen it coming when..."

Ralph Pederson did not wish to call the police, however. Perhaps he saw Helga as a potential customer. His thoughts were hidden to Philip.

Philip thought that the soft collar suited Monica, adding physical inflexibility to her already formidable air of self-righteousness and endowing her with a regal bearing.

She would turn her entire body in order to regard Philip. "If she thinks she is going to scare me, she has another think coming," she would say. "I will not be intimidated by a crazy woman."

Monica maintained that she could have taken Helga in a fair fight. "I was off balance," Monica exclaimed. "I didn't see it coming."

With a paste-up artist gone and Monica physically impaired and a sudden surge in the demand for résumés and business cards, Philip was asked to come in early. He hated arriving early, when the battle raged on all fronts.

Ralph Pederson grew more overwrought as his employees worked longer hours, accruing dreaded overtime. "Dear Jesus," he would say to a harried employee, "are you still here? No, no, keep working, but couldn't you work just a little faster?"

Distraught, Pederson would rush into the back room and fire a printer in an attempt to vent his frustration. Philip kept expecting

Bingham to get the axe—his attitude was bad—but Ralph Pederson seemed not to see the man, his eye instead alighting on some younger printer just in the act of taking a personal phone call or botching a three-color job.

The Texas heat stretched into September and then violent thunderstorms vandalized the city. Philip's ceiling sprung half a dozen leaks, and management sent a maintenance man with a large desperado's mustache who regarded the dripping water sadly and said, "She rains inside," and left without offering hope. Philip covered the floor with pots and pans and grew accustomed to the syncopated plops and dings.

"I feel like I'm underwater," he told Amelia. The phone had a bad connection, and Amelia replied in a rush of static. "What?" Philip said.

"Like your monsters," Amelia shouted back. "They live under the ocean, right? So that the other monsters from outer space can't get them easily."

Philip didn't answer. Amelia began to cry.

"Aw," Philip said.

"What?"

"Don't cry."

Amelia sniffed. "I'm sorry," she said. "That was mean—about your monsters. It's just that I didn't get another job, and I really need a job." Amelia sobbed, regained control quickly, and said, "I hate this weather. I better talk to you some other time." And she hung up. Philip started to call back, thought better of it, and dialed his therapist instead.

Lily listened until Philip got to the end of it.

"She loves you," Lily said. "Poor dimwitted girl." There was a pause. "Good hearing from you. Come by sometime." She hung up the phone.

Philip continued to read Henry James, medicating himself against the frenzy of Ralph's One-Day Résumés and the rebuffs of his ex-lover, but even the soporific tones of the Master could not quiet the rising anxiety. Philip longed to go to Amelia's door, to stand there in the rain until she took pity on him and let him in. He did not do this, primarily because he felt that something dire was about to happen, and he did not want to bring his true love into the sphere of this evil event. The past was mustering grim forces. He could feel it. The past was a dark, black pit, and if he peered into it, something could turn its baleful eye upward and spy him there, frozen against the light. Then it would come rushing up to greet him with a mouthful of dirty razor teeth and malice on its black breath.

When it came it was no real surprise, so Philip was able to lie there in the parking lot and stare at the overcast sky and console himself with the thought that the universe did follow certain laws of cause and effect.

This is how it happened. He had just gotten out of his car and was walking across the parking lot when he heard a scream and saw Monica running toward him. Her arms were stretched out in front of her. Her soft collar did not in any way impede her progress, and she was traveling at a good speed, her short brown hair jumping on her head. A stout, low-to-the-ground woman in slacks, she crossed the slick asphalt gracelessly but with surprising dispatch. She saw Philip at the last minute, acknowledging his presence with a widening of her eyes and a quick, sideways leap.

The pickup truck was right behind her, and Philip saw Helga's round, oddly placid countenance behind the windshield. Philip jumped, but the car's right fender caught him and he was thrown, spinning, in the air. His mind clutched at scraps of the known world: an upside-down tree, parked cars, two karate students in their white pajamalike uniforms turning to look his way, their expressions unreadable but no doubt critical of his floundering passage through the air.

His left leg broke when he hit the ground, a cold, ungainly sound echoing in his teeth, and he did not pass out or even scream, but watched with his head sideways to the wet pavement as the pickup roared on in pursuit of the fleeing Monica.

Monica would have made the curb and the safety of an alley formed by two warehouses, but she fell and as she scrambled to her feet, the truck was upon her and sent her hurtling into the air. Not an aerodynamically sound woman, Monica nonetheless moved with some grace, holding her arms stiffly out from her body and appearing, indeed, to fly. Philip, fresh from his own scrambling, ungainly dive, felt something like admiration and, to his shame, envy.

Monica hit the pavement with the flat smack of a sack of feed hurled from a barn's loft. She did not move.

The Ford turned sharply with a squeal of tires and roared back onto the highway and the young men in their karate garb raced toward the immobile Monica.

As the young men fretted and flapped over the body, they seemed to multiply, becoming a crowd of luminous angels, and then Philip lost interest, overwhelmed by a kind of philosophical calm and disinterest. He heard a long, thin siren wail and wondered, as he always did, what strangers were in jeopardy, what tragedy elicited that plaintive cry.

Lily visited Philip in the hospital. For a moment, Philip did not recognize her. She was disguised as someone's grandmother, in a blue-print dress and one of those small, black hats with tiny pink flowers.

"That's some cast," she said. Philip's left leg was entirely wrapped in plaster and surrounded by a sort of wire scaffolding, as though it were under construction by tiny elves. A silver rod pierced the plaster just above the knee, like a magician's trick.

Lily was holding a large, tropical-looking green plant. "I called your work and they told me what happened. Are you okay?"

Philip said that he was fine. He did not tell

her how much he hated hospitals, how the labored breathing of the air conditioning made him feel as though he were in the lair of Dagon or Cthulhu himself.

Lily put the plant on the windowsill and turned back to Philip. Just then Amelia came into the room. Philip's heart jumped.

"Hey Philip," Amelia said. She was wearing a dark suit—no doubt she was out job hunting—and sunglasses.

"Hey," Philip said.

"You're Amelia, right," Lily said.

Don't listen to her stomach, Philip thought, but the fear was unwarranted.

Lily shook Amelia's hand. "I'm Lily Metcalf. I'm Philip's therapist."

"Wow," Amelia said. "Good luck."

Lily told them what she had learned in her call to Philip's office. Monica was still in a coma, and Helga had disappeared, although the police had found her truck at the airport.

"Your boss asked if you could call," Lily said. "He has hired some temps, but he says they are nothing but slackers and cretins, and that if there were some way you could come in... I guess he hasn't visited you or he would know better."

Lily looked at her watch. "Hey, I've got to be going," she said. She kissed Philip on the cheek, then turned and hugged Amelia. Still holding Amelia's shoulders, the old woman looked steadily into the girl's eyes. "Well, well," she said. She let go of the girl's shoulders but continued to study her face. "Not what I would have guessed at all."

"I beg your pardon," Amelia said, flustered by this close scrutiny.

"You saw something too," the old woman said, and then she turned and walked out the door.

Amelia frowned at the empty doorway. Then she turned and regarded Philip. "What was that about?"

"My therapist is very intuitive," Philip said.

"Great. Sounds like your kind of therapist. Does she read entrails?"

"Huh?"

Amelia rolled her eyes. "Forget it. Are you in pain?"

"I would never call anything pain that brought you to my side," Philip said, surprising himself with the nobility and poetry that flew, with such felicity, from his lips.

It was that sort of genuine, heightened and faintly stupid moment that only lovers, long parted, know and appreciate.

"Oh Philip," Amelia said. Twin tears bloomed in her eyes. Her eyeliner, a new, unproven product, bled instantly, giving her a haunted, tragic look.

She went to Philip's bedside, knelt down and kissed him on the lips. He kissed her back, in the hallucinatory ecstasy of an invalid on strong painkillers.

Amelia had to leave—she did indeed have an interview—but she promised to return the next day.

Philip felt joyous beyond belief. And what a curious, convoluted path toward joy. He wished

Bingham, that natural philosopher, were here to share the feverish thoughts that filled his head. He fell asleep, fully expecting dreams of unalloyed happiness. Instead, he dreamed of his father.

"You'll scare the child senseless," his mother said. His father looked up from the tattered copy of *Weird Tales* and said, "You don't know a thing about it, Marge. It's in a boy's blood to like this kind of story."

"An older boy," Marge said. "Not a child."

"Oh, just leave us be," Walter Kenan said, and he turned back to the child propped up by pillows and read, *"Then came a noxious rush of noisome, frigid air from that same dreaded direction, followed by a piercing shriek just beside me on that shocking rifted tomb of man and monster. In another instant I was knocked from my gruesome bench by the devilish threshing of some unseen entity of titanic size but undetermined nature…"*

Philip listened to his father read. His father was a great fan of the reclusive New England writer, H. P. Lovecraft, whose horrific tales of loathsome, monstrous entities from beyond the stars had thrilled the teenage Walter Kenan. The stories first appeared in pulp magazines with lurid covers, and the originals were Walter Kenan's most prized possessions. He never lost his love for the tales, and chose them as bedtime reading for his son. Perhaps his wife was right—no doubt, she was—that they were not proper fare for a child of six or seven, but what harm could there be in stories?

And that was true enough.

And there was no telling how it happened, how Philip's father descended into the same madness that was the lot of most Lovecraft narrators, and opened the black abyss and let them in, a grotesque, unholy crew, the monstrous Old Ones that waited in eternity at the gates of Sleep and Time—Cthulhu, Nyarlathotep, Yog-Sothoth, Dagon, and the ones whose names were lost to time and to their own forgotten languages.

They were creatures the mind could not quite encompass. Their shapes possessed an unholy geometry that shattered human reason. Often, it was not the monster itself that was perceived, but that truncated section that writhed in the visible world, the rest remaining in shadowy dimensions.

Perhaps the drinking did it, or perhaps the drinking came after. In any event, a bitterness descended on Walter Kenan and he grew angry and violent. He would sit at the kitchen table drinking. He would be leaning forward, all his weight on his forearms, his straight dark hair falling over his eyes, hiding their haunted intensity. The hum of the refrigerator would fill the room. He would still be in his office clothes, his tie loosened, his white shirt wrinkled, the sleeves rolled past his elbows. He would talk to himself or turn and shout into the living room where Philip's mother was ironing.

"It's the System," he would mutter. "The goddam, dog-pissed System." He would stand up suddenly, the frail kitchen chair falling and clattering behind him, and he would lurch to the refrigerator and wrench the door open and shout into it. "You goddam sons of bitches! You whoring, lying, cheating bastards."

He would spy Philip, standing silent by the backdoor and he would shout, "You don't know shit about it. You think the System ain't gonna get you. It'll hold you down same as the rest. I don't see no wings sprouting from your backside."

When not drunk—and sometimes, rarely, he was sober in these nightmares—Philip's father would be full of sadness and weariness. He would put an arm around Philip and say, "Don't lose your dreams, boy. Don't let any bastard steal your dreams, or trick you out of them with a pension and a promise. Don't let the System eat your soul."

The System. The Old Ones, crouched at the beginning of time, malevolent and patient. They thwarted all aspiration, all true and noble yearning. Ironically, the System bound Lovecraft himself to a life of poverty—so Philip's father raved, in drunken, lunatic eloquence—forcing the reclusive New Englander to eke out a near-starvation existence revising the dreadful scribblings of lesser writers and finally killing him with a cancer in the guts.

The System was ubiquitous and merciless. Its minions were everywhere, from the President of the United States to the clerk at the hardware store to Claude Miller, who was Walter Kenan's supervisor at the office where Walter worked in the accounting department. The System's creatures were fellow office workers, mysteriously generated regulations, numbers, signs on the walls, one-way streets, radio announcers, movies. These were the puppets of the Dark Gods. The distinguishing feature of a creature of the System was this: It bore Walter Kenan malice and worked diligently to confuse, demoralize, and destroy Walter Kenan.

Had it not been for the System, Philip's father would have been Somebody. The System had weakened Walter Kenan, had driven him to daily drinking, had saddled him with a shrill, ungrateful wife and a whining momma's boy for a son. Walter Kenan, who could have had a major league baseball career if the System hadn't set him up, would clutch tiny Philip's shoulders and lift him up and thump him against the wall, and say, "Are you listening to me? Look at me. I am trying to tell you the way it is. I am trying to prepare you."

After his father's attempts at education, Philip would lie in bed and his mother would come in and put her hand on her son's forehead and tell him that his father was a good man who was under a lot of stress.

One day things would be different, she said. She was a small woman with a round face and sad eyes—and it was only years later, when he found a photo of her in her high school yearbook, that Philip realized those eyes might have been capable of reflecting something other than pain.

Sometimes Walter Kenan would hit his wife. Philip understood that the System was responsible for this. Once Philip had seen his mother on her knees on the kitchen floor, her hair in her face, her body shaking with sobs, a garish splash of red on the floor—which proved to be tomato soup but lay forever in Philip's mind in the terror of spilled blood. His father, reeling over his kneeling wife, had looked up at Philip and said, "Damn woman can't even cook soup."

That night Philip's mother had again reassured her son that Walter Kenan was a good man and that one day things would be different. They were just having bad luck.

"The System," her son said. Philip was nine years old.

His mother smiled down at him.

"I wish—" Philip said. And he stopped. He was not sure what he wished. And then it came to him: "I wish the System would kill him."

"Oh Philip," his mother said. She leaned over and hugged him, and he could hear her labored breathing and smell the perfume she wore and feel the scratchy fabric of her waitress uniform. "You don't really mean that."

But he had meant it. "Now I lay me down to

sleep..." he prayed in the darkened room. But when he had finished his petition to his mother's invisible god, he turned to the one of power. He prayed to the System. "Kill him," he hissed. "Please." He prayed to Yog-Sothoth and ancient Cthulhu.

After Philip had been in the hospital a week, Al Bingham came to visit.

"I don't like hospitals," Bingham said. He was wearing a hat, something a gangster in a forties film would have coveted, and a brown rumpled suit. No tie. "My wife went into a hospital for a routine check-up once, and that was the last of her. Doctor calls and says the test is positive, and I say, well that's a relief and he says no, positive isn't good. Negative is good. Positive means they shrink you with chemicals until you are small enough to bury in a shoe box."

"I'm sorry," Philip said.

Bingham waved a hand. "That was a long

time ago. I just came to cheer you up. Was that your girlfriend I saw coming out of here?"

Philip said that indeed it was, and that it looked like they might get back together again.

"Hey, congratulations," Bingham said. "It's always good to see young folks resolve their differences. Life is short, et cetera."

"It's not absolutely for sure yet," Philip said.

She wants me to throw out my novel. She wants me to chuck 2000 pages. She wants me to rip my heart out and feed it to the paper shredder.

"I'm sure it will work out," Bingham said. Like many old people, the tone of his voice seemed to add that it would not matter in the long run.

"I got to get back to work," Bingham said. "Old Ralph is losing it. He keeps telling everyone that the typesetting broad will be back next week, when the way I hear it she is still unconscious. Eddie Shanks says our boss is just being optimistic, but I say he is losing it big time. He fired two printers last night, and this morning he hired some guy who doesn't speak

English and spends three-fourths of his time in the bathroom."

The old printer left, and Philip drifted back into fitful sleep.

Well? Amelia had asked.

I don't know. I don't know if I can do it.

Ralph Pederson always said, "Insurance is a racket," and, since he did not want his workers to appear to be gullible fools, he did not offer them health insurance until they had been with him two years. Consequently, Ralph's One-Day Résumés had very few employees who actually were insured. Philip, a new employee, was most definitely not insured.

The hospital administration, running a cool

eye over Philip's physical and financial health, decided the former was far better than the latter, and they had Philip on crutches and out the door in five days.

Amelia drove Philip back to his apartment. She drove a small, maroon Honda, zipping through traffic with her usual flat-out, solemn concentration.

The day was overcast with occasional tremors of rain. In Philip's apartment, the pots and pans were full of water and the air had a thick, mildewed flavor of defeat. Fortunately, Philip's stay in the hospital had coincided with mostly clear skies and good weather, the rain arriving late last night. Had it been otherwise, the carpet would have required more than Amelia's industry with towels and a hair dryer.

Amelia helped him up the steps and into bed, a wobbly enterprise. His cast had been cut to mid-thigh, but it was still a huge, ungainly weight and Philip was weak and dizzy from the days of lying in bed.

Amelia started setting the apartment to rights

immediately. She found cans of soup in the cupboard.

"You're welcome," she said, handing Philip a hot mug of chicken and rice soup. She went out the door and came back minutes later with the hospital plant. She put it down next to the sliding glass doors that led to the small deck and a view of the highway.

"This is a nice place," she said. "Sort of basic. I think the plant helps. I see you've got a new computer."

"Yes," Philip said, turning his head to look at the desk and the computer and printer that dominated it. "It really helps with the writing."

Amelia looked at him with her X-ray eyes. "I guess so," she said finally, turning away. "Well, I better be going," she said. A hand on the door, she turned back to him. "Are you going to be all right here without anyone?" she asked. "I don't feel right about leaving you."

"I'll be fine," Philip said. "Lily, my therapist, you met her, said she would come by. And I've got a phone, after all. The world is at my fingertips."

"Okay. Call."

And she was gone. No kiss this time. She had issued an ultimatum in the hospital, and he had not replied. They were in limbo now, waiting. Philip waited himself, waited to see what he would do.

"Throw that awful novel out," Amelia had said, "and I'll come back."

The suspense was killing Philip. Would he do it? Could he?

Philip could not sleep. The pain increased, and he had to struggle out of bed, balancing awkwardly with his crutches, and hobble into the kitchen to fill a glass with tap water and swallow the two yellow pills. By the time he was once again in bed and had elevated his leg with pillows, he was exhausted. Life was going to be an ordeal until the cast came off.

The next morning Philip was awakened by a telephone call from Ralph Pederson.

"They told me you were out of the hospital," Ralph said. He was shouting, no doubt in order to hear himself over the din of the presses. "I'm glad to hear it. That Helga was sure nuts. I would have called earlier, but I figured you could use some rest. I can tell you we could use you down here."

Philip explained why he could not come into the office.

"I won't lie to you," Ralph said. "I'm disappointed. I know you are probably not one hundred percent, but I was hoping you could manage at least a few hours down here. That's the mark of a real trooper, that willingness to go the extra mile, to make a few sacrifices when the business is in a jam."

Ralph went on at some length, pausing only to shout orders to others in the shop.

"I can't make it," Philip said. "Sorry." He hung up.

Philip had just finished the elaborate business of washing himself without getting his cast wet, when Lily knocked on the door.

"Just a minute," he shouted. He dressed and let her in.

"I got some groceries," she said.

Lily fixed breakfast: eggs and bacon and grapefruit and toast and cereal and coffee and juice. Philip did not tell her that he never ate breakfast. Eating breakfast always made him feel the way he imagined a python must feel after devouring a rabbit.

"Okay," Lily said.

Philip knew what was coming.

"Counseling time," Lily said.

Philip hated talking about his life. It was not a good story, full of loose ends and implausibly motivated characters. There seemed to be no unifying theme, although perhaps that was the point of the whole exercise—to discover such a thing.

He had gone to a small college in northern Virginia, and he had met a girl named Elaine

Gregson his sophomore year, and they had lived together for a couple of years. They were married in June, the year they graduated. The wedding was large, most of the guests being friends of Elaine's—she was a popular girl—or members of Elaine's substantial stock of family and relatives. Philip's mother came, as did several of Philip's friends, bookish misfits who huddled together, a dark-suited and sullen clump amid the brighter celebrants.

Philip's father was dead, but he was represented by Philip's grandfather, a dour, gray-bearded man who looked a little like Philip's father but did not drink and almost never spoke. It was never clear to Philip whether grandfather Kenan liked or disliked him.

Philip showed Lily photos of the wedding.

"She's very pretty," Lily said, looking up from the album. In the photo inspiring this observation, Philip's bride was lying on the ground in her green wedding dress, looking skyward, her smile demure. Her hands are hooked behind her head and her shimmering black hair is spilling out to the limits of the frame. You can see to the bottom of her dark eyes, and what is there is a white, pure contentment—a serenity at once arrogant and innocent—as the rich green grass springs up through her hair, and everything (the weather, her new husband, her friends) conspires to ensure her happiness.

"She's dead," Philip said.

"I'm sorry."

"Well," Philip said, realizing that he was uttering the precise words that Bingham had used in the hospital when similar condolences were offered, "that was a long time ago." He understood then that the hollowness was intentional, that the words were not meant to indicate healing or indifference, that they were, indeed, bitterly ironic.

"How did it happen?"

"She killed herself," Philip said.

Lily opened her mouth. Philip thought she might say it, might say, "That makes two," but she didn't.

She didn't say anything, but she looked so sad,

so stricken, that Philip sought for words to comfort her, poor old woman.

"I don't think it was intentional," Philip said. "She was drinking a lot, and she was always going to all these different doctors, and she never really thought that pills and alcohol could harm her."

"Can you tell me about it?" Lily asked. She had moved to sit on the bed, and she rested her arm on Philip's armored leg.

Philip said, "Elaine was going to be a world-famous painter. Her degree was in fine arts and she painted these oil paintings that were terrific."

They were hard-edged, violently colored canvases, abstracts within which photorealistic details existed, a door knob, a tennis shoe, an apple. She was very serious about her work, and a professional; she worked every day. Whenever Philip thought of Elaine, he saw her in a gray apron, the pockets of which bristled with gaudy brushes. Her cheeks or forehead would usually bear some mark of the day's work, a splash of yellow or orange or some other primary color.

When they made love, he would smell the turpentine in her hair.

Philip told Lily that he had majored in English literature. He was, he said, one of that vast horde of post-war baby boomers that went to college as a matter of course (in Philip's case, primarily to please his mother). Philip had always been a good student, and he had gone on a scholarship.

Philip never thought of the college world as remotely connected to the mundane, dimly perceived world of employment, and none of his professors ever suggested that the two were connected. Philip was going to be a famous novelist. People like Norman Mailer were going to review his first novel.

Philip, closing his eyes, quoted Norman Mailer's review: "I just finished reading Philip Kenan's stunning novel, and I am frankly overwhelmed. This man is a genius, and I applaud his arrival on the literary scene, but I confess that I can no longer look at my own efforts with any joy or pride, and I doubt I will be able to write anything in the shadow of this profound talent. I am paralyzed by Mr. Kenan's monumental achievement, and I must retire from the field with what dignity I can summon."

Lily smiled. "Pretty impressive," she said.

"Oh, I've memorized my future reviews," Philip said. Philip lay back on the pillow and looked at the ceiling, studied its ominous bulges where yet new leaks threatened to sprout.

"Artists should not marry artists," Philip said. "And young artists are the worst. We thought we were protected, that talent was some sort of shield against reality."

They had ten thousand dollars in the bank, money from Elaine's trust fund, and that seemed more than enough to keep them going until fame and fortune arrived.

They rented a small house in Falls Church, Virginia, a suburb of Washington, D.C., and they planted a garden in back and acquired two cats, Seth and Jesus, and worked as diligently as young artists could amid the distractions of the late sixties and the confusion between lifestyle and actual work. Many of their friends, fellow artists, seemed to remain on the preparatory, research side of their art, expanding their minds with LSD, seeking enlightenment in communes, smoking dope and developing long raps about the nature of reality.

Compared to their colleagues, Philip and Elaine actually did considerable work. They smoked dope and listened to Bob Dylan and learned to play the obligatory folk instruments (guitar, harmonica, autoharp) and drove into Washington to protest the infamous war that was raging in Vietnam, but they also wrote and painted. Elaine even found a gallery in Georgetown that was willing to exhibit her paintings.

The war tried to claim Philip; he was called up for the draft. But his knees saved him. They were inclined to dislocate on whim, and the right knee had undergone corrective surgery after a nasty fall Philip had taken while ice skating with high school friends. The night of the day Philip failed his physical, Elaine threw a party for all their friends. Philip wore shorts displaying knees that Elaine had painted white and emblazoned with four red F's apiece.

"One day the money ran out," Philip said.

All of a sudden, it seemed. They had to get jobs. Philip hadn't finished his novel, and Elaine had made a few hundred dollars from her paintings—spent immediately in celebration—and the bank account was empty and the rent was coming due.

Potential employers (discovered through the help wanted ads in the Washington *Post*) were far less enthusiastic than college professors when contemplating fledgling artists.

Philip got a job working in the research library of a large government contractor. His job was to help catalogue the library by typing endless notecards.

Elaine got a job as an admissions clerk in an orthopedic hospital. She worked the three-to-eleven shift, and Philip worked from eight in the morning until five at night. During the week, they saw each other only briefly, in passing.

They tried to pack all the work and play they could into the weekends, and there was a kind of giddy excitement to those early months when they took some satisfaction out of having saved themselves from financial ruin and eviction. They had needed money, and they had gone into the bourgeois world and gotten jobs. They had done the adult thing, and it had been easy, actually, and it was, of course, an expedient measure, nothing for the long run.

Elaine quit the hospital after working there six months. "I don't want to work in a hospital," she said. "I don't like sick people. And nurses are worse than sick people. And the only thing worse than nurses are doctors."

She said that she would get a different job, but the next day, when Philip came home from work, she had set her easel up on the porch. She did not look for other employment for the rest of her life.

ne night, two years and two months after Philip had begun work at the research library, he heard his father's voice, choked with self-pity and outrage.

"I knock myself out for nothing," his father's voice muttered. "I am getting nowhere except older. I do not deserve this. It is a rigged game."

Philip was in the kitchen, nursing a beer. Elaine had gone to bed hours ago, and Philip was alone with his father's querulous voice and the flickering fluorescent light.

Philip felt a cold, crackling terror. In a moment of despairing clarity, he knew what he had heard. He would have preferred a ghost, a moldering ghost with broken teeth and dirt spilling out of its eye sockets. This transformation was more dreadful.

Philip had spoken the words himself.

"No," he said, trying to regain his voice, his own inflections. "No."

It was his father's bitterness that possessed him. It was the implacable weight of the System.

Less than a week later, Elaine asked him how the novel was going. Later she said she had asked in good faith, that she had been curious, interested, nothing more. Philip knew better. She was drunk and mean, mean with the failure of her own art, and he had answered her with his frustration and rage. He had told her that he was not writing a novel, that he was working at a rotten job in order to keep a wife with artistic pretensions supplied with booze and tranquilizers.

Elaine responded by saying that *he* had spent *her* money writing what had to be one of the most unengaging monologues ever written, and that pity and horror had kept her from voicing her true assessment of his novel. He needed, however, to hear the truth, and the truth was that *The Unraveling of Raymond Hart* (the working title) was one of the most insipid and bloated creations ever spawned. More succinctly, it was shit. And, while a publisher might publish sensational shit, a publisher would not publish boring shit, and *Unraveling* was boring enough to kill an accountant.

Once the battle lines were drawn, they fought often.

The research library was located in the basement of a gravy-colored, three-story brick building that squatted in the middle of a parking lot, its tiny windows like the glittering eyes of a mechanical spider. It was a big shoebox of a building, aggressively ugly inside and out and inhabited by unhappy people: secretaries who had lost all hope, narrow-shouldered men in cheap suits who lived in fear of being fired, fast-striding men in better suits who lived in fear of dying before they had fired their quota of timid underlings, and the real bosses, grim, self-assured men, ever vigilant to screw before being screwed.

Every morning, Philip would park and walk through the glass doors and smile at the security guard who never smiled back and get into the small elevator that smelled like dirty wet towels and ammonia and go down to the basement and walk down the green hall to the library. Mrs. Walston would already be there.

She was a dumpy woman, Mr. Grodinov's secretary, and as soon as Philip sat down at his desk, she would begin talking.

"Well Philip, it's good to see you," she would say. Then she would tell him in detail what she had had for breakfast that morning. She would describe the nuances of thought that prompted certain decisions (*I thought, I'll have Grape Nuts, and then I thought, No, I had Grape Nuts two days ago and anyway I'm out of skim milk and only have the regular, which I don't care to use with cereal, and I thought, I'll have a grapefruit with maybe some toast and jam because I just the other day went to the supermarket and...).* Philip would listen. Her words would fill him up, like wet concrete, and he would experience a sense of deep despair, brought on in part by Mrs. Walston's narration and in part by the knowledge, born of experience, that the day offered nothing better, that, in fact, the drama of Mrs. Walston's morning repast would be the highlight of his office hours.

Mr. Grodinov, Philip's boss, would come in an hour or so after Philip. Mr. Grodinov was an old man, bald and small, shrinking daily it seemed into a dusty suit so old that its original color was now a matter of conjecture. Mr. Grodinov had come from Russia a hundred years ago or so, to the basement of AmMaBit, Inc.

"The old man is crazy as a shaken-up soda pop," Mrs. Walston would confide. "He don't do nothing but the crosswords in the newspaper, and they pay him for that. And he don't even do the crosswords right; he puts in extra letters and makes words up."

Philip actually liked Mr. Grodinov, who almost never spoke and did, indeed, spend most of his time doing crossword puzzles. Occasionally the old man would sigh or laugh.

When Philip was new, he had been logging in papers and abstracts with some speed and sense of purpose. Mr. Grodinov had picked up the stack of typed notecards, thumbed them like a card shark taking the measure of a new deck, and said, "This is very good, Mr. Kenan, but please remember the turtle is the winner."

This cryptic statement came clear over time. "The truth," Mr. Grodinov said one day, "is that he is nobody that comes here. Nobody cares about this libraries. They spit in it as a toilet."

Mr. Grodinov had sighed and taken off his shoe and absently scratched his ear with it. "This is a job of work, you see. This is a doing every day over and over of the same thing, and throwing out the old and putting in the new. It is not a thing for finishing, but only for doing. It is the System here, and that is our jobs."

Philip was aware that he had stopped talking when he heard Lily urging him to continue.

"The Old Ones were trying to come through, but the building wasn't properly located, maybe, or maybe there was too much individuality, too many nut cases like Mr. Grodinov. Sometimes, when I worked late, I'd notice a wet trail down a hall or hear a noise like a high, shrill whistle. I was writing on my H. P. Lovecraft novel a lot. Elaine hated the book, and somehow that made the writing all the more urgent."

"You were writing about monsters at home," Lily said, "and seeing them out of the corner of your eye at work."

Philip smiled ruefully. "That's what Amelia thinks too."

"But that's not it," Lily said. She pursed her lips, frowned. "So enlighten me."

"Writing isn't a cut-and-dried, cause-and-effect sort of thing," Philip said. "They were there to begin with, the monsters. I wrote about them. The writing came, as it does for all writers, from some deeper, more observant me. And then I took that back into the office. And, of course, Mr. Grodinov knew they were there, although he was unfamiliar with Lovecraft and didn't call them the Old Ones. But if you don't have the name of a thing, it is still the thing. I knew what he was talking about.

"Mr. Grodinov died, and they closed the library down. I was out of a job."

"They are after me," Mr. Grodinov had confided, the last day Philip saw him. "First they are after me in Russia because I say this is very wrong. Then to this countries they are after me but I am no fool." Mr. Grodinov tapped a throbbing vein in his temple to indicate the presence of brains. "I hide here in this undergrounds, safe from the secret police and the CIA and the FBI and the other letters, and I see right away that it is here too, but I think, 'It is nothings here, just small crappers, little mice things that cannot kill.' Ha ha. I forget and it grows and grows and now it comes out of the pipes, and it puts poisons to my brain so I dream about being already dead and my mouth sewed shut." Mr. Grodinov waved the half bottle of wine in the air. His gold-rimmed glasses flashed with some of the mad fire of his revolutionary youth. "They say, 'Mr. Grodinov, Mr. Grodinov, you are too old, go and die,' but I say nothing. I say nothing so they will not hear me and find me." Grodinov clutched Philip in an embrace of alcohol and stale old man. "You are like me, young Mr. Kenan, you think they don't come if you be very, very quiet and clever. But still they come. They smell the dream in you. They smell it and they, little tiny crappers at first—make you laugh to see them—they come."

Mr. Grodinov left early that day, and Mrs.

Walston, scowling after his departure, said, "Well, the old fool's drunk."

Mr. Grodinov's wife called the next day. This in itself was extraordinary. "The way he talked," Mrs. Walston said, "I thought he was a widower."

Mrs. Grodinov had less English than her husband. "No come," she said. "Dead." She had broken into sobs then, and Mrs. Walston had had to wait until the old woman collected herself again. "Stuck," the woman said. "Stuck dead."

Mrs. Walston got the hospital's name and was able to confirm that the old man was dead of a stroke.

"Mark my words," Mrs. Walston told Philip, "they'll close this office."

And she had been right.

"And you think that, somehow, the Old Ones killed your boss," Lily said.

Philip nodded. "Yes."

After Philip lost his job, he did not seek another one. And when the rent came due and they could not pay it, Elaine said, "I am moving in with Susan." Susan was an old college roommate, and she had never approved of Philip.

Philip nodded. "Fine." He moved back to his mother's house, and he slept in the bed he had slept in as a child, waking with a start when he thought he heard his father's footstep on the stairs.

One day Susan called. "Elaine's in the hospital," she screamed. "You son of a bitch." She had hung up then, and it was only when Philip arrived at the hospital that he learned his wife was dead, that she had died of an overdose several hours before her arrival at the emergency room.

"How awful," Lily said.

Philip looked up, was surprised to see tears in his counselor's eyes, and said, "Too many tranquilizers. She was drinking too. Booze and downers don't mix. Elaine wasn't suicidal, just a kind of negligent, don't-give-a-damn person."

"I'm sorry," Lily said, leaning forward and clutching Philip's hand.

Philip nodded. "After she died, I felt... it was

anger. I remember standing in the emergency room lobby thinking, 'This is such a lot of shit.'"

Philip stopped.

Lily waited, nodded her head, waited some more. "Yes. Yes, Philip. It must have been terrible."

Philip exhaled slowly. "This is exhausting, you know. I mean, I don't think it is doing any good. She was dead then. She's dead now."

"Yes," Lily said, with a compassion that Philip found terrifying, "but you aren't, Philip. You aren't dead."

A routine was established. Lily would arrive in the morning, letting herself in with a duplicate key. Sometimes Philip wouldn't even be up yet, would be sleeping soundly, and the smell of frying bacon would wake him.

Philip told Lily about the jobs.

"We are looking," Lily said, "for patterns."

"Are you sure that's a good idea?" Philip

asked. "I mean, H. P. Lovecraft would say that the unexamined life is probably the best bet for humans."

The hideous machinations of Cthulhu and his monstrous overlord, Yog-Sothoth were not suited for the daylight of reason.

"I've taken the time to read about your Lovecraft," Lily said. "Face it, the man wasn't in the pink of mental health."

"Exactly," Philip said. "Lovecraft stared too long at the abyss."

"Be that as it may," Lily said, folding her hands in her lap, "examining is my trade. You don't want an old lady to wind up out of work, do you?"

Philip didn't. He talked about the jobs. He talked about the boredom, the boredom that he came to see as the sign of the beast, its sour, suffocating reek.

There was boredom at the community newspaper where Philip pasted down advertisements for pizza parlors and car dealerships (*WE WILL BEAT ANY DEAL OR GIVE YOU*

THE CAR!). There was boredom working at the state agency where Philip corrected addresses on a computer that logged his every keystroke. There was boredom at the insurance company where Philip typed checks and filed forms in huge, gray banks of file cabinets. There was boredom at the several printing companies where Philip typeset brochures and flyers and business cards and waited on customers and encountered what he came to think of as "copy people," humans—often elderly and confused—addicted to photocopying various scraps of paper, recipes, Ann Landers' columns, letters, tax receipts, thousand-page novels. These people were always shocked that a copy cost eight cents—or whatever—and knew of a store, generally in another city, where copies could be obtained for half as much money and the atmosphere was altogether more pleasant. You could always see a copy person coming, spy them through the window as they hobbled across the parking lot. A copy person would be moving very slowly, but with a dread inevitability, clutching boxes filled with copy fodder. Philip's heart would wince when he saw them.

There was boredom in the dozens of jobs obtained through temporary agencies, tasks of such stupefying tedium that the regular employees could not be coerced into performing them even under threat of being fired. "Temp!" the regular employees would scream. "Get a temp!"

And so Philip would stuff envelopes and file unreadable documents, and enter data, row upon row of x's, and white-out zeroes and ones on mountains of government documents bound for warehouses, and sit in rooms with dozens of other temps wearing headphones (*"Hello? I'm calling about a new, economical way to ensure your family's financial well-being in the event of sudden death."*).

There was boredom in the custom photo lab where eight-by-tens of dogs and squinting children and Washington tourist attractions were generated relentlessly, until the pointlessness of all life was starkly revealed, and the sickbed smell of the processing chemicals followed you into sleep.

And there was the boredom, and worse, of MicroMeg Management Systems.

"I think we are making progress," Lily said.

"I feel a hundred percent better," Philip said. "I think this talking has really done the trick. It has clarified everything. I'm ready to get on with my life."

Lily had frowned then. "Not so fast, buster. We've got a lot of ground left to cover."

It was the second week in December before Philip was able to return to work. The cast on his left leg had been replaced by a smaller and lighter model, but Philip still needed crutches in order to get around. Driving would have been out of the question if it had been his right leg that had been broken.

In the interim between being run over and returning to Ralph's One-Day Résumés, Philip had been fired four times. Ralph Pederson would call, beseeching Philip to come in and help out, and Philip would explain that he was incapable of doing that. Ralph would then say, "I'm sorry, Philip. I am going to have to get someone else. The business can't wait until you feel absolutely tip-top, you understand. This is nothing personal."

Philip would say he understood, and when the conversation ended, Philip would lie back on his pillow with a sense of relief. A few weeks later, Ralph would again call and beg Philip to return; Philip would again decline. Reluctantly, Ralph would let Philip go.

Philip understood that Ralph was having difficulty finding people who could operate the ancient typesetting equipment and Philip sympathized with his employer's plight. Still, he felt that being fired once per job was sufficient, and he resented this repetition of the experience.

Ralph continued to call, however, and one day Philip surprised himself by saying, "I could come in next Monday."

The day of Philip's return was a day of freezing rain. Negotiating the parking lot on crutches was a perilous venture, and Philip was certain he would fall, but he made it in the door without doing himself injury.

In the lobby a Christmas tree (decorated with business cards) reminded Philip that the holiday season was upon him.

Ralph Pederson came running up. He looked thinner than when Philip had last seen him, and more disheveled. "Philip, Philip," he said. "Come on back, I'll introduce you to everyone."

Had they forgotten him already? True, he had always arrived at the end of the day, when everyone was leaving. And he was not, he knew, the sort of person who made a lasting impression. He was quiet, of average height and features, and he was inclined to utter the stock phrases of social commerce.

Still, he had only been gone a few months, and his leavetaking was, in itself, spectacular enough to keep his memory alive.

On entering the long room, Philip realized

that he did not know anyone. All the employees he had worked with were gone, replaced by a new crew. Later that evening, when Philip was alone with his thoughts, he remembered Ralph saying that morale had been low for awhile, but that recently it was much higher.

Philip had attributed this elevation in morale to particularly eloquent motivational pamphlets or a decrease in the workload, but now Philip understood that morale had been improved by the simple but effective measure of firing all the low-morale types (i.e. everyone) and hiring new blood.

The new crew was obviously frightened, displaying the large, wild eyes of headlight-hunted deer, but their adrenaline reserves had not yet been depleted, and so they were not sullen or apathetic.

Monica was not there, although Ralph said she would be back next week. Surprisingly, Al Bingham had survived the purge.

The old printer walked into where Philip was typesetting at about eight in the evening.

"Yeah," he said, when Philip expressed his delight in seeing him, "I'm an old-timer here now. Don't take long to get seniority at this joint, does it?"

Philip agreed that it didn't, but his surprise at seeing Bingham was obvious, and the old man read his expression and answered the question there.

"Ralph don't fire me because he can't smell the fear," Bingham said. "I'm invisible. He is always coming up, ready to give me the boot, but then he falters, gets this baffled look, and I know he can't see me. He wonders what he was about to do and marches off to ream some poor Mexican working in the bindery."

Philip called Amelia at nine in the evening. His inability to destroy his novel—or even to lie and say he had destroyed it—had set their relationship back to one rationed phone call a week. Philip knew that Amelia was waiting for him to make the next move, but he couldn't find the internal resources to act.

"I'm back at work," he told her.

"I've found a job myself," Amelia said, excitement in her voice. "I start next week."

"Oh." Philip felt a flutter of panic. "Well."

"Hey, congratulate me." Amelia giggled with good spirits.

"Hey, congratulations."

Oh, be careful, Amelia. I know you don't want to remember, but please, please be careful.

They talked briefly. Amelia said she had to get up early the next day, some sort of orientation thing in preparation for her first day of work, and she hung up.

That night, Philip dreamed the dream of his father's death in the coils of the System.

This is how it went, as it always went, a dream as unvarying as a documentary unwinding:

The kitchen is silent and cool and Philip, who has just come home from school, walking through one of spring's first truly hot days, goes to the refrigerator and finds a carton of milk and drinks the cold, headache-inducing milk standing in the light of the open door which sheds the green-tinged light that aliens use to immobilize teenagers making out in cars. The refrigerator hum is, of course, the hovering spacecraft.

Today the refrigerator is louder than normal, and when Philip closes the door, he discovers that a second sound pulses behind the familiar drone of the fridge. The sound comes from the door to the garage, and, as Philip opens the door, he realizes that it is the sound of the car engine, the muttering machine-speak of his father's souped-up black Chevy.

Philip does not want to encounter his father. Just yesterday they had fought. (*"My God, Philip's bleeding!" his mother screamed. "It's just a scratch, Marge. He's got to learn what he's got to learn. Baby him now, he'll bruise easy later."*)

Philip pushes the garage door open and the sound blooms—*rumble, blat, rumble, rumble, blat!* The garage is dark, smelling of oil and earth and metal. A coiled garden hose hangs from a hook like a sleeping snake. Tools and engine parts and cans of paint and boxes bursting with old newspapers lean against shadows.

Ordinarily, the bare overhead bulb would be on, throwing everything into cold, dirty fact, and it is this darkness that draws Philip, this mystery. He approaches the car, his sneakers sliding over the dirty concrete, a scraping, zombie-hiss of a sound.

He peers in the window of the car, which is shaking slightly, like some black, armored monster in a sleep of fevers. No one is behind the steering wheel. No one is in the car, he thinks, but then presses his face up against the window and sees him. His father is sprawled in the front seat, flat on his back, a dark brown bottle cradled against his chest. His white T-shirt is stained with the whiskey, and his face lies pressed against the back of the seat, his mouth open. His legs are bent, and his brown suit pants are pulled up to reveal bare ankles gliding into ceramic-shiny black shoes. The bare ankles frighten Philip, suggesting strange and unpredictable thought processes.

He is dead, Philip thinks, but then his father stirs, as though rocked on a sea of drunkenness.

The whiskey bottle rolls and a thin trickle of the dark liquid bleeds a new stain on his father's pale, soiled T-shirt.

Philip backs away from the car window.

He is aware suddenly that the room is full of writhing shapes, monstrous, coiled bodies that drop from the ceiling and begin to move. A black serpent crawls from the car's exhaust pipe to a window on the passenger side. And there are other, thicker serpents, some brown, some mottled as though by mold, moving rhythmically.

Yog Sothoth!

Philip runs out of the garage, slamming the door behind him. He runs through the bright, sunlit kitchen and up to his room.

He lies on his bed, heart beating wildly.

The Old Ones, he thinks.

He lies in bed, staring at the ceiling. His heart does not slow at all, and the bed seems to be lifting in the air.

He wakes, not from real sleep, but from the sleep of the dream, and he hears voices, and he walks down the stairs. The front door is open, and the sky is darkening, and the red lights of an ambulance wash over his neighbors, fat Mrs. Odell, and Mr. Warden in a suit, and the Clarks' German shepherd, Ripley, and the skinny Bausch twins, and Mrs. Odell looks up and sees him and jumps like a roach has run up her leg and hollers something into the crowd, and a lot of people stumble back and his mother comes running toward him, her arms outstretched.

She is crying and she hugs him and he is suddenly full of terror, because she is going to know, but instead she says, "Philip. Oh Philip. I was so afraid..." and he realizes that her fear is for him.

"I am all right, Momma," he whispers.

He wants to say, "I didn't mean it," but he doesn't, because he did mean it, and he knows what happened and he knows that his father is dead. His father is dead because his father's son, yes, Philip Kenan, has prayed to the System that it be so.

The next day, Philip told Lily about the dream.

"These monsters have been around a long time," his therapist said.

"Eons," Philip said. "They arrived on earth six hundred million years ago, but of course that tells us nothing about how ancient, as a race, they actually are."

Lily ate a brownie, sipping tea to wash it down. She raised one eyebrow and offered a wry smile. "I meant these monsters have been around a long time in your personal history."

"Ah. Well, yes, I suppose so."

Lily said, "You can't live with a child's guilt forever. You didn't kill your father, he killed himself."

"I wanted him to die," Philip said. "That's where the awfulness is. I wanted him to leave my mother and me alone. If he had to die to do that, that was okay."

"Oh," Lily said, "we all think a lot of dark thoughts. And from what you've told me, it's not even clear you knew what he was doing."

"I knew," Philip said. "Maybe I didn't know about carbon monoxide poisoning, maybe it wasn't clear what he was doing, but I knew he was dying. I went upstairs and went to sleep. I didn't try to get help."

It was a payday at work, and the motivational pamphlet that came with the check was entitled "You Matter!" and Philip effectively resisted reading it at work, but when he returned home and was emptying out his pockets, he saw it and read it while standing up, and it was every bit as bad as he suspected.

It began, "Successful people are people who always give one hundred percent, who understand that a company's success depends on an individual's determination to excel. You may say to yourself, 'I am an insignificant person in this big company. I could be laid off tomorrow along with five hundred of my fellow workers, and no one would care.' The truth is, what you do is important to people who *are* important. While you may, indeed, be one of many, your labor can benefit someone who is, in fact, *genuinely* important. You can..."

Philip put the motivational pamphlet down. The writer had gone too far this time, Philip thought.

On the weekend, Philip did his Christmas shopping. The stores were crowded, and Philip found his spirit buckling as he moved through scenes of gaudiness and decay. Bikini-clad elves touted a lingerie store. Coming out of a bookstore on Sixth Street, Philip saw two Santa-suited men brawling, rolling on the sidewalk.

"Mutherfucker, mutherfucker, mutherfucker," they yelled, as a crowd gathered.

Philip hurried along as fast as his crutches would permit, refusing to look back. He bought his mother a knick-knack to add to the vast collection of knick-knacks that he had been giving her—dutifully—since childhood. He thought perhaps he had given her this piece before, but he knew she wouldn't mind. He bought Amelia a Cowboy Junkies album. That group's female vocalist had eyebrows similar to Amelia's, which made the purchase somehow inevitable, although it did not ensure Amelia's delight.

Philip bought books for his few friends in Virginia. The books he bought as gifts were novels he loved, and he was fairly certain they would go unread. He thought of all the unread novels sitting on shelves or packed in cardboard boxes, and he was assaulted by something like grief. He was certainly wobbly these days, both emotionally and mentally.

Of course, it could be that all this was simply a sign of advancing age. Brain cells, like time bombs arriving at their appointed hour, were being sprung; various creatures of remorse and despair were crawling from their blown cells.

Philip spent all of Sunday lying in bed and thinking about old friends and acquaintances, wrong turns taken and opportunities missed and words uttered in the heat of anger. He missed Amelia, missed her with fierce longing. He closed his eyes and conjured her image. He saw her black, clipped hair, her smooth, intelligent forehead, her mouth, orange or red or purple, her dark eyes outlined boldly. She loved make-up, indeed, she would occasionally get so carried away with the application of face powder and eyeliner that strangers would be startled when she spoke, mistaking her for a mime. Amelia had been a graphic artist at MicroMeg. That's where they met.

Philip thought about old Ronald Bickwithers, his immediate supervisor at MicroMeg. Bickwithers, always poised to go with the corporate flow, no more trustworthy than a Hollywood agent, a sly glad-hander, dodging and ducking like a long-abused dog when a superior entered the room. But even Bickwithers didn't deserve the fate that came to him.

Philip thought about Ronald Bickwithers' wig, which was unabashedly false, and which abandoned Bickwithers in death, leaping from the man's smooth pate to the floor where it lay curled on its back like some small mammal smacked by a fast-moving Greyhound.

Philip thought about his friend, Todd Tillick, who worked for three years on a full-size statue of J. D. Salinger, a statue made entirely from silver gum wrappers and superglue. During that time, Todd had only left his house to purchase fast food and rent horror videos.

Todd once told Philip that he had enough money in a trust fund to live at his current rate until he was sixty-two. If his genius was still unrecognized by then, he would kill himself. He had already purchased the shotgun he would use for self-destruction. He didn't want to be caught short of cash on the day of reckoning. He calculated that he would have to kill himself on August second of two thousand and fifteen.

He wasn't worried. The last time Philip had seen Todd, his friend was doing some sketches for his Thomas Pynchon project, and was composing a letter to ex-underage porn star Traci Lords, speaking of his admiration for her work in Roger Corman films and inviting her to his exhibition, *Writers Who Shun the Limelight*, which was tentatively scheduled for July 12, 1998.

Todd was the happiest man Philip knew, and Philip often surprised himself with mean-spirited envy.

Philip lay in bed and thought about the people he had met at various jobs, malcontents like angry John Miller, a born-again Christian who hated those Christians who had only been born once, and old Mrs. Meadows who believed that her coworker, an equally ancient woman, plotted against her and slept with the boss; workers like Edith Profitt, a mannish woman in tweeds who worked in accounting and played an easy listening station at heavy metal volume, and Honey Gee, a young receptionist at Blink-Of-An-Eye Placards and Signs who was always on the phone to her boyfriend and laughing helplessly at his wit. She would interrupt these conversations to wait on customers, and she would remain cheerful, while making it clear, the way a mother might instruct an importunate child, that she was being inconvenienced.

Workers were not all miserable and driven by economic necessity. "I like getting out of the house and meeting folks," a coworker would confide (at a sweatshop too frenzied for even the most perfunctory sort of social commerce).

There were workers who insisted they would continue working if they had a million dollars. Philip doubted the truth of these statements. But, he reflected, even the horror of war had its addictive side.

Offices were not tribes, sharing common rituals and beliefs. Offices were random collections of people, washed aground on islands of limited resources, battling for sustenance. Philip had seen grown men wrestle over a stapler. He had watched a dowdy, elderly woman scavenge paper clips and candy bars from a rival's drawer. If Eloise took an overlong lunch break, Glenda ran to their boss with the news. Nick Petigrew deleted Mel Tucker's customer list from the computer's hard disk after a dispute over a commission.

Philip thought about Meg Jensen, who he had kissed once in elementary school. Meg had been a sleepy-voiced, wonderfully vague girl who had moved to Atlanta halfway through the school year. Her mouth had been slightly open when they kissed. Philip's tongue had licked her small, perfect teeth, and it was under "teeth" that his memory filed her, so that television toothpaste commercials would unlock a vision of her and while some announcer droned on about plaque and statistical studies, Philip would see her gray eyes and the blond curve of her neck and hear her say, in a voice from some exaggerated, fantasy South, "Philip Kenan, whuhut kind of girl do you think ah am?"

Philip's thoughts came full circle to Amelia again. He would destroy his burdensome novel and marry her. No. He couldn't.

Could he? He wished he were a more decisive human being. Although, of course, so much was preordained.

Philip, a tortured realist, longed not for free will but for the illusion of free will.

onica returned to work.

"I see they fired all the slackers," she said, smiling savagely. Her grin was a little ragged; she had lost a couple of teeth, others were chipped, and her jaw had been reconstructed with a new truculent thrust.

Because the workload had increased, Monica stayed on into Philip's shift. He could see she had changed, but he could not, at first, identify the precise nature of the change. She still worked with a frenzied intensity, screamed imperially at paste-up artists and talked loudly to herself ("Look at this! They want a whole Webster's dictionary on this card!").

She was altered physically, of course. There were a number of nasty scars on her face. One angled laceration had required the shaving of her left eyebrow, and the hair had not grown back. Her outthrust jaw and a tendency on the part of her left eyelid to droop created an expression of simple-minded cunning. Her right ankle had been broken, necessitating a brace and an orthopedic shoe and producing what in a normal person would have been a limp but which, in the hyperactive Monica, was a bird like hop.

All these physical changes were nothing compared to a mental shift that Philip found unsettling.

On the third day of Monica's return, a chance remark by Bingham unlocked some internal door, and that night Philip dreamed of MicroMeg. The old printer's remark had been uttered casually into the cool night air. "Old Ralph has got himself a model employee in that Monica. She's twice as efficient since she got run over. Let's hope Ralph don't put two and two together or we will all be having accidents."

Philip dreamed he was in the men's restroom on the fifth floor of MicroMeg. He knew it was the fifth floor restroom, because Ray Barnstable was brushing his teeth at the sink. Ray spent most of his office hours in this restroom.

"Is Jennings still in the building?" Ray asked.

"No," Philip said. Jennings was Ray Barnstable's hated rival and they shared an office.

"Good," Ray said, and he left the restroom. He would now go—as Philip knew from office gossip—and search Jennings' desk drawers for incriminating information.

The restroom expanded suddenly, growing to the size of a train station. Indeed, there appeared to be a train at the far end, a great, black blur of an engine surrounded by a milling crowd. A line of stalls, dozens of them, stretched down the long white expanse in the direction of the train.

Philip's bowels cramped and he flung open the first of the stalls and availed himself of the toilet. As he sat there, dizzy and oddly hollowed by a sudden liquid evacuation, his eyes fell upon the door and the scrawled writing there: "Phnglui mglw'nafh Cthulhu R'lyeh wgah'nagl fhtagn." He knew the translation, of course, which was "In his house at R'lyeh dead Cthulhu waits dreaming."

He felt a numbing horror, a sense of his insignificance amid black, cosmic forces. He yanked his pants up and stumbled out of the stall as he heard the unholy wail of the train.

The crowd that surrounded the train rose like burnt leaves swirling on an autumn bonfire. Not men at all, but winged creatures, and—for with this knowledge came the realization that they were much more distant than he had at first assumed—creatures of a far greater size than men, the least of them perhaps twelve feet tall and some twice that.

And then the black engine in the midst of the swarming horde turned, a sinuous, immense unwinding, a flowing of its intention, and Philip felt its baleful scrutiny, knew that he was regarded by something malevolent and ancient, a shifting viscous mass. And his reason, like a slippery city shoe coming down on a newly-mopped linoleum floor, skittered and he sought to give the creature a name, and his mind said, "Shoggoth" for those were the ghastly, golemlike creations of the Old Ones and surely that was what now turned a cold and palpable scrutiny upon him. These creatures had, for a time, broken free of their masters and waged a terrible war. Perhaps this was one of the renegades.

Philip turned and ran toward the door. In an instant, the distant monster was racing toward him, accompanied by a horrid rending sound, as though its own protoplasmic flesh were tearing as it moved. Philip looked back and saw the sputtering green eyes burn on the crest of its motion. Like a black cloud of flies, its loathsome winged compatriots hovered over it.

A strange, musical scream filled the air, "Tekeli-li! Tekeli-li!" and Philip felt volition abandon him. The door in front of him shrunk to the size of a cigar box, and as he watched, it swung open toward him, and poor Amelia, attired primly in a brown suit, entered the room. A doll-sized version of Amelia, with long eyelashes and clownlike circles of rouge on her cheeks.

"Philip," she began, and then her eyes widened, comically, the overblown acting of a silent film, and she said "Aw shit."

And the raging Shoggoth overtook them both, tumbling them into the fetid dark of the waiting abyss.

Philip awoke sweating and blinked at the clock on the end table. Glowing red numbers announced that it was three o'clock. It seemed that it was three in the morning more often than it was any other time. The explanation was no doubt sinister and had something to do with the control the System possessed over time itself.

Having thought this, Philip groaned. Why fight cosmic forces?

He got up, turned on his computer and sat

before the green screen. The cursor pulsed like a drugged, rectangular heart.

He wrote for awhile on his novel. He had been writing on this novel for so long, through so many incarnations, that he thought of it as a beast he fed. *Why couldn't Amelia understand?*

Today he wrote, `"They slept in the woods that night having fled the giant, ravening dogs. In the morning, they set their faces into the sun and marched, at a good clip, toward the cliffs of Leng."`

Philip wrote for two hours and then saved what he had written. The blank screen remained, and on that he typed, in all caps, `MONICA IS A ZOMBIE. THEY ARE HERE NOW! THEY HAVE SNIFFED ME OUT. THEY COME AT ME, AS ALWAYS, IN DREAMS. BUT I SENSE THAT THEY WON'T SETTLE FOR JUST RUINING MY SLEEP. THEY HAVE LOST PATIENCE, I THINK.`

Philip saved this too, under the file name "zombie" and turned his computer off. He went to bed then and did not wake until noon when Amelia called.

She was excited. "I just got back from orientation," she said. "I think this job is going to be great."

"I hope so," Philip said.

Amelia heard the caution there. "Hey, come on. Be positive."

Before brushing his teeth, before shaving, before taking a shower, Philip turned his computer on and added this to the zombie file: WHEN THEY COME, THEY COME IN A RUSH. THEY ATTACK ON ALL FRONTS.

Once Philip understood Monica's altered state, he marveled that none of the other employees saw the obvious. Bingham, of course, had remarked on the change, but even he missed the darker truth.

You could even see the stitched incision where they had gone in and tinkered with her brain. It was at the nape of her neck, a two-inch straight line, and while it was generally hidden by her hair, it was easily visible when she leaned forward to study her computer screen.

And didn't anyone notice that Monica Gibson was no longer interested in Lucille Ball? Well, no, of course not, because these were *new* people. They did not know that Monica was an insufferable fan of the original *I Love Lucy* show and all its interminable incarnations. Monica could—and would—quote entire episodes. Like all fanatics, she found it inconceivable that others did not share her enthusiasm, and she even had audio cassette tapes of Lucy material which she played incessantly.

Not anymore. No Lucy tapes. No Lucy stories. No Lucy dialogue. And anyone who had known Monica prior to hospitalization would not have missed this transformation, as noteworthy as, say, a born-again Christian suddenly forswearing mention of Jesus or salvation.

As soon as Philip understood that Monica was now externally operated, much became clear. Her zombie-hood explained her boss' new, cavalier manner with her. In the past, Ralph had always been a little frightened of Monica, fearing she would quit. Now he spoke to her without cringing or wringing his hands, and he abandoned all the wheedling body language and facial expressions of supplication that he had previously used to urge her on.

"I need this, this and this," he would say, dumping the papers on her desk.

Monica would nod rhythmically, like an addled geriatric on a porch swing.

One weekend several weeks later, Philip talked Amelia into going to a movie. Her resolve not to see him until he destroyed the novel that came between them had been weakened by her delight in her new job. The movie they saw was about a lot of postwar baby boomers who were living in California and experiencing mid-life crises that caused them to drive expensive cars very fast, have sex with shallow people, and question the value of their jobs as movie directors, fashion designers, and architects.

After the movie, Philip and Amelia went to The Magnolia Cafe.

Amelia looked different, her features sharper somehow. He realized that her hair was newly cut. Pale-orange lipstick made her mouth seem oddly childlike, and when she briefly put on large, round glasses to study the menu, Philip felt a pang of protectiveness and something approaching panic.

Amelia talked about her new job at Pelidyne.

"I'm learning all about computer graphics," she said.

Philip listened with a growing sense of dismay.

Amelia told a humorous anecdote about her coworker, Thelma, who had worked at Pelidyne for thirteen years.

"Don't," Philip wanted to shout, "become too attached to your coworkers."

Philip studied the restaurant's walls, which were covered with the watercolors of a local artist who appeared to be obsessed with frogs and their relationship to extremely large, nude women.

"Mr. Grayson says I'm a very quick learner," Amelia said. "He says most people who already know about computers can't figure the database out because..."

"The Dada base?" Philip said. "Ah." Worry muddled him. When the waiter came to the table and tried to engage them in a discussion of Umberto Eco's latest novel, Philip waved the man away.

"Philip, are you okay?" Amelia asked.

"I've had a bad week," Philip said. "Bad dreams."

Amelia frowned. "I'm sorry. I still think you might look into some group therapy."

"I have a therapist," Philip said, noting some coolness in his voice.

"Yes, I met her, remember. She's kind of old, isn't she? And just what are her credentials?"

"Well, she's still alive," Philip said, wondering just why he was growing suddenly irritable. "She's old and still alive, those are certainly credentials."

Later, he drove Amelia to her house and

kissed her on the cheek under the porch light that was exploding with fat white moths and brown beetles that pinged against the screen door. In the past they had been lovers. He had stuck his tongue in her belly button. Now he planted a chaste kiss on her cheek. It was depressing.

When Philip climbed back in his car and shut the door, he said, "I love you Amelia Price." There was no comfort in the statement, which was, in truth, only an acknowledgment of the increasing scope of his dread.

Philip found Pelidyne's address in the phone book and drove by the building on his way to work. It was a shiny black building, windowed with cold black glass suggesting hostile takeovers, a towering, five-sided, arrogantly modern structure on San Jacinto. The sides of the building were not of equal length, and this added to its sinister aspect. Was this the loathsome, non-Euclidean geometry of ancient R'lyeh, that reason-defying, accursed city where dread Cthulhu waited to be reborn?

Philip didn't have time to stop and examine the building's interior. He was already late for work.

The job was uneventful that night. Monica worked throughout Philip's shift and was still there when Philip left. She did not look very good; there were dark circles under her eyes and her brown hair had lost what lustre it once had. She had, if Philip wasn't mistaken, worn the same black jeans and tie-dyed T-shirt for a week now. Philip was not surprised. Zombies, of course, take no pride in their appearance.

"Moving right along," she said to Philip when he first sat down. It was the only thing she said directly to Philip during the course of his shift.

Ralph came into the room several times, snatched illegible orders from an ancient fax machine, and handed them to Monica without a word.

After work, Philip picked up his mail from the P.O. box at the apartment complex's main office.

Philip lay in bed and opened his mail. There was an advertisement for cut-rate computer software, a bill for utilities, and a package from his mother. She had sent a belated Christmas present.

"I hope you are well," his mother wrote, "and that all your self-destructive behavior is behind you."

The present, wrapped in cartoon cats, was a thin, hard-backed book whose title Philip had seen on recent bestseller lists. The book was entitled *A Wind Through My Heart*, and it was about a free-spirited woman (Leslie) who travels the Midwest selling cosmetics door-to-door. She meets a man (Mark) whose wife, a wealthy businesswoman, is away on a business trip. Mark and Leslie have a brief affair, making wild love, quoting the poetry of Rod McKuen, and recreating each other with eyeliner and lipstick. In the course of their affair, they utter lethal amounts of bad poetry. Leslie, breathless with lovemaking, says, "I am the wisp and the willow and all the perfumes and all the nostrils in the rain and the sun."

Mark replies, "And I am old movies and the popcorn you don't eat for fear of getting fat and wet, mushy kisses in the rain."

Their love is doomed, however. Mark's wife is about to return. He can't leave her; the whole town would say that he only married her for her money. That is, in fact, why he married her, but it would be cruel to make it known, and Mark is nothing if not sensitive.

So they part, Mark and Leslie, never to see each other again. They both drift about in post-romantic swoons until Leslie dies in her late seventies. Mark dies soon afterward, and his children discover that he has kept a diary, reeking strongly of perfume, and a picture of himself dressed as Marlene Dietrich. In the diary, he analyzes his old lover's poetry at great length and urges his children to make his love affair known to the world. The children, having as little sense of decorum as their father, do just this.

Philip closed the book. He felt dazed, disoriented. It was a thin book, perhaps thirty-five thousand words.

His mother had written, "It is good to see that literature is still being written in these cynical times. I'm sure you will enjoy this as much as I did."

Philip *had* enjoyed the book. He had laughed heartily, startled into outloud guffaws by certain inflated passages. But this, alas, was not the response the book was supposed to elicit.

Philip eyed his own manuscript, or rather the large box it rested in, and thought, not for the first time, that he was out of sync with his times. His book was probably half-a-million words and its vision was bleak.

The next day at work, during a late-night break, Philip told Al Bingham about *A Wind Through My Heart*.

Bingham, who looked unhappy and older, glared at Philip. "You want sympathy or what? You read some crappy little book, some emotional cheesecake, and you say, 'What is this? How come people are buying this?' I'll tell you why. Because they like it. People are getting dumber everyday. Television is shrinking the brain back to a streamlined, reptile model. Evolution has come to its senses and realized all the fancy bells and whistles just take up space. You didn't notice this was happening?"

One printer had quit that night and another had called in sick, so Bingham was snowed under with print jobs and consequently in a foul mood. Philip knew better than to argue with him. He went back to his computer terminal and sat down next to Monica. He typed for about fifteen minutes and then realized that Monica was staring at him. He turned and looked at her.

"I love you," Monica said.

Philip, who had been working diligently on a résumé for a young man whose employment experience consisted of delivering pizzas and newspapers and who was seeking a mid-level position with a high-tech firm, blinked into Monica's dark, rapt gaze.

"I beg your pardon," Philip said.

Monica was leaning forward slightly, like a drunk about to vomit or confide some awful crime. "You heard me," she said. There were dark shadows under her eyes and her forehead was white and shiny and dotted with small, bright beads of perspiration.

Before Philip could reply, Monica returned to her terminal and began typing furiously. Without looking at Philip, she muttered, "There, I have said it. It's done."

Monica said nothing else to Philip the whole shift, and when he left, she did not look up.

The next day, Philip drove to Pelidyne and waited in the lobby for Amelia. The lobby was big, way beyond human scale, and Philip imagined tall, conical creatures from the cold reaches of space sliding on their pseudopods across the marble floor.

Dear God, not again.

Amelia came out of the elevator wearing a brown suit. She came walking briskly across the wide room with the preoccupied smile of a novice tightrope walker. New job, new shoes.

They ate at a nearby delicatessen. Amelia talked with great animation about her job, about the eccentricities of her boss, Mr. Grayson, about the confusion caused by the updating of a software program, and Thelma Karnes' outburst during the meeting on the upcoming office picnic.

Philip was unsettled by Amelia's regular use of the first person plural. "We had to decide whether or not it was worth it to make a concentrated effort with the Briggs account. We came to the conclusion..."

"There is no 'we'!" Philip wanted to shout. *Watch out!* The landscape was littered with traumatized ex-team players, mice the cats enlisted for feline enterprises.

Slowly, during the course of the meal, Amelia shook the spell of Pelidyne.

Philip told her about Monica's declaration of love.

Amelia giggled, which was a legitimate response but which depressed Philip somehow.

He changed the subject. He asked about her sister.

Amelia said she hadn't been getting along with her sister. It wasn't her sister's fault. It was just time to move out.

"You could move in with me," Philip said.

"How's the novel coming along?" Amelia asked.

He dropped her off at Pelidyne and drove back to his apartment under grim, overcast skies.

He entered his apartment and emptied the pots and pans and put them back on the carpet in preparation for the approaching rainstorm. He called the apartment's management office.

"They still haven't fixed that leak?" a woman asked. She was sympathetic, but incapable of doing anything about the matter. Maintenance, like the government of a foreign country or the price of gasoline, was sadly beyond her human control. "Tomorrow is supposed to be sunny," she said, by way of consolation.

Philip hadn't expected anything to come of the call, and so was not disappointed. Indeed, disappointment would have required hope. The room had a dank, moldy smell these days, and the ceiling had bloomed with brown shapes suggestive of monstrous creatures and unholy alliances of peeling plaster and rotting flesh.

The damp accounted for a respiratory infection that afflicted Philip, causing his breathing to be labored. The thin notes that sounded in his chest would wake him out of a fitful slumber, terrified that what he heard was not of this earth.

He made himself work on his novel.

They reached the dark red sea and came down to the beach, as white and terrifying as typewriting paper. Masters reached down and scooped up a handful of sand.

"My God," he said. "Look."

"What is it?" Daphne asked, but the professor said nothing. She saw the horror in his eyes, and then discovered the same within her soul as the white pebbles and dust came into grim focus.

She looked upon teeth, a handful of bleached, shattered teeth, mixed with a rubble of bone shards and a fine, gray grit of blessedly unidentifiable origin. A vast, white arc of this material stretched out beneath their feet, and Daphne found herself thinking, quite against her will, of the sea itself, and what might lie beneath it.

The writing cheered Philip up, and he found he was able to go to work despite the sure knowledge that Monica would be there, full of funereal love.

That night when he went down the hall to the vending machines, she followed him.

They stood watching the wheel lurch forward.

Without looking at Philip, Monica said, "If you was to try to kiss me, I wouldn't stop you."

"Well," Philip said. He got a Snickers and returned to his computer. He could feel Monica's eyes on him. He saw himself kissing her—the curse of an irrepressible imagination—and felt his body grow numb and cold, paralyzed with icy dread.

"See you," Monica said when he left that night.

hen Philip entered Ralph's office, Ralph hurriedly shoved the book (a massive, brown tome as battered and frayed as a seminarian's Bible) into a desk drawer. The book, Philip was certain, was the *Necronomicon*, that dark book of forbidden knowledge written by the mad Arab Abdul Alhazred. Ralph Pederson's expression, equal measures of guilt and diffidence, seemed to confirm this.

Philip's employer was looking particularly disheveled. He wore a tie, but it was loosened and tossed back over his shoulder. His eyes were red and every hair on his body, including his eyebrows, seemed to bristle. His suit coat lay on the floor, a brown, enervated off-the-rack garment that seemed destined for a soup line.

Ralph stood up. "I'm going to have to ask you to knock before you come in here," he said. "I try to maintain a casual atmosphere. I want my employees to feel they can come and talk to me whenever they have a problem, but knocking is a small courtesy."

Philip said that he had knocked.

"You are going to have to knock louder," Pederson said. "My hearing is not what it used to be. This is not a quiet profession I'm in. Printing presses are louder than a whisper. Not that I'm complaining. They are silent enough when there is no business. I'm grateful for the roar of the presses."

"Yes," Philip said.

"Well, what is it?"

Philip sat down. He was already doubting the impulse that had sent him to his boss' office. Why make an issue of it? No one else seemed to mind. Indeed, Philip suspected he was the only one who read the things.

"It's this," Philip said. "This motivational pamphlet."

Philip handed it to Ralph, who smiled and read the title out loud, "Loyalty Counts" and nodded his head. "Yes, that it does."

Ralph smiled and leaned forward on his elbows, shoulders hunched to indicate a listening mode.

"Well," Philip said, "I've just thought that whoever your vendor is for these pamphlets... well, he may have... the tone of these things has become increasingly shrill, and I am not sure that they are really serving a positive function anymore."

"Oh really?" Ralph Pederson's eyebrows lifted. "I haven't heard any other complaints."

Nobody else reads them, Philip wanted to say. But he didn't; he said, "Well, this one, for instance—"

Ralph interrupted. "You know, I believe strongly in these messages. They are brief, certainly. We are all busy here and no one has the time for lengthy tracts, but I think that an occasional thoughtful word can make all the difference. They don't give me these things for free, Philip. If I didn't think they had a morale-building effect, I wouldn't spend good money for them. I could take that money and throw myself a party, I guess, hire a couple of hookers, a case of beer, balloons, the whole works. But I spend that money on my employees, and, by and large, they are grateful, I think."

"Well," Philip said, "I appreciate that. But I'm not sure—"

Ralph interrupted. "Times are hard," he said. "The economy here is not what you are used to. You're from California, right?"

"Ah, no. I'm from—"

"And I know you've got a wife, and she has got a right to be worried about your career, and—"

"I'm not married," Philip said.

Ralph waved this away with a scowl, as though it were an argument unworthy of Philip.

Ralph stood up and came around the desk. He put an arm around Philip's shoulder. "We've all got to work together or we'll all go under. It's as simple as that. I can't tell you how sick I am of being thought of as the villain. My God, I work long hours; I buy pizza for the whole crew when a little extra money turns up in the till, and I, for one, treasure and appreciate loyalty. I don't think loyalty is a joke, and I don't think it is any great inconvenience to ask you folks to spend just a minute thinking about the concept yourselves."

"It's not that," Philip said, "It's this. Listen."

He read the beginning of the motivational pamphlet:

How would you feel if, right after the wedding ceremony, your wife turned to you and said she was leaving you for the best man? If your answer is "discouraged" or "betrayed" then you can sympathize with the plight of many modern employers. For far too many employees, loyalty is a dead word. Employees are job-hopping at the first sign of adversity. If they aren't given a raise during their first month on the job, they are out the door. If the economy takes a turn for the worse and the boss asks everyone to be patient and hang in without a raise, all he gets is a lot of blank, cold stares. "Tough luck," Mr. Gimee says, "I'm out of here."

But if you think loyalty is dead and buried, you just might have another think coming. One disgruntled employee, let's call him Bob, quit his job when his employer, suffering heavy financial losses from real estate deals gone sour, was forced to cut employee salaries in order to meet the overhead. Bob left and found himself being interviewed by another employer. This employer said, "I see, Bob, that you have lots of experience, but I see that you have rarely worked at a job for over two years. I am afraid this sort of job-hopping is not what we are looking for. We suspect that you won't be happy here either, that the minute the going gets rough, you will be gone. Frankly, we are looking for people who have worked at one place for a very long time, and who are now seeking employment due to a layoff or the dissolution of their company. I wish I could hire you, but I can't. If you are fortunate enough to find an employer that will overlook this record of discontented drifting, I hope you will give him the loyalty he deserves. That's loyalty spelled L-O-Y-A-L-T-Y."

Philip stopped and tossed the pamphlet on the desk, resting his case. There was more, in the same vein, but surely the portion he had read was sufficient.

"Well?" Ralph said. "Are you suggesting that loyalty is spelled differently? Are you suggesting that it is an outmoded virtue, and that these pamphlets are old-fashioned or corny?"

"No, of course not," Philip said, wondering just what sort of mental aberration *was* responsible for this interview. "I am just not convinced that these pamphlets are really that positive. They seem to be weighted toward—"

"Phil, it's a hard world we live in. It's getting harder all the time. I guess there are some hard truths in these little pamphlets"—here Ralph picked the tract up and waved it between his thumb and index finger— "but we can't just stick our heads in the sand. No sir, we have to come to grips with the issues. I offer an honest wage for an honest hour, and I don't think it is too much to ask for a little goddam respect and loyalty because it is my goddam money that is paying the goddam salaries and there is not a goddam day goes by that I don't worry about letting everyone down. You see me in this office late at night. You think I am sitting in here reading goddam *Penthouse* magazine or snorting cocaine? I am in here working my ass off so that we don't go under. I'm doing it for all of you. Why hell, if anything, this pamphlet isn't strong enough. It doesn't talk about the kind of loyalty we employers have. It's a kind of loyalty that burns your guts out, I can tell you that. My doctor says I've got an ulcer that could win prizes."

Ralph ran a hand over his face, as though testing to see if his features were still intact and not irreparably distorted by emotion. He sighed. His shoulders sagged.

"I'm glad we had this talk," he said. "I think it has helped clear the air." Philip realized he was dismissed.

Philip returned to his computer terminal.

In all caps, on the screen, someone had typed,

I'M NOT WEARING ANY UNDERWEAR

Philip turned and saw Monica, her ragged smile full of salacious intent. Philip cleared the screen.

He left work early, punching out without saying goodby to Monica. It was raining hard and the highway was crisscrossed with small, treacherous rivers. Philip took an early exit—to avoid an accident, he thought. When he found himself on the street where Amelia was rooming with her sister, he realized his subconscious had plans of its own.

The lights were on in her house, so he pulled up to the curb and got out. He'd just say hi. Maybe she'd offer him a cup of coffee. It was a little after nine, not late really, and maybe he could talk to her about MicroMeg. They never talked about it, and—really—they had to.

It wasn't Philip's novel that had torn them apart. It was MicroMeg—and what had happened there.

Philip darted out of his car and into the earnest rain. He made the porch and was pushing the doorbell when he noticed, out of the corner of his eye, that the driveway contained a second car, something silver, low to the ground and polished.

A broken gutter uttered a thin stream of water that licked the back of Philip's neck.

A reservation, a doubt, flared like an arsonist's match. Then the door opened, and Philip blinked at a broad, muscled chest.

"Yeah?" The man was wearing red briefs and nothing else.

A woman, dark-haired and wearing a blue negligee, clung to the man's right arm. Philip knew Amelia's sister from his days of watching the house. She looked at Philip and said, "Who's this?" She turned and licked the man's bicep.

The man said, "You got me."

"Rita? Who's there?" Amelia pushed past the two of them.

"Philip," she said.

"Hi," Philip said.

Amelia was wearing a yellow bathrobe. The make-up was gone from her face, and she looked defenseless. A dab of cold cream adorned the end of her nose.

"I got off work, early," Philip said. "Thought I'd drop by."

"Yeah," Amelia said.

The man and the dark-haired woman had gone away from the door. The woman suddenly laughed, a piercing, lascivious shriek, conjuring, somehow, an explicit and precise image of oral high jinks.

Amelia flinched slightly, shoulders rising as though someone had clutched the back of her neck. "That's Robert, Rita's boyfriend," she said. "You can see why I want to move out."

"Yes," Philip said.

"Are you okay?" Amelia asked.

"I'm fine," Philip said. "I guess I should have called. I'll talk to you later."

He left, driving home in a state of heightened misery.

He could not sleep and so worked furiously on his novel, as though he might actually flee to that fictional land where he ruled—admittedly over a disenfranchised crew that no one wanted and that one editor had called "implausible, unmotivated madmen."

He sat typing furiously, crouched over his computer as the rain came through the ceiling and an army of pots and pans uttered froglike exclamations of delight.

The novel could not shelter him. He kept seeing Amelia's face. The thought bloomed wickedly in his mind, inspired by the arrogant male loutishness of bikini-briefed Robert: *What if she finds someone else?*

In the morning, Amelia called. "I'm sorry," she said. "You can see why I have to get my own place."

He could.

After the call, he got out of bed and showered. The cast had been removed two days ago, and its absence felt unnatural. He still couldn't move his leg at the knee and had been instructed in various exercises to restore muscle tone. He scrubbed the pale flesh and the bright scar at the knee. He thought about the general flimsiness of human beings, and the specific, blown-glass fragility of Philip Kenan.

As he came out of the shower, the phone rang again.

"Philip Kenan?"

"Yes," Philip said, instantly wary, always ready for bad news.

"My name is Richard Klausner, and I'm an editor at Wingate House here in New York."

Wingate House, Philip thought. Maybe the second biggest independent publisher out there.

"Sorry we took so long getting back to you, but nobody here knew what to make of your book. I loved it, but you know how it is, you have got to get a lot of heads nodding in unison these days before you can do anything. Everyone said, 'Yeah, sure, Richard, maybe you didn't notice, this book is two thousand pages long. And this guy Kenan is nobody, not Norman Mailer, not Stephen King, not Jackie Collins. We are talking an unknown author, with no track record, dropping a thirty dollar plus book on a sluggish market. Forget it.'" Klausner paused, chuckled.

"They had a point," he said. "But I was ready for them. Listen. See how this sounds. I said, 'You're right. We can't do that. I understand that. So forget a two-thousand-page book. Think five books.'" Klausner stopped speaking abruptly. Philip leaned into the receiver's silence, expecting more. The silence expanded.

"Well, what do you think?" Klausner finally asked.

"I don't follow you," Philip said.

"Five books," Klausner repeated. "We take *The Despicable Quest*, and we chop it into five neat, marketable, repeat-business, cycling sales fantasy novels. That's what I told them. And guess what, Philip?"

"Ah—" Philip said.

"Yep, they loved it. You are in. Congratulations."

Philip hardly heard the rest of the conversation. He had sold his novel. After years of labor, after it had developed a bloated life of its own and had come to seem more of a parasite than a potential breadwinner, it had sold.

Philip called Amelia back but got no answer. He realized, then, that she was at work, had probably called from there during a break. He didn't have that number. He decided he would call her from Ralph's that evening.

With a moment to think, he realized that Amelia might not be delighted with this news. She hated the book, after all.

That night, Bingham congratulated him, shaking his hand gravely. "May it bring you no grief," he said. They stood in the back door of the shop while Bingham smoked a cigarette. Rain hissed across the parking lot and the sky trembled with lightning. Thunder was a constant, no-nonsense, mean-dog growl rolling from massive cloud-speakers.

"I can't believe I have finally sold this book," Philip said.

Philip was so cheered by his sudden good fortune that he even announced the news to Monica.

Philip hadn't expected much enthusiasm, zombies being notoriously reserved. Her reaction was heated. She glared at Philip.

"I guess you'll get famous now," she said. "I guess you will quit here. I guess it is all over between us."

She turned quickly back to her keyboard and began banging the keys with savage fury.

Yes, I'll quit, Philip thought. Editor Klausner had suggested a ten-thousand-dollar advance for the first in the series. "I'm sending along a contract and the names of a few agents. You might like to get an agent before going ahead on this. This sort of multiple book series deal can be a little trickier than the standard contract."

Ralph Pederson flew by, snapping an order from the fax and dropping it on Monica's table.

I'm quitting, Philip thought. The impulse was to grab Ralph as he raced by and say, "I quit," but Philip found an equal exhilaration in holding the knowledge within him where it sang with self-contained power.

Philip had had a lot of jobs in his life. The euphoria of quitting a bad job was rivaled only by good sex. In the endless series of job interviews that were a direct consequence of this quitting ecstasy, Philip had often fantasized of a time when he was rich. He would continue, he thought, to go on interviews. He would listen to the fat man with three chins say, "We are important people handling important documents written by important people, and it is imperative that we work efficiently. I want you to tell me why you feel you would be a real asset to our team. What skills and insights could you bring us? What...."

He would let the words wash over him. He would nod his head and look rabbit-scared and at the end of the interview, he would shake the man's hand and thank him, as unctuous as Uriah Heep, and he would walk out of the office, past all the desks of bored secretaries and clerks and typists and photocopiers, and he would take the stale elevator, crowded with men in wrinkled, sweat-permeated suits. He would land in the air-conditioned moonscape of the lobby, and he would walk quickly across the marble floor, push the glass doors open, and step into the sunlight, the slow, ponderous heat of Austin's summer, and he would shout, as though calling down angels, "I'm rich. I don't have to work there. I don't *ever* have to work there." He would feel as clean and clear as a pilgrim purged of sin at a holy shrine.

"Dear God thank you," he would shout, falling to his knees in a green square of city park. And by that means, he would never grow jaded or indifferent to his freedom.

The computer screen in front of Philip flickered, and Philip's heart jumped, as it always did at such moments. If the electricity went out, the computer went down and the file was lost if it hadn't been saved. Quickly, Philip saved the job and continued keyboarding. Thunder shook the building.

To Philip's left, Monica typed quickly and angrily. He could observe her blurred, stocky form out of the corner of his eye. As Philip watched, she banged the keys with one last dramatic flourish, saving the file and clearing the screen. Then she got up and marched out of the room.

Philip remembered that he had intended to call Amelia. He punched her number and she answered on the first ring.

Her voice cheered him instantly, and when he told her the good news she shouted with genuine delight.

Philip felt a sense of intense relief. "I thought you might not be happy for me. I mean, I know how you feel about the book."

"No," Amelia said. "I don't think you do. You think I hate it, and I don't. I've just hated the way it *ruled* you. Now, you see, they will be taking it away from you. It will be finished; it won't be so suffocating... so dominating. It will be just a novel in a bookstore."

Philip didn't entirely understand her reasoning, but he was pleased that she was happy for him. "Great news, isn't it?"

"It is."

"Bitch."

"What?"

"Bitch. Cheap little cunty bitch..."

Amelia's voice faltered. "Philip. What..."

"Monica! Get off the line!" Philip shouted. "This is a private conversation. Get off."

"Bitch, bitch," Monica muttered. She sounded as though she were speaking through mud.

"Amelia," Philip shouted. "Look, I'll call you back. I'll call you right back, okay?"

"Sleazy cheap dirty slut bitch..."

"Philip?"

"Amelia, I'll call you right back."

"Well, okay."

"Bitch cunt..."

Philip heard the click as Amelia hung up. He dropped the receiver and ran out into the hall. He paused, listening. He could hear her voice, rolling on in a guttural litany of invective. He ran toward it.

She sat behind Mrs. Burrell's desk, muttering into the phone.

"Monica," Philip said, standing in the doorway. "What do you think you are doing?"

Monica looked up. She grinned and giggled evilly, the phone poised at her ear. The only light in the room came from a small desk lamp that sent its yellow rays upward into her eyes. Her single eyebrow, in combination with the long, blasted shadows, created a sardonic, ghastly effect.

"I'm giving your bimbo a piece of my mind," Monica said. "I'm telling her to fucking mind her own fucking business."

"There's nobody on the phone," Philip said. "She hung up."

Monica scowled, dropped the receiver. She swept the phone off the desk. It clattered impressively, made a single *jing* sound.

"What do you want with a bitch like that? What can she type? Maybe forty words a minute, max, I bet. Ha! You are not saying different because it's true. I bet she couldn't tell Helvetica from Times. What do you want with a bitch like that?" Monica laughed, leaping an octave in mid-laugh as though goosed by invisible demons of injustice.

"Don't apologize," Monica screamed—a superfluous injunction. "I don't know why I bother. You fucking men are all the same. Probably she's got a bubble ass and tits like headlights on a jeep and that's plenty to make you forget about me. But you couldn't just come right out and tell me there was someone else. I had to find it out. I had to pick up the phone and there she was, breathing and squealing like one of those nine hundred numbers."

"Monica," Philip said. "You are insane. There was never anything between you and me."

"Ha!" Monica said. She yanked the desk drawer open, fumbled through it, looked up. "Ha," she repeated. She looked down again and returned to her search of the desk drawer. A third "ha" brought her head up with a smile of triumph. "We'll see about what's between us."

She waved the brass letter opener in her right hand.

Just then a loud bark of thunder made the window pane hum, and the desk lamp and the hall light faltered and failed. The room dove into darkness except for the small, stuttering square of the window where lightning seemed to jump in sync with Monica's choked laughter.

Philip pushed away from the office door, for he had seen, in the jerky, strobe-parsed images of the storm, Monica's raised hand and unmistakably murderous intent.

He stumbled backward, heard her in front of him, moving fast. He pushed away and ran, as fast as his gimp leg would allow, down the hall.

Slam! His nose flared with pain. What was that? Of course. The goddam, monster filing cabinet that reduced the hall to a one-man corridor for about ten feet. The goddam, awful—

His shoulder erupted in pain. Monica leaned forward and screamed in his ear.

Again. She jabbed him again, the blade glancing off a rib.

Jesus God. He flailed wildly. His elbow connected with something, her jaw, he thought. She grunted and lurched backward.

Philip scrambled forward, each file drawer knob banging his injured rib with that petty love of torture that characterizes inanimate objects. He burst into the lobby; vinyl sofas pulsed with the beat of the lightning. It was after office hours. The doors would be locked. He had a key, but it was the fourth or fifth generation, and it required some jiggling and Monica was behind him and filled with insane, scorned fury and strength.

Philip fled toward the back of the building, banging through swinging doors in the dark, bouncing off more cabinets. There were people back in printing. Charlie and that new guy Owen, Mowen, whatever. And Bingham, of course.

Strength in numbers. *Put that goddam shiv down Ms. Gibson. As you can plainly see, you are outnumbered. You are—* This hope, bright and energizing, lived for perhaps two seconds. Lights rolled across the far wall, twin orbs, headlights, and Philip followed their course to the window as the car rolled by through the rain. There went the printers. They would be doing what they always did when the electricity went off. Taking a break. Flying down to the local Seven-Eleven for a couple of cold ones.

Down time in the storm.

Philip heard something crash behind him. "Hey!" Monica screamed. "Philip."

Philip banged through swinging doors and into the back storeroom. He collided immediately with stacked boxes of paper, toppled forward, righted himself. It was before-god dark here, no windows, and there was an overpowering burnt-sulphur reek.

The acrid scent of the Old Ones, the smell of Time itself.

No. This was not a good time for exercising the imagination. The dirty lung-clogging smoke came from the thermography presses, overheated again.

He heard the doors bang behind him, felt a gust of cooler air.

He needed a weapon, something to hit with. He felt the shelves behind him. Something shifted, tipped, and it seemed then like a hundred, a thousand cockroaches tumbled over him, danced across his face, his neck...

"Ugh—"

He brushed them from his face. *Business cards* Surprise.

What a mess you are, he thought. *What an inept, dismal buffoon. What—*

Monica embraced him.

He fell back against the shelf and more boxes shifted, a rain of small, cardboard appeals.

Monica pushed her face toward him. Her breath was coated with the licorice cough drops she ate like candy.

She kissed his cheek.

There were hissing things in the dark now, things possessed of alien teeth and talons, and although the darkness was absolute, Philip could sense their writhing, feel the darkness folding and looping upon itself and hear a sound that was not the wind or the rain or any of the scuffling sounds he made as he struggled on the concrete floor, and he *had to get out of there*.

Monica sought his lips.

He was no longer afraid of her. He was not afraid of her deranged passion or the possibility that she still had the letter opener and meant to thrust it into his heart. The fear of Monica had been trumped, effortlessly, by the hideous things that floated over her, the minions of Yog-Sothoth, the outcast, star-headed creatures, the Shub-Niggurath, Yig, the Mi-Go, Tsathoggua.

He had to get away.

He struggled to his feet in the dark. She clung to him. He clutched her shoulders, shook her savagely, and hurled her from him. He ran, colliding with more boxes, sprawling forward. He could almost see the cold, lidless eyes, the size and shape of dinner plates.

Someone was shouting; not Monica, a man's voice.

Boxes slid under him as he crawled forward. His palm touched the dirty concrete floor; he pulled himself forward and stood up again.

Just then the lights went on. Machines, alert again, fidgeted mechanically, hummed.

"Philip! Monica!"

A figure strode toward Philip.

"Ralph," Philip said.

"Philip—My God!"

Ralph darted past Philip. Philip turned. Monica was flat on her back between two metal shelves. Ralph clutched her ankles and dragged her forward.

Philip ran to help.

"What the hell happened?" Ralph asked.

Monica was unconscious and she did not appear to be breathing. There was blood on her forehead. Several quarter-sized red bruises decorated her cheek.

Ralph was shaking his head and muttering. Philip leaned forward and sought a pulse.

She's dead, he thought, reaching to touch her throat. The carotid artery was silent. Something flickered under the corner of one of the metal cabinets, a last segmented tentacle withdrawing. Of course. The symmetry of those welts on

Monica's cheek could be one thing only, the mark of biting suckers, the track of a monster's caress.

"Let's get her down to my office," Ralph said.

They staggered and dragged her down the hall to the office, cleared a space on Ralph's desk, and laid her out on her back.

Ralph wiped sweat from his forehead. "I don't need this," he said. "I goddam don't need this. We are already behind schedule."

Philip picked up the phone, punched 911.

Ralph grabbed the phone away from Philip. "What the fuck do you think you are doing?" he asked. He slammed the receiver down.

"I was calling an ambulance," Philip said. "She's—" *She's dead.* "She's really hurt."

"She's fine," Ralph said, absently patting her head. "She just fainted or something. She'll come around."

"No."

Ralph leaned forward across Monica's still form and shouted in Philip's face, propelling flecks of spittle. "Look, I can't spare her! I goddam can't spare her. This is a goddam business, and it can't have everybody lying around in bed recuperating from one thing or another—pleasant as that might be."

Philip shouted back, "She's dead!" There. He had said it.

Ralph shook his head. He shook his head like a dog shaking off water. "No no no no no no no no." He came around the desk in a flurry of arms. "Go home," he shouted, shoving Philip toward the door. "I'll handle this."

Ralph proved to have surprising strength, and Philip found himself colliding with the hallway wall. The door slammed behind him.

Philip turned, tried the doorknob. The door was locked. Philip hammered with his fist. "Let me in!" he shouted. "Come on."

Philip threw his shoulder against the door. Nothing.

He heard it then, heard the voice. It rose and fell. He pressed his ear against the door panel, but he could not decipher a word. It was his employer's voice, rolling in a kind of liturgical cadence, but the language was—

My God. Was this the corrupt Latin of Olaus Wormius, the forbidden translation, the—

Go home. That was the ticket. Go home. Unlock the lobby door and walk out into the safe haven of thunder and lightning and rain.

Philip moved away from the door. He walked back to his computer. Always the good, always the dutiful employee, he turned the computers off. He turned off the hot wax machine and the photocopier. He punched out and donned his raincoat.

He pushed his collection of pens, his X-acto knife, his ruler, his calculator into his briefcase. He wouldn't be returning.

Walking through the lobby he could hear a deep, humming noise, and the sound of some whispery, flutelike whistle. He jiggled his key in the lock and opened the doors. He stepped out into the rain, which had slowed to a steady, businesslike drizzle.

He turned and saw the green light that poured from the window.

Don't. In Lovecraft it was always the same. They always paused too long. Curiosity always drove them forward. Once the ancient, hideous knowledge pierced them, they were lost.

Don't.

They never had the power to resist.

Philip walked to the window and peered in.

Monica floated in the air above her employer, who held a luminous box in his hands. No, it was a glowing book, that book...

Powerless.

It seemed to Philip that he was not looking at a window at all. He was peering down at a small, rectangular swimming pool. Its green water rippled hypnotically. He stared, leaned forward. He fell.

The window shattered, and the roar of vast engines filled his ear. He hit the floor and rolled, glass crackling in the wet folds of his raincoat. He thrust out a hand to regain his balance; a bitter shard of pain found his palm.

He clutched his bleeding hand and looked up. Monica hovered over him, airborne again. Déjà vu. A green sheath of light surrounded her ample form. She turned slowly, like some inflatable mobile jarred into motion.

Ralph Pederson's hair stood on end. Each word he spoke seemed to erupt from his mouth, a silver, mercurylike bubble that blipped instantly ceilingward as soon as it slid from between his lips.

Philip's eyes turned upward. A loathsome nest of such bubbles spread across the ceiling. At their center was a bright, vertiginous hole. A *rift*.

Ralph Pederson, desperate for good help, was attempting to reanimate Monica Gibson.

As Philip watched, Monica raised one of her arms, and Pederson, heartened by this success, spoke yet more rapidly, the abhorred words ripping from between his teeth like viscous bubbles in molten lead.

Rift.

The hole in the ceiling widened; its radiance filled Philip's head with strange voices, voices grotesque and terrible but also—dear God—familiar.

They were trying to come through. Pederson, that fool, was summoning them.

Philip tried to rise to his knees.

Don't bother, a voice said. *You'll be light as air soon. Trust us.*

Invisible forces held him down. He tried to push upward, and his hand screamed. He felt lighter. Then, instantly, the thick, dead weight returned.

Pain. Pain was the antidote for this unnatural gravity. He reached his good hand across and gripped his bleeding, savaged hand.

I don't want to do this, he thought.

He squeezed. *Jesus!* He stood up. *All right. Okay now.*

The pain abated. His shoulders sagged under sudden pressure. His knees buckled. Back on the planet Jupiter's bone-cracking gravity.

He squeezed again. Screamed. Hurled himself toward Ralph Pederson, who was roaring like Hell's own evangelist as the ceiling cracked open and plaster began to fall like snow from a cement sky.

Philip struck Ralph Pederson with his damaged hand, howled, they both howled, cosmic dogs. The accursed *Necronomicon* slipped from Pederson's grip. Looking like one of the creatures it conjured, it flapped its leathery pages to impede—but not halt—its fall.

Monica also fell, slamming down behind the desk, lost to Philip's line of vision. Philip looked up as he rolled on the floor under his employer's frenzied assault. The ceiling was closing again; the Call had been incomplete.

There was no time for triumph, however. Something in the narrowing crack peered out and saw Philip. An animate darkness, trembling with malevolent rage, it recognized Philip. And he recognized it. Sundered in Time and Space, they had come together again.

Tendrils poured from the ceiling, like the entrails from some unimaginable beast.

Philip might have screamed as the first cold, impossibly cold, pseudopod licked his face, but he was already removed from the place of screaming, floating above the floor where he saw, beneath him, the top of Ralph Pederson's head, thinning hair, narrow shoulders, and beyond Pederson, on the other side of the desk, the dark form of Monica Gibson, moving slowly (but quicker, far quicker than dead), a hand reaching up toward the edge of the desk, pale moon-face staring up at him with an unreadable expression, terror, perhaps, or joy.

She opened her mouth to form a scream or shout, but the world was soundless now in this receding space, this diminishing, this—*No! God Jesus not there!*—this Returning.

PART TWO

THE DOOM THAT CAME TO MICROMEG

e was staring at the horrible gray flesh, long
dead and pocked with Swiss-cheese-like
holes. This was a Wednesday, then. They
always served meatloaf on Wednesdays.

He knew the place, of course. It was the hated
cafeteria at MicroMeg.

But where, exactly, precisely, was *he*? That is,
himself? He had no sense of a body. Was he
incorporeal, a ghost? Was this cafeteria of milling

office drones his purgatory, his hell? A tremor of pure white panic threatened to dissolve his reason.

Just then, he saw a hand—his own; he would have recognized it anywhere—enter the sphere of his vision where the meatloaf and the paste-like mashed potatoes resided dismally on a pea-green plate. The hand held a fork, which speared a square of meatloaf, skated it through tan gravy, and lifted it in the air.

It was clear to Philip that he lodged somewhere in that Cartesian theater that science had abandoned.

Hello? Hello? No answer.

Think.

He knew what had happened. Perhaps that was just enough consolation to keep him from going insane. What had happened was of almost inconceivable horror—but it did have its precedent.

What had happened to Philip was similar to the fate suffered by the narrator of Lovecraft's *The Shadow Out Of Time*. The Great Race had, in the case of that unfortunate man (a professor at Miskatonic University), hurled him back across millions of years to reside in a monstrous, alien body.

In Philip's case, the time leap was only a matter of a few years, and he had landed in his own body.

Thinking of the professor's plight, Philip could summon some measure of gratitude. Things could be worse.

It was disorienting, however. *Hello*. Nothing. He appeared incapable of communicating with himself.

The camera of Philip's consciousness lifted away from the meatloaf as a man approached the table carrying a tray. The man sat down opposite Philip.

It was Ray Barnstable, looking as unsavory as ever, his pale forehead bulging, his eyebrows bristling, his thick glasses enlarging his eyes into orbs of brown incredulity. Philip encountered the old, uneasy sensation that those extraordinary long black hairs that rose above the eyebrow thickets were the antennae of sequestered insects, mole crickets or bugs indigenous to body hair, flat, sinister eyebrow roaches.

I'm really back. Oh Jesus, I'm back.

Maybe he *would* go insane. Locked inside his own mind, he would lose his mind. How would that feel to this Philip Kenan from the past? Would he hear some thin, brief note of gnat-hysteria? Would he experience a brief shiver of disorientation, of vague disquiet? Would he think, "What was that?"

WHANK WHONK WAY.

The noise boomed in an echoing vault.

What? What?

Philip heard himself speak, but the words were an unintelligible roar. He was too close, somehow. Where was the goddam volume control?

"Hey Phil," Ray said, "how's it going?"

WOBAY. *Okay*. You could translate. It was possible. You just had to listen a little differently, a little *distantly*, like seeing in the dark with your peripheral vision.

"You seen that new girl?" Ray said. "The one works down in Personnel? Whoooeeeee." Ray stuffed a forkful of meatloaf in his mouth and washed it down with iced tea. "I might just ask her to take a look at my résumé." Ray laughed. "You reckon she'll say,"—here Ray put a hand under his chin and wriggled fat fingers as he launched his voice an octave higher than usual and imitated a coy maiden— "'Oh, Mr. Barnstable, this résumé is *too* long for little old me.'" Ray laughed, a fat man's body-rocking series of snorts. He stopped abruptly and quickly shoveled meatloaf into his mouth, cleaning the plate with sudden savage fury. Finished, he patted his mouth primly with a napkin.

He leaned forward. "Well, I heard Cowell is out. He pissed in Woodson's pool once too often. He's got nothing, and that talk about going to IBM is a lot of crap. He's finished and he knows it."

WHAB NOT BONE. *I've got to be going.*

Oh it was all familiar. It poured into him with gruesome clarity, with every detail, every footfall on the blue-gray carpet. He was in the basement of MicroMeg, where the cafeteria was lodged, where banks of cold-room computers pontificated, where the storage rooms presided over outmoded equipment and file cabinets of entombed documents, where janitors smoked the nubs of old cigarettes, tossing them out—with a killed-serpent hiss—in the overcast water of dirty mop buckets, where security guards read old copies of *Penthouse* amid guttural bursts of officious two-way radio static, where—where the rituals were performed in preparation for the great Leap.

Dear God, wasn't once enough?

He was staring now at the bulletin board next to the elevator. Someone had cut the article about Merv Wiggins' retirement from the *MicroMeg Monitor* newsletter. There was old Merv, smiling, a death's head grin in the clairvoyant flash of the camera. Old Ronald Bickwithers had his arm around Merv and was waving a glass of champagne in the air.

Okay, Philip thought. *Just where the hell in time have I landed?*

He could figure it out. He could narrow it down. Obviously, he had been transported to a time after Merv's retirement. How long after? Things could stay pinned to the bulletin board for an indefinite amount of time, but in this case, Merv had died less than a month after retiring, so someone would have taken the article down by then, replacing it with the obituary.

Philip studied the contrasty newsprint photo. Merv Wiggins had worked with Philip in the Graphics Support division of MicroMeg. Old Merv. Merv with his crisp white shirts, sleeves rolled up, his harried smile, his crew cut, and his dauntless team spirit. "We can do it," he would say. "It would be nice if they had given us some warning before springing this project on us, but we've got the weekend, and if we all make that extra effort, we'll be golden on this one."

"Golden," Merv would say. "Golden."

Philip remembered the retirement party, held at a Ramada Inn. Ronald Bickwithers, Merv's supervisor, had delivered a rousing testimonial to the man's spirit.

"Old Merv," Bickwithers said, squeezing the man's shoulder. "I hate to see him go. If I was to look in the dictionary under 'dedication' I would find the name Merv Wiggins written there."

Bickwithers told the story with real drama. "It was right after the Ellison Naval project that Merv went into Fairfax hospital. I remember it like it was yesterday. We were just getting the completed boards out the door, and I look around and there is Merv curled up under the drafting table, and I lean under and ask if he is okay, and, you know Merv, he says sure he is just fine but if I would call up an ambulance he would greatly appreciate it."

That was the time they took out half of Merv's stomach. "I figured we wouldn't see him for six months, but three weeks later he's back. It's two in the morning, and I ring up the office expecting to get one of the younger folks, and it is Merv that is there working on a last minute proposal for BeeSams. I tell him to go slow, and he says,

'Going slow didn't make us number one.' I guess if you looked up the word 'trooper' you would find Merv's name there too."

Later Merv had had to have a substantial part of his upper intestines removed. He had been back on the job in less than a month. A number of health problems plagued Merv.

Ronald Bickwithers spoke at length and with some eloquence on Merv's hospitalizations, cataloging, with a pathologist's zeal, the various organs that had been pared down or completely removed from Merv's system. Each time some new physical catastrophe would strike the man, office gossip would have it that he was out for the count. But, invariably, Merv would return and work the youngest and hardiest of them under the table.

"But he came back!" Bickwithers would shout, rising up on the balls of his feet like a preacher full of Good News. "Yes sir, he heard MicroMeg cry out, 'We need your expertise and enthusiasm,' and he didn't turn his back on that cry for help.

You look under 'loyalty' and you'll find the name Merv Wiggins written large there too."

Philip remembered the speech, remembered old Merv bent over and smiling and saying he just did the best he could. It seemed now that when Merv waved his hand in a self-deprecating gesture intended to quell the audience applause, a blue wristband from his last hospitalization was visible next to his watchband, but this may have been one of those details created by a memory more in love with aptness than with accuracy.

In any event, Ronald Bickwithers' words proved so inspirational that two members of the graphics staff left that very day, one of them a paste-up artist, a thin, blond woman who said, "Wow. I'm out of here. I'm hanging on to my spleen."

They filled the vacated paste-up position with Amelia Price.

So, think. When did Amelia get hired? How soon after Merv left? Not long, they were dreadfully understaffed and...

The elevator door opened. It made all the

usual noises, the fanfare of electrical industry: *Hoooooeeeeeeee waaaaaaahummmmmmm*. The door opened.

GO ON AHEAD. I'M WAITING FOR SOMEONE.

Philip could translate now. He had found the secret of parsing the roaring sentences of his host. And Philip knew, of course, why this Philip had lied.

You did not get on the elevator when it was already occupied by Fred Linquest, more commonly referred to as F.F. (Flatulent Freddie). Freddie was a large, shy young man who worked in the mailroom and who, like certain species of fish in tropic waters, kept potential predators at a distance by secreting various noxious poisons. Being paranoid, Freddie saw *all* his fellow workers as dangerous.

Freddie, dark hair hanging in his face, mail cart in front, nodded grimly and pushed the button, closing the door.

Philip caught the next elevator to the fifth floor.

Amelia. She was standing in the middle of the workroom, turning slowly as Bickwithers spoke in her ear and indicated the various graphics computers and equipment.

This was her first day. Philip had been transported into the past to the very day of Amelia's arrival at MicroMeg.

Philip actually remembered this first day. He remembered her standing there before, just so, a small, heavily made-up girl with a round face and a page-boy cut to her black hair, her chin thrust forward with a certain challenging air (the mustered-up toughness of a shy kid), her small body compactly enclosed in a brown suit, a formidably-sized briefcase in her left hand. And he remembered something else, something so extraordinary, in light of his present circumstances, that he threatened to lose himself in the ramifications of this revelation.

When he had first seen Amelia he had thought, *Her name's Amelia.*

He had told her that later, and she had said, "No way. Really?"

A tiny voice had told him her name.

He tried not to think about the mind-boggling notion of such a circle in time. In any event, he was being introduced.

PLEASED TO MEET YOU.

God, what a formal asshole. Transmigration to an earlier self could be embarrassing.

Amelia didn't seem to notice this rod-up-the-ass behavior, however. She was, herself, shy and consequently somewhat stiff. She extended a hand and said, "Nice to meet you. I'm Amelia Price."

Philip loved the way her mouth, bright with orange lipstick, formed and expelled words with more animation than the average mouth. There was something tentative about this, as though she were improvising an entirely new language and might, at any minute, be unmasked.

"Those are lovely sounds," someone might sternly declare, "but they aren't words, my sly girl."

She would be flustered then, silenced in mid-sentence, staring at the floor.

And Philip, like hormone-addled Romeo, fell in love with her instantly—in the loutish, superficial manner of all romantics.

Except that now he wondered. That love-at-first-sight that his memory served up might be something quite different. Perhaps he had come to love her slowly over time, to dote not merely on the music of her voice or her exotic use of mascara, but on her soul, which was fearless when encountering injustice and full of quick compassion for the less fortunate.

It was possible that his love had grown solid and deep over time, and that now it was this experience-born lover, this ghost from the future, that influenced their first meeting.

Once again, Philip felt disoriented by all the implications of such influence.

"Let's meet the rest of the team," Bickwithers said, and he led her away. Philip watched as Bickwithers introduced her to a printer named Lonnie Hark, who took his baseball cap off and shook her hand slowly.

Philip went to his own drafting table and

began creating another flow chart, box upon box of names and titles, locked in the labyrinth of MicroMeg, one of the world's largest corporations.

He did not see Amelia again that day, and although he would have liked to seek her out, he was not in charge. Quitting time came, and the container of his consciousness crowded into an elevator with other exhausted workers and rode it to the ground floor.

That night in his apartment, he watched as he typed his novel. He did not yet own a computer—although he would buy one soon; he had been saving to do so—and he typed cautiously, slowly, since any error carried with it a sense of failure, and the cumulative effect of botched words or x-ed out sentences could engender an almost suicidal sense of defeat. He would look up sometimes, and Philip would take advantage of these moments. He was not privy to his host's creative ruminations, but the stares into space (although fuzzy thanks to the out-ofkilter focus the muse required) allowed Philip to study the room. His memory was all the resolution he required to identify certain objects.

The apartment, an efficiency, saddened him. It was smaller than his memory's version, and shabbier. Hanging on the wall was a picture of Elaine and him at the beach. They had prevailed upon the man who ran the hot dog concession to snap the picture. Cameras were not that old man's long suit, and he had barely managed to fit them in the frame. So the subject of the picture appeared to be a yellow dog, a mangy stray that growled when Philip tried to pet it.

And granted that Elaine's smile was winsome, there in the corner of the frame, and that Philip himself appeared to be caught in a moment of rare, open-mouthed laughter, still, the question remained: What had possessed him to hang such a picture? Masochism? Hiding a stain perhaps?

That's me. That's my dead wife. A suicide. I have an eight-by-ten of my dead father—another suicide— around here somewhere. It was hanging up for awhile

but one night it shattered—inexplicably I think,
although I may have actually thrown something at it.

There were the bookcases full of paperback
books, and the inexpensive stereo system, the
turntable of which had to be given a spin with a
forefinger to overcome some mysterious internal
inertia. There were several of Elaine's paintings,
full of an energy that seemed to hurl the rest of
the room into desolate shadow. A sofa, whose
missing leg had been replaced by hardback books
unworthy of shelf space, looked less welcoming
than a sidewalk grate and the end table next to
it was flimsy beyond belief.

It didn't take long to exhaust this study, and
when his host began typing again, Philip studied
the faint, marching characters—a new ribbon
was in order—with interest.

He read,

They scaled the side of the bleak
mountain, pausing to look back on the
abyss.

"What's that?" Professor Rodgen

asked, pointing to a rock some forty feet below, a rock from which a shadow detached and moved into the sunlight.

"Why, I believe that's Dr. Patterson," Weaver said.

"I thought he was dead, crushed in that rock slide."

"I could have sworn he was," Weaver said. "But it's him. I can see him clearly now. And he looks none the worse for wear, except for that curious hat and cape."

"He always was a bit of a dandy," Professor Rodgen said.

"Wait," Weaver said. "That's not wearing apparel at all, that's—"

Wearing apparel? Philip sighed. *Forget it,* he thought, straining in what he hoped passed for the telepathic equivalent of a shout. *You are going to throw this whole scene out anyway.*

SHIT.

A hand reached up, tore the page from the

typewriter, and tossed it toward the wastebasket. Philip found himself moving away from the typewriter, across the room, into the bathroom. Philip watched himself brush his teeth. Philip saw himself in the mirror. He looked younger and dumber.

Philip felt oddly detached, alienated. Well, why not? *It might even be a definition. Alienated: Having been transported back in time by aliens.*

The bedroom was a tiny room containing a bed, a floor lamp, and a narrow bookcase for paperbacks. Somehow a scruffy dresser had insinuated its way into the room, pathetically pretending to be a legitimate piece of furniture.

Philip watched as a dresser drawer was opened by artful jiggling. A copy of *Hustler* magazine was extracted.

Great, Philip thought.

Can you be, Philip wondered, *your own voyeur?*

Clothing flew into a lump on the floor. Underpants were removed.

The slick, shiny pages flicked by. Then paused.

Her? Come on, she's not even our type.

It was over quick enough, foreplay being optional with two-dimensional women.

Philip felt faintly disgusted, and as the portals of his world shut, enclosing him in darkness, he thought of how unpleasant it would be to reside with his younger self for any substantial period of time.

And he thought of Amelia, dear, sweet, large-hearted Amelia.

Look out! he wanted to scream. *This guy is a moron.*

"How did you sleep, Phil?" the woman asked. Her name was Dr. Ann Beasley, and she was a gray-haired, middle-aged woman who managed to look a little like the young Abraham Lincoln.

"I didn't sleep at all," Philip said. "I was back at MicroMeg."

The woman nodded. "You dreamed you were at MicroMeg."

"No, I was at MicroMeg."

"Philip, do you know why you are here?"

"Ah—"

"You were standing on the highway. It was late at night. Cars were swerving to avoid hitting you. The police were called. When they got there, your employer, a Mr. Pederson, had taken you to the side of the road. He was trying to calm you down. Do you remember any of this?"

"I'm afraid not," Philip said. He looked around the office. It was small, dominated by the psychiatrist's desk. Various official documents hung on the walls. A small window offered a view of a city street, bright sunlight, traffic.

"You were not coherent," Dr. Beasley continued. "When you were brought in, one of the ward clerks said you were speaking in a foreign language."

"That would be Latin," Philip said. "The corrupt Latin of Olaus Wormius who translated the *Necronomicon*. There is no extant version in Arabic, you know."

The woman leaned forward across her desk. "You have an explanation then, for your behavior?"

Philip nodded. "I appear to be caught in a reverberating time loop," he said. "It may have something to do with the Great Leap planned by the Old Ones. MicroMeg was to be the nexus for that jump, but that was thwarted by other influences."

"You feel you are caught in some cosmic war, then?" the doctor asked.

Philip sensed that she wasn't entirely with him on this, but then it wasn't an easy concept to get your mind around. His own mind did not embrace it willingly.

"It's not a war exactly," Philip said. "The Old Ones are taking a telepathic leap from pre-Pleistocene times. The Pnakotic manuscripts suggested that they would leap beyond the reign of man, into sentient crustaceanlike beings, the next dominant life form on the planet. I think Lovecraft was mistaken on this. I think they are coming into our world, what you could loosely call 'now.' My own involvement is peripheral. I was just in the wrong continuum at the wrong time. I got pulled along. I'm nothing to them."

Dr. Beasley nodded her head.

Good, Philip thought, *I'm getting through.*

But this was not, in fact, the case. Dr. Beasley said that she had talked, by phone, to Philip's friend Amelia Price who was quite concerned.

And Amelia's interpretation of events was, alas, dismally skewed.

"She tells me," the doctor said, "that you have written a very long book about these monsters."

"It's a novel," Philip said. "I hadn't intended it to be so long; it just got away."

"Got away," the doctor mused, tilting her head backward for a second. "Your choice of words is in keeping with your friend's belief that the years you have worked on this book may have caused some blurring of the boundary between fact and fiction. There are clinical conditions, forms of schizophrenia, that operate in this fashion. She says you have taken medications for such conditions in the past. Let's see." The doctor flipped the page on a legal pad. "Yes. You were hospitalized at Northern Virginia Mental Health in 1982."

Philip sighed. This interview wasn't going at all well. That morning when he had awakened and determined that he was in a psychiatric hospital, he had rejoiced. To live in that past, to haunt the armageddon halls of MicroMeg, would have been more than he could have borne.

But now he saw that he was not out of the woods, not yet a free man.

He would try a reasoned approach. "Mental health," he said, "is a relative term. I think I have come through pretty well, considering. Do you mind if I quote Lovecraft? He says"—here Philip leaned back and studied the ceiling, to give his mind a clear screen for the scrolling of internal words— *"The most merciful thing in the world, I think, is the inability of the human mind to correlate all its contents. We live on a placid island of ignorance in the midst of black seas of infinity, and it was not meant that we should voyage far. The sciences, each straining in its own direction, have hitherto harmed us little; but some day the piecing together of dissociated knowledge will open up such terrifying vistas of reality, and of our frightful position therein, that we shall either go mad from the revelation or flee from the deadly light into the peace and safety of a new dark age."*

Dr. Beasley smiled. Philip felt a sense of triumph. It was always satisfying to see logic triumph.

"We'd like you to stay with us for a little while," she said. "There is often a physiological basis for this sort of thing, and it can be controlled by medication."

Philip sighed. *Be philosophical*, he counseled himself. You can't expect someone who has never gazed on the naked visage of Yog-Sothoth to understand the mind's essential fragility.

That afternoon, Philip found himself in a circle with other crazy people. The group was led by a pretty, dark-haired woman who insisted that people call her Olivia.

"Why don't we all begin by telling something about ourselves," Olivia asked. She said she would start, and she talked about her cats and how she went to school and got a Ph.D. but still didn't feel like a grown-up.

When it was Philip's turn to share, he said, "I'm forty-five years old, and I came to Austin to win back my girlfriend. She refuses to believe that an ancient, super-intelligent race of cone-shaped beings inhabiting pre-Pleistocene times are responsible for the breakup. I've got to convince her; I've got to recover her love." He admitted that he didn't feel adequate to the task.

Although it was difficult to tell—Philip had very little experience reading crazy people—the group seemed to accept this without shock or incredulity. Indeed, it was the next person to share, a middle-aged white woman, who elicited some argument and anger.

"I'm Michael Jackson," she said. "You all

know who I am already. I'm depressed because everybody is always after me."

"You done betrayed your people," shouted a large black man in a blue tank top.

"See there!" she screamed. "See there! Just like I said. Everybody is after me."

"I'm not sharing in no room with a traitor," the man said, folding his arms and glaring at the ceiling.

That evening after dinner, Philip went to his room and lay down on the bed. One of the residents knocked on the door and told him he had a phone call.

It was Amelia. She asked how he was doing.

"I'm fine," he said.

Amelia began to cry then. Philip hated that. He stood there in the hall, cradling the phone's receiver to his chest and rocking it. Her sobs penetrated his rib cage and battered his heart. He lifted the phone again and spoke into it.

"Amelia," he said. "It's not hopeless. I promise you it is not hopeless. I won't let anything happen to you."

But she just cried louder at that, and finally, when she began to wind down, she said, "I've got to go, Philip. I'll talk to you later." She hung up.

Philip went back to his room, heartsick, and lay on the bed. He closed his eyes, and when he opened them he was at MicroMeg again. He wasn't even surprised.

FREELANCE.

Philip stared out from behind his eyes at a large, broad-shouldered man with a very smooth face and rudimentary features. Philip could not remember the man's name—the man had been fired shortly after hiring Philip—but he remembered the day.

I WORKED FREELANCE DURING THAT PERIOD.

Actually, Philip thought, *I was in a mental health facility, going to group, reading paperback books, forming a long-term game plan.*

The man was nodding his head, smiling. "Self-motivated," he said, and he checked a box on a piece of paper.

This was the day of the interview. The second interview. The first interview had been with a mousy woman in Personnel who had said, "This is just a screening interview. There are a lot of candidates for this job, so what we are looking for here is anything that might eliminate candidates right off. Can you think of anything, offhand, that would be a really good reason for not hiring you?" She had laughed brightly. "Joke," she had said and winked.

They had called him for a second interview. Here he was. He would get the job, of course. No suspense there.

"This company believes in keeping the workplace drug-free," the man was saying. "Would you be willing..."

No. Tell him no.

"... would you be willing to be stripped naked, sodomized, and videotaped during the procedure? We would want you to sign something authorizing us..."

OF COURSE.

Was this an alternate universe? He did not remember those precise words. But then, he had been nervous, and much of what the man had said slid past him. He had been broke and desperate.

Even now he was drifting away, following his thoughts to the unhappy precipice of despair. He had been transported further back this time, to the very beginning of his MicroMeg career. He had worked for MicroMeg for eight years. Eight. If he were left here, he would have to slog through eight long years, eight years in which he would note every sign, every tremor of the approaching horror.

Trapped in his ignorant, younger self he would see the dread significance in each event, see the inevitable darkness thicken, and be powerless to act.

WILLIAM BROWNING SPENCER

No. God, don't let this happen.

He was standing up, shaking the hand of the thick, smiling man in the dark suit.

"Thanks for coming in," the man was saying. "We'll get back to you the end of this week."

The next morning, in group, Philip said, "Yes, I think I can talk about fear. I think I can share on that one. I'm bouncing back and forth in Time. I figure it will have to slow down. There is probably some law of inertia for Time, too. Right now I'm ping-ponging back and forth, but I think the energy will go out of it. And then, then I'll be stuck... either here or in the past depending upon exactly when this ricochet effect exhausts itself. If I'm stuck in the past... I can tell you, the thought of getting stuck at MicroMeg again scares me to death."

"Thank you Philip," Olivia said. "Would anyone else like to share on fear?"

Bob, a thin, timid man wearing a jump suit

and tennis shoes without socks, said he was afraid of snakes.

"Shit," grumbled the balding man next to Bob, "you missed the point entirely. You can't share any better than that, you should get out of this group. You ain't no asset to this group if all you can say is, 'I'm skeered of snakes.' That's bullshit sharing."

Bob began to cry, his shoulders shaking inside his jumpsuit. The man next to him hugged him. "Hey, I didn't mean anything," he said.

I hate this, Philip thought.

Lily Metcalf came to see him that evening. She came into his room and sat on his bed.

"Flipped out, did you?" she said.

"That's not a very professional diagnosis," Philip said, huffily.

"You're right. I apologize." She studied her hands as they knotted together in her lap. She was wearing a large, bulky gray dress and a straw hat. Strands of dry, gray hair drifted across her ravaged cheeks.

My therapist is ancient, Philip thought.

Lily looked up. "I get glib when I'm worried. I knew you would be a heartbreaking client."

"I'm sorry," Philip said.

Lily waved away his apology. "I only put that ad in the paper one day. I was retired, and I thought, maybe just a few clients wouldn't hurt. You are my only client, you know."

"I'm sorry."

"Dr. Metcalf?"

Lily turned. Dr. Ann Beasley was standing in the doorway.

Lily smiled. "Hi, Ann."

Dr. Beasley came into the room and hugged the older woman. "I was just walking down the hall and I saw you. Obviously, you've met Mr. Kenan."

"He's my client."

"Oh." She looked at Philip with new interest. "He didn't mention you."

"He's probably ashamed of me," Lily said.

The younger woman laughed. "Dr. Metcalf was one of my professors at UT," she said. "She's the best."

Philip smiled, pleased. Frankly, he had thought of his therapist as an economy measure, the best he could do on a budget, and, while he liked her, he had not suspected she had any real professional standing. And yet here was the director of his present psychiatric abode saying that Lily Metcalf was the best.

Amelia called later. She sounded better, more controlled. She talked about her job at Pelidyne.

"I'm time allotment manager this week," she told him; he did not ask her to elaborate, although he was concerned. It was always a bad sign when an employee began speaking of job arcana as though it had life and relevance outside its System. Nowadays, Philip always looked for the incision or the plug-in module when he encountered someone who said something like, "We are having a hell of a problem distributing the T jags on the Nimbus net." It was symptomatic of zombies to believe that everyone shared the same information lines, that everyone was on the team.

Time allotment. Perhaps the time ricochet was governed by free association links. Philip was sitting at a long table with Amelia, explaining MicroMeg's time accountability table, referred to by all employees—most of whom had long ago forgotten what the acronym actually stood for— as a "tat."

YOU GET A NEW TAT ON THURSDAYS.

Philip studied the side of Amelia's face. She was listening to the instructions with the focused attention of an A student. Her straight black hair drifted forward slightly; her mouth was pursed in a small, pink bow of concentration. He longed to push one errant strand of dark hair back into place, and he could even remember wanting to do so before—*again and again this strange overlapping of the then and the now.*

EACH BLOCK REPRESENTS A SIX-MINUTE PERIOD.

Philip watched himself describe what each color stood for, picking up the colored pencil and filling in a block. The idea was to account for every six-minute period of time by coloring in a block with a color that indicated the nature of the task.

"Is there a color for the time required to fill in this form every day?" Amelia asked. Everyone asked this.

No, there was not, but management applied a formula to the number of colors used on any line, determining an average time for the filling out of that line, and subtracted that amount from the totals per line.

Amelia asked another question.

JUST LIE, was the answer.

"Lie?"

CERTAINLY.

Amelia had wanted to know how this rather complicated time accounting worked under the pressure of deadlines. How could she keep such a precise account while racing to complete a job before deadline?

An employee's familiarity with the business world could be judged by the response Philip's answer (LIE) engendered. People who had been employed by a corporation simply nodded their heads—or, more often, didn't even ask such a question.

Amelia was obviously new to the world of corporate employment and, consequently, dismayed by Philip's answer. Randomly filling in blocks with whatever colored pencil came to hand would render the data worthless, wouldn't it?

WELL, YES. IN A WAY.

Philip was saddened to see the look of reproach in his true love's eyes. Time and experience would, of course, soften that expression, but that didn't make it any less painful.

Philip listened to himself explain. It was a dismal business, this explaining. The truth could sometimes seem like the worst sort of cynicism when that was not what it was at all.

The data acquired wasn't exactly worthless. True, it was not accurate, but it was more important to have data than to have accurate data. If you did not have data, you could not manipulate it, you could not determine how efficient people were in January as opposed to July or what percentage of in-house jobs took time from outside clients or whether instructional, unbillable time was up or down. Without data, MicroMeg's entire Quality team would have nothing to do, would look like irrelevant staff, would be fired. We were talking here of human beings with families to support.

Amelia told Philip that she intended to be as accurate in her accounting as humanly possible. She raised her chin in a challenging manner as she said this.

The course of true love never runs smooth.

After work, Philip visited his friend Todd Tillick. Todd lived in a small house in Sterling, Virginia, a twenty minute drive from Fairfax.

Todd was just recuperating from an unrequited love affair with a topless dancer named Doris, and he was cynical about male/female relationships. He wasn't optimistic about Philip's chances of winning Amelia's heart.

"Women don't want to do anything but dance naked and drink beer," he said. "You should forget about that bimbo and concentrate on your art."

It was chilly in the house, and Todd was wearing several sweaters and a stocking cap. The floor of the room was covered with paperback books, magazines, beer cans, record albums, and unrecognizable, gutted electronic equipment.

I LOVE HER, Philip said.

Todd sucked on a beer and glowered. "It's your funeral," he said.

Whup. He was in group. The topic was relationships. The time jumps really might be thematic, flying across the years to a kindred idea. If so... if so, could he control them?

"Philip," the group leader Olivia asked, "are you with us today?"

"Yes," Philip said. "I'm right here." He had a flitting, disheartening thought. When he wasn't here, who was? Was his physical body inhabited by one of the Old Ones? Did impossibly ancient eyes study these surroundings, gaze coldly at his companions? And, if so, did his fellow patients notice anything different?

A woman in her late twenties was talking about her abusive boyfriend.

"He doesn't mean it," she said. "He's just passionate in every way. It's a tradeoff."

He had tied her to a bed, poured gasoline over her, and threatened to set her on fire, striking matches and blowing them out when they were inches from her nose.

"He was just trying to get a rise out of me," she said. "I know him."

The woman who was Michael Jackson

interrupted. "My hair caught on fire once," she said.

Several people shouted at her to shut up.

The bald man, who seemed to have a penchant for platitudes which covered a deep, solid craziness that probably trumped the insanity of everyone else in group, said, "I cried for not having shoes, until I saw a man who had no feet."

Al Bingham came by in the evening. He brought a card signed by everyone in the office, including Monica and Ralph Pederson, both of whom were just fine.

"Stress," Bingham said. "You were just under too much stress. I read an article about stress once. It's a mutherfucker. It's a matter of concentration. You got to focus on a very narrow band, you know. Otherwise, there is too much stuff to look at and think about, like being fired or your car breaking down or getting cancer or losing your mind—whoops—or being called up for jury duty or being arrested for socially unacceptable behavior. Thinking is a dead end.

Look at mice. What if a mouse was always thinking, 'Jesus God, I am on everyone's food chain. Owls, foxes, cats, snakes, you name it. What was that!'? The thing is, you can't dwell on your situation."

"Monica is dead," Philip said.

"She is setting a lot of type for a dead person," Bingham said. "Her fingers are flying."

"She may be productive," Philip said, "but she isn't alive. I should know. I killed her. It was an accident, but that doesn't make her any less dead."

Lily Metcalf arrived while Bingham was still there. She introduced herself.

"I've never met a psychiatrist," Bingham said.

"You still haven't," Lily said. "I'm a psychologist."

Bingham seemed very impressed with the woman. He stayed while Lily asked Philip how he was doing.

"I'm okay," Philip said. He leaned past her and said, "It was nice of you to come by, Al."

The old printer smiled.

"Your friend doesn't have to leave," Lily said.

"I can only stay a minute. I just wanted to check in. How are you feeling?"

"I keep being flung back to MicroMeg."

Lily nodded. "Got to stop that," she said. "Maybe I can haul you back permanently with some hypnosis. But not today, I've got to run."

Bingham followed her out.

Philip could hear Bingham speaking as they moved off down the hall.

"You think I'm too old for therapy?" Bingham was asking.

"You are never too old for therapy," Lily answered.

he basement. He was in the basement.

He had run out of eight-inch photo paper for the typesetting machine, and he had come down to the basement, but the supply room wasn't where he remembered it. He had peered into two ill-lit rooms full of mop buckets, floor waxers, drums of chemicals. Now this third room... another clutter.

He knew what was going to happen. He remembered.

He was in the seventh year of MicroMeg. Amelia and he were living together now, fighting about the time his book consumed, wrestling with the nature of commitment. They owned a cat named Speedo. They had purchased a car together. The car was not running very well.

He pushed open the door. At the end of the room a figure hunched over a table. On the table itself, an oscilloscope's screen displayed an undulating snake of green. A rubble of machinery extended spiky wires. The figure stood up, silhouetted against the bright ceiling lights, and moved swiftly toward Philip.

WHO'S THAT?

You know. F.F. Flatulent Freddie.

His black hair hanging down in his face, sweat rolling off his cheeks, eyes rolling, F.F. stood in front of Philip.

"You shouldn't be in here," he said.

I'M LOOKING FOR THE STOCKROOM FOR GRAPHICS.

F.F. reached forward suddenly and grabbed Philip's right hand, tugging it forward. He turned the hand palm up and studied the wrist. He grunted.

Philip remembered the fetid stink, F.F.'s usual noxious emissions combined with fear-brewed sweat and a sulphurous, hot metal smell. Sheltered in the quarantined cubicle of his host's mind, Philip did not have to endure the suffocating stench again. He was grateful for that; it was vivid enough as a memory.

"This ain't no stockroom," F.F. muttered, dropping the wrist. "You shouldn't be in here."

SORRY TO BOTHER YOU.

Philip was turning to leave.

You know what he's doing, Philip thought. *He's making bombs. He has been sitting down here in the basement, in this fart-infested mailroom, making bombs for Jesus. Are you just going to turn around and walk out?*

Philip was moving down the hall.

The voice came from behind him. He knew it would, of course. He remembered.

"You don't have the mark," F.F. hollered. "I thought you would have the mark, seeing as how your girl has it, but you don't. You ain't lost to the sweet love of Jesus. I got something to show you."

Whup. He was in group. An acne-scarred kid named Sammy Phelam was talking about how his girlfriend was cheating on him. He had found a bunch of Polaroids of her and this guy having sex. What bothered Sammy the most was that the guy was wearing a baseball cap in all the pictures. That was a low, cheap thing to do and—

Philip interrupted. "They were all wearing the mark. It looked a little like a starfish, a wiggly, blue tattoo on the wrist. Amelia said it was just a motivational thing, something Quality cooked up, but I was uneasy about that, from the very start, I thought—"

The counselor, Olivia, said, "Philip, I believe

Sammy was trying to share about his anxieties regarding—"

Whup. "'You got to bring it all down, Fred.' That's what Jesus said to me. 'You got to topple Satan's tower.'" The fat mailroom clerk showed Philip the bombs, showed how the switches made solenoids snap forward with the cold precision and speed of mechanical serpents. "I polish every bit of metal. Some might say that was crazy, seeing as how it is all going to go up in roaring thunder, but the Eye of God don't miss a thing, and He appreciates attention to detail, you know. You can go to the backside of a tree that is hunched up against a mountain, and you can scramble in through brush and vines and snap off a hidden leaf, and you'll see that it is as labored over as anything on view. God don't cut corners."

Flatulent Freddie waved a hand above his

head. "Like stars in the sky," he said. "Seventeen floors of firecrackers. What do you think of that?" F.F. had strewn bombs throughout the building, in vents, taped to concrete pillars, under desks, behind vending machines, resting precariously on the acoustical tiling of ceilings.

"It's all linked through the mainframes. I can go to any computer in this joint, execute the command, and *Kablam!* the Philistines are dust again, and Jesus is hugging Himself for joy."

JESUS WOULDN'T WANT YOU TO BLOW UP MICROMEG. HE WOULDN'T WANT YOU TO KILL INNOCENT PEOPLE.

F.F.'s eyes grew wide. When he shook his head, his hair danced over his eyes. "You don't know poop about it," the fat boy said. "Jesus ain't happy about it, but He knows you gotta break a few eggs to make an omelet."

YOU CAN'T DO THIS THING.

"Yes I can. I see now that you are one of them. Jesus washed me clean of all ambition and doubt and lusting after power, and said, 'You are the only vessel I got for this job. You are the only one been virginized by the blood of the Lamb. You are a Sword and I am Wrath.'"

Philip hit the fat man in the nose with all his might. He dove forward, pushing Freddie back against a wobbly table that instantly collapsed, envelopes of all sizes leaping in the air.

Whup. Dr. Beasley was leaning forward, a look of concern on her noble if unattractive features.

"You are particularly anxious today, Philip."

"I seem to be really bouncing, doctor. One second I'm in MicroMeg with crazy F.F., then I'm back here, in group or, like now, talking to you."

"You may be experiencing some anxiety with the new medication," Dr. Beasley said.

"I'm on new medication?"

"Well, yes, we discussed it before."

Philip sighed. "I think I missed that discussion, doctor. Look, I think it is a bad idea to put me on any—I mean, *any*—medication right now. That could stop me flat on the wrong side of the tracks. I don't want to get stuck in MicroMeg. Doctor, I can't get stuck in MicroMeg!"

"Philip, please sit down."

Whup. Amelia was walking in front of Philip, out into the parking lot. A security guard named Hal Ketch accompanied them. The security guard was a thin, cold man who said he had once worked for the CIA. His uniform was black, immaculately pressed; the creases might have been crimped metal.

He lifted his static-wheezing radio and spoke into it, "I've escorted emps Price and Kenan to lot 9. I'm taking a tour, west through BuSubs. I'll be reentering through CS-One."

The radio coughed an acknowledgment.

The security guard nodded at Amelia and Philip and turned away. They watched him move across the empty parking lot, through pools of weak lamplight.

OUR VERY OWN NAZI.

Amelia laughed.

This is the night, Philip thought. *I wouldn't be confused about the night.*

They stood by the side of Amelia's Honda. She had a hand on the door.

"I'm exhausted," she said.

FOURTEEN-HOUR DAYS WILL DO THAT TO A PERSON.

"Yes. I guess so. Well, good night."

He walked across the lot to his own car. He got in, turned the key, and drove toward the exit.

Wait. There is a mistake here. This was the night. She was wearing her gray suit, and when she took it off, revealing her white, surprising flesh, Philip felt that he had stumbled to the heart of some extraordinary mystery—like the discovery of hope or renewal. She came out of the bathroom, the makeup washed from her face to reveal a less precise, more generous and wanton woman, and she smiled as though they had both been party to some deception, out there in the faceless, machine-hearted world, and that, having pulled it off, they were free to revel like children.

He pulled up to the exit, fumbled for his encoded card that would open the gate.

You asshole. Look!

The camera of his consciousness shifted. He was staring into the rearview mirror.

Yes.

Amelia's car sat in the desolation of the empty parking lot. Headlights glowed, then dimmed; flared again and sank to weaker, smaller orbs the color of weak tea.

Philip turned and drove back to Amelia.

HI.

"I think the battery is dead," she said. They both listened to the sound the engine made when she turned the key. A sound like a man with rusted lungs, hacking up handfuls of dirty pennies.

The coy sound of sudden romance.

I CAN DROP YOU OFF AT YOUR PLACE.
IT IS WAY TOO LATE TO DO ANYTHING
ABOUT IT TONIGHT.

"Thank you," Amelia said.

"Last night," Philip told Lily Metcalf, "I was
back with Amelia the first time we made love."

"That's nice."

"Well, it was a little disturbing, actually."

"Oh." Lily Metcalf struck a match and lit her
cigarette. You weren't supposed to smoke in these
rooms, but Philip figured the woman had some
clout. Her old student was the director, after all.

"Well, there was a voyeur quality; I wasn't
really participating, of course. There were no
physical sensations, so... I don't know."

He didn't really know just how to explain it.

Suffused with sadness.

Amelia had moved under him, her mouth a

surprised, delighted O. She had reached a hand toward his face, touching his forehead as though checking for a fever.

He watched his own hand glide up her ribs and come to rest on her breast, more voluptuous and slightly larger than he had imagined it—and yes, he had been imagining it for fourteen months—and his other hand sought the black, clipped tangle of her hair, still wet from the shower.

She opened her mouth and spoke. "Amelia," she said.

He leaned forward; her marvelous eyes bloomed, full of dark intensity. Again, this time speaking each syllable slowly, she said, "A... meel... e.... ya."

Say it, you idiot. She wants you to say her name. She is here with you and she wants you to say her name, to tell her it is her and not blind sex that animates you.

AMELIA.

"Yes. Philip."

AMELIA. AMELIA.

The sadness came like a descent of locusts. He watched as the wildness grew, saw her shoulders glisten.

AMELIA.

I will win you back, he vowed. *I will save you.*

Whup. Olivia, their counselor in group, was a morning person. That is, she was aggressively cheerful in the morning, her voice containing a lilt that made Philip wince.

"Well," she said, slapping her hands on her blue-jeaned thighs, "This is Mr. Hatfield's last day. Would anyone like to say anything to him?"

Mr. Hatfield was a small, weary man who had never said anything in group. He was in the hospital for depression, and if appearances counted for anything, he was as depressed as he had been on the first day, his thick lips jutting out in an exaggerated pout, his eyes sunk into folds of despair. His reserve and misery were so great that even Olivia was incapable of calling him by his first name.

"Hang in there, Mr. Hatfield," the bald man said. "It's always darkest before the dawn."

"Lighten up," Sammy Phelam said.

"Find Jesus," Michael Jackson advised.

Flatulent Freddie had found Jesus, and Jesus had said, "MicroMeg is a satanic cult. You must tear it asunder. I will tell you how."

Jesus had revealed his plan to the devout mail clerk, who then constructed dozens of explosive devices. How often, when Philip had spied F.F. in an elevator, had that young man been busy doing the Lord's bidding? How often had polished engines of destruction resided at the bottom of the ubiquitous mail cart?

Whup. Flatulent Freddie had surprising strength. He came off the floor with a rush and lifted Philip off the ground. The room tilted, spun. Philip got up and lunged.

F.F. backed away, laughing. "Jesus is sharper than that," he said. "You can't sucker punch the Son of God."

JESUS DOESN'T WANT YOU TO DO THIS THING.

F.F. laughed again, shaking his head. "I can be fooled. I'm mortal and frail. I thought you might be okay, cause you don't have the mark, and I've never spied you at their vile worship. But you are one of them, sure enough."

The mail clerk backed against a file cabinet, dragged open a drawer, and pulled out a revolver. The gun seemed almost comically large, a steel-blue, long barreled weapon.

THOU SHALT NOT KILL.

"That don't apply to Satan's Spawn," F.F. said. "Good try, though."

The room exploded.

Even knowing what was coming, the sound made the time-transported Philip jump, as though his soul might bang the roof of his mind.

The fat man's head flew back, spraying blood, hair, skull fragments.

Someone shoved past Philip to stand over the sprawled form of Flatulent Freddie. The uniformed man looked down at the corpse and spoke.

"Son of a bitch," the man said. "Thought you'd make me look bad, did you? Look who is looking bad now."

Hal Ketch turned and grinned at Philip. He blew on the end of his revolver, winked. "Guess he thought I was beating off in the furnace room."

Ketch put his gun back in his holster and walked over to Philip. He put an arm around Philip's shoulder. "Let's get out of here," he said.

In the hall, he leaned into Philip. "Look in my eyes," he said. Although Philip could not feel or smell, he knew that their noses were touching, and that the security guard's breath smelled of Listerine. He remembered.

"What do you see?" Hal Ketch asked.

I DON'T KNOW.

"What you see is a man who wants things to run smoothly. A man who was hired to do that, and who is doing it. Smoothly. This incident is closed. This incident didn't happen. You don't even talk about this to your girlfriend. You don't say, just making conversation, 'Guess who got his head shot off today?' You don't do it because you don't want anything to happen to her. Do you understand all that?"

Philip understood.

Whup. Lily Metcalf and Philip were outside, walking on the grounds. The sky was bright. A cool breeze rippled the leaves of the live oaks. The light under the trees skittered like a school of fish being chummed.

"You saw this mail clerk get killed, and you couldn't tell Amelia. That created a strain in the relationship."

"That was certainly part of it."

Lily came to a concrete bench and sat down.

"Well, that would be enough, I would think. What else?"

"Amelia really hated my novel."

Whup. Amelia's voice called down the hall. "Philip. Philip. What are you doing? Come to bed."

JUST A MINUTE, HONEY. I'M FINISHING THIS CHAPTER.

Philip watched the green letters appear, glowing, on the computer screen.

Thank you, God, for inventing the word processor during my lifetime. I know you might have used the same time to alleviate poverty, or end war and disease, but I personally applaud your priorities here. I am, after all, a writer. Thank you.

They were living together now, the both of them working long hours at MicroMeg, and time away from the office was at a premium.

The letters formed words, the words, a paragraph:

A kind of green-grayish mold dripped from the walls and covered all the furniture, like kudzu on a hillside.

Professor Rodgen swung his flashlight in a slow arc. A damp, dismal miasma choked him.

"There!" Weaver exclaimed.

Something shaped vaguely like a man sat at the gray, feathered desk. What were once hands floated upward, shielding the hollows where eyes might lie from the glare of the flashlight.

"Approach no further," the creature said, each word laboriously expelled as though breaking flesh and tooth and bone in its effort to come free from the rotting body.

"If you value your sanity, professor, come no closer. We were colleagues once. I was your intellectual superior, and I outran you, and this is the prize I won."

WILLIAM BROWNING SPENCER

Something in the ruined voice was familiar. Professor Rodgen, with misgivings, edged forward.

"Dr. Armitridge? Is that you?"

Amelia came up behind Philip and put her arms around his neck. She leaned over and kissed him on the cheek.

"Come to bed, Philip," she said.

FIVE MINUTES, he said. He reached back and touched her shoulder.

"Right now. I know your five minutes," she said.

OKAY. I'M COMING.

He saved what he had written, exited the program, turned the monitor off.

Philip watched their lovemaking which took place in the country of fatigue amid the small, tiny betrayals of living together and the slow, crafted affection of their daily intertwining.

And the sadness assailed him again.

melia woke him in the morning, and he had a moment of disorientation when he saw her there, dressed in her tan suit, poised for workday battle.

"Why didn't you wake me?" he muttered. Amelia always arose without an alarm clock, took the first shower, and then woke him. They drove to work together, although their jobs had diverged and they no longer worked on the same floor of MicroMeg.

He came fully out of sleep and saw the room, its fraudulent brightness, its air of brief, transitory inhabitation by this Philip Kenan and his small store of identity-confirming possessions: the books, the Cezanne poster, the picture of Amelia feeding seagulls at the beach.

"I apologize for waking you up," she said. "Last night when I went by your place to get your mail, there was this. It's from your agent. I figured you'd want to see it." Amelia extended her hand with the bulky envelope. "I thought I would swing by here before going to work. I didn't know what time I'd be getting off work."

"Thank you," Philip said. He felt sleepy and at a disadvantage, a middle-aged man awakened in a psych ward by his ex-girlfriend. He had become what Lovecraft would call a "decayed" member of the Kenan tribe, his hair sticking out in unfortunate clumps, his face in the mirror pale and slack-jawed and stupefied, like a drugged killer rousted out of sleep by the cops.

"Agent?" he said, blinking at the letter. He said it much the way a muddled felon might have said, "Murder?"

He read the return address, "James Pierce Literary Agency." He remembered then, surprised himself with the memory. He had written to one of the agents Wingate House had suggested when the editor there sent along the contract. "Oh yes."

He put the envelope on the end table. He smiled at Amelia.

"How's Pelidyne?"

Amelia smiled. "Busy. Really crazy. I've been working a lot of overtime."

Whup. An entirely different set of colored pencils were used to chart overtime on the mandatory TAT form.

Overtime was charted with the complement of the color used to chart normal time. Should one forget the color scheme for overtime, a simple look at a color wheel could set one straight (provided, of course, that one could remember the regular scheme). It was a bit complicated at first, but it was ingenious.

Philip sat on the low bed and colored in three TAT forms. He'd gotten behind. He had been working a lot of overtime recently. So much so that he had adopted the Quality Domicile incentive program, spending his nights in one of the minimal converted living quarters which constituted the entire fourteenth floor and part of the fifteenth and sixteenth.

Amelia had also been closeted in the building for the last couple of weeks. Philip had not seen her, although he had talked to her on the phone. The fourteenth floor was a male dorm, closed to women.

A memo stated that this sexual segregation was an "efficiency" measure, although what that meant was unclear. In practice, it meant that Ray Barnstable could walk nude down the halls to the showers. And if that was efficiency—a view of Barnstable's hairy, pocked butt—then inefficiency, chaos itself, had much to recommend it.

Each room was supplied with a computer, and Philip had brought a disk with the last chapter of his novel. He worked on it for awhile.

When he tried to save the disk, the screen uttered a green error message: **DISK FULL.**

SHIT.

Just save it to the hard disk, Philip urged his younger self.

At the time it had seemed critical that he find a blank disk. Why? A foolish question. As Philip was learning, bad decisions never made sense in retrospect.

He went into the hall.

Some kind of tarlike residue covered the carpet. He entered the elevator where the usual reek of strong cleaning agents was dominated, that night, by something dark and fetid, a stink of slaughtered animals and stagnant tidal pools.

Philip did not reexperience the odors, but they had been so strong that his memory conjured them instantly.

Don't you smell that? Aren't you just a little bit concerned with the goddam originator of that stink?

The fifth floor, where Philip worked, was locked. The elevator doors refused to open, and he had forgotten to bring his access card with him.

SHIT.

That's when he had rolled his eyes upward. Philip watched again as this action of petition or dismay brought the lurid graffiti into focus. On the elevator's ceiling, someone had spray painted a purple scrawl, the jagged script reading, *e'yaya ngh'aaaaa YOG-SOTHOTH!*

Yog-Sothoth, the accursed gate-keeper, the one who would usher in the Old Ones, the blight from black Space and Time.

Philip experienced the same sharp fear that had occurred when he first saw the writing. But then he had been able to allay the fear with reason. Some practical joker, no doubt. Someone who was aware of Philip's fascination with Lovecraft.

Now reason could not quell the fear, for Philip

had been here before, and he knew what lay ahead.

Back to the fourteenth floor, he urged.

But he did not heed himself. He stepped out into the basement.

The lights in the hallway were flickering wickedly, accompanied by a dull hum and something else, the rolling liturgical sound of voices speaking in unison.

Had he recognized the sound as voices then, or only now, knowing what was to come?

He followed the voices, past a room of coiled wires and large, steel barrels and blind computer screens and the peeled nervous systems of unidentifiable electronic components, and past glass-enclosed banks of white computers. The hall was long, and—a trick of perspective—seemed to narrow as it stretched in front of him. He had been in the basement before, of course—and didn't he *know* that bad things happened in the basement?—but none of what he saw seemed familiar. The walls were speckled, a gray and black reticulation that suggested those optical illusions that appeared three dimensional if stared at long enough. From the corner of his eye, he sensed motion and sudden pockets of swirling translucency.

He passed another bank of glassed-in computers. These computers were black and showed signs of corrosion and disuse, as though they had been repaired endlessly and in a slipshod, expedient way. The massive machines rested in a tangled sea of cable and rubber tubing. A junkyard for old technology, Philip thought, but myriad small lights, green and blue and red, flickered, and tire-sized wheels whirred, transporting tape. The machines were running.

On-line to the Other World, he thought.

Then he was moving away from the sound. He stopped, turned back.

He tried a black, unmarked door, and it opened to reveal a descending flight of concrete steps—a basement beneath the basement. The sound rose up, a mournful chant, conjuring the horror of forbidden rituals in the dark— implacable, cruel deeds that shunned the light.

Always, poised above an unwelcoming flight of stairs that led into darkness and the threat of death or worse, the Lovecraftian hero shivered and marched downward. Philip, a writer himself, was powerless to resist the call. Unreasonable, unmotivated, plain stupid by the standards of even the most rudimentary of single- or several-celled creatures, all this could be said of these descents into the abyss. But it was a tradition older than reason that willed Philip into the dank, noxious depths of MicroMeg. It was the tradition of pulp fiction, the tradition that his father had instilled in every fiber of his being, the tradition that Philip carried on in the grueling narrative of his own novel, *The Despicable Quest*.

Down.

It went, of course, a long way down. And somewhere, light ceased to exist, and then the walls seemed to speak, to form his name with something other than human tongues, and there was a large, inhuman wheezing noise mixed with the chanting voices, and some of the concrete steps did not appear to be concrete at all but of living flesh, or, more precisely, once-living flesh that had reached a state of unpleasant mortification.

Then the walls lightened again, and he saw that they were covered with ancient, violent graffiti. He made out the names Cthulhu and Azathoth and Tsathoggua and some drawings that the mind tripped over rather than attempt to correlate into the known universe.

He entered a vast underground hall, the ceiling of which dripped with huge, round-bodied heating ducts and thick cables. On the lighted stage, in front of a twelve-foot-high, silver sculpture of that same writing star that Philip had observed on Amelia's wrist, stood a gray-haired man that Philip instantly recognized as MicroMeg's chairman, Alastair Stern.

The hall was crowded with business-suited men and women, all attired as they would be for a workday at MicroMeg. They took no notice of Philip.

Chairman Stern was speaking with his arms stretched out, a stance familiar to Philip, who had attended numerous Monday morning motivation rallies at which awards were made for various employee achievements (records of long attendance without a sick day, projects brought in under cost, slogans invented, clients enlisted, et cetera). Stern stood in a circle of squat, white photocopiers. Between each photocopier was a small white table upon which sat a fax machine.

Now Stern was intoning, "...with a great binding and dreaming, Yog-Sothoth came. The Old Ones who were, who are, and who shall be. Who throw shadows between the stars. Yog-Sothoth."

"Yog-Sothoth!" the crowd responded, the words rolling and echoing in the vaulted room.

Stern coughed, let his shoulders sag slightly, his arms fall to his side in the classic manner of a preacher winding down. "'Bind all of them,' Yog-Sothoth said. 'From the greatest to the smallest.'

"'The Leap is at hand,' cried great Nyarlathotep from the watery depths. 'The path is cleared. All the dreamers are aligned.'"

Stern raised his hands over his head. "Facilitators, approach."

Men and women in business suits climbed the stage, and stood, in military stances, next to the copy machines, one person per machine.

"Dream to dream!" Stern roared. "We shall incorporate the very stars with the aid of our mentors. Come up, bask in their radiance."

Philip watched the scene unfold, wondering how it lost so little of its strangeness from being replayed. His fascination and horror was untempered by his knowledge of what was to come.

He watched as the crowd, sedately, in what was obviously a practiced ritual, approached the stage from either side. The facilitators then went to the edge of the stage and brought individuals to stand by the photocopiers. At a nod from Stern, these pilgrims bent forward and pressed their faces against the glass of the machines, hunched under the lids with varying degrees of grace. Philip recognized old Filmore from Accounting and Personnel's obese Meg Smathers, her wide buttocks thrust upward in straining black slacks. Then the multiple explosions of white light occurred, and a faint hum of electric industry filled the air.

The supplicants backed away from the machines, adjusted their clothing, and exited the stage. More of the faithful were led forward.

When all of the crowd that cared to come forward had done so, the photocopied images were gathered with great pomp and brought to Stern, who raised the thick sheaf over his head and said, "From three dimensions to two. From thick to thin. From sleep to dream."

He nodded his head and the facilitators approached him and took the photocopies and divided them between themselves and fed them into the fax machines.

"From two dimensions to four. From thin to thick. From dream to the mind of Yog-Sothoth."

YOG-SOTHOTH! the crowd screamed.

YOG-SOTHOTH! YOG-SOTHOTH! There was a collective shivering, an undulating frenzy that seemed to travel through the crowd, each member convulsing as though part of some fused chain, electrified and then released, the air thick and silver. And in the liquid-mercury air, hidden by its reflective properties, things moved. And without seeing their true form, Philip knew their terror and otherworldliness. The Old Ones.

YOG-SOTHOTH! the crowd roared. *YOG-SOTHOTH!*

The Old Ones were coming through, summoned in some damnable bargain between vast corporations, souls faxed on a number that was, most certainly, a row of 6's.

They are not coming through. They are not because that isn't what happens at all, because—

And what if this were not the past, were, instead, an alternate world? Perhaps these cold and implacable Architects of Time had altered the outcome this time.

A dozen, two dozen articulated legs, scrambling wildly, pierced the void and sought purchase in this human realm. A leg touched one of the photocopiers, which burst instantly into flame. A second copier was lofted into the air.

They are—they are coming!

A dark, oblong shape obscured the ceiling. A noise, like laughter in the center of some shattering, all-destructive explosion, shook the underground cavern.

Here.

Too late. Too late.

A hissing. Rain. Not rain, but the sprinkler system. And not an alternate universe but the one that Philip had lived through before.

Thank you, God.

Something howled in frustration. Chairman Stern shouted vainly, "Wait."

The falling water tore holes in the silver fabric of the atmosphere. Thick, undulating bodies shivered and rained black scales that decayed and disappeared even as they fell. The silver air poured into invisible drains, once again revealing the dirty, dripping ceiling.

Philip laughed wildly, the laughter of

shattered reason, of relief. He laughed in unison with his old self, stumbling toward the stairs, pushing his way through the dazed crowd, moving in the clarity of utter exhaustion, his only goal his bed, sleep, forgetting.

Whup. "So," Lily was saying, "these Old Ones, these all-knowing super monsters, were scared off by the sprinkler system."

"I think," Philip said, "they may have misinterpreted the falling water. They may have identified it as rain, and thought they were emerging under open skies. They would not want to do that, of course. They would not want to be so exposed, not before they had regrouped. Their old enemies, the Mi-Go, had come from the sky and forced them to seek refuge under the ocean. They were naturally skittish about open spaces."

"Makes sense to me," Al Bingham said.

Lily frowned at her companion. "Why don't

you wait in the lobby?" she said. Al shrugged and left the room.

"Tell me," Philip's therapist said, moving to the dresser and fluffing her unruly hair in the mirror, "what do you think of me and Bingham as a couple?"

"Is this question pertinent to my therapy?" Philip asked. "I mean, will my answer determine your treatment modality?"

Lily shrugged. "No, I guess not."

"I want you to talk to Dr. Beasley about my medication. I think it is sapping energy. I believe I could actually be caught in MicroMeg if I jump one more time—"

The old woman reached forward and gripped Philip's shoulder. "I'll do that, Philip. Tomorrow, I want to shut the door on MicroMeg. I want to hypnotize you and end these nightmares, achieve closure on those events."

"We are not talking about nightmares," Philip said, feeling a sense of hopelessness.

Lily squeezed his shoulder. "Just let me try."

"Okay."

"Good." Lily nodded, turning to go.

"You could do worse than Bingham," Philip said.

A new woman had arrived in group, a stout, brown-haired woman with small, angry eyes. Her name was Caroline Trout.

"I am a goddess-empowered menstrual warrior," Trout told the group. "I only want justice; I only want the yoke of oppression lifted."

She had attacked a middle-aged man named Richard Milton, biting him on the wrist.

"I didn't do anything," he grumbled.

Olivia said, "Does anyone here feel Richard had a part in this?"

"We might not know all the facts," Sammy said. "Maybe he goosed her or something."

"He wasn't sensitive to her needs," Michael Jackson said.

"I just won't be railroaded by male-sexist power rhetoric," Trout growled.

"It's my goddam name!" Milton roared, jumping up.

"You should change it then," Trout said. "I won't be responsible for my actions if you call yourself an imperialist, territorial, invasive phallus."

"I'm not following any of this," said a timid woman who seemed uncertain of just where she was, having been in a number of psychiatric wards for depression.

Olivia smiled. "We have some boundary issues here, don't we? Does anyone feel that Caroline has overreacted?"

Either no one felt that way, or the question was simply beyond them. Silence.

"How about you, Philip?"

"I'm sorry," Philip said. "I can't seem to think of anything except the end of the world—well, the end of humanity, in any event, which I realize isn't the same thing at all. I think that end is approaching. I believe it is inevitable, and that the arrival of the Old Ones will render Ms. Trout's objections to Richard's nickname irrelevant."

Olivia continued to smile, but her eyes narrowed and lost what little warmth they held. "Well, I suppose we all think our personal problems are the center of the universe, but I want you to try very hard, Philip, to listen to others and empathize with them. I'll ask you, during the course of group, to be as attentive as possible."

Philip was about to say something, although he couldn't later remember whether it was in the nature of a rebuttal or acquiescence.

Richard Milton, speaking low in a taunting singsong and smiling grimly said, "Dick Dick Dick Dick Dick." He began to shout as Caroline leapt from her chair and raced across the circle.

"Stinking semen sack!" she screamed, hurling herself into him.

His chair slammed backward, but he continued to scream. "Dick Dick Dick!"

They rolled on the floor. Two orderlies came running.

Someone grabbed Philip from behind and dragged him backward. His chair tilted over. Bang. He struck out at his assailant, the lunatic bald man.

The bald man embraced Philip in a rib-cracking bear hug. "I been watching you," the bald man screamed. "You don't fool me. Thou Sower of Dissension, Thou Betrayer, Thou Vile Anti-Christ."

Whup. They rolled on the floor. Philip had his hand on her mouth. PLEASE, AMELIA, PLEASE. JUST BE QUIET. JUST LISTEN TO ME. YOUR MIND IS PRESENTLY IN THRALL TO POWERFUL ENTITIES TRANSMITTING ACROSS SIX HUNDRED MILLION YEARS. YOU ARE NOT—

She bit his hand.

OW!

Philip watched himself struggle with his lover, watched with some of the same sadness that hovered over their lovemaking.

Perhaps trickery would have worked better than force. But he had never been able to fool Amelia.

Amelia, I'm sorry.

He watched himself bind and gag her.

Don't hurt her.

What else could he have done? There was no time to spare, and although the Old Ones might wait to attempt a second crossing over, it was not something Philip could count on. He had to act. Reasoning with Amelia was out of the question. She had been subverted by Quality Management. Her wrist bore the tattoo, the writhing star that was the mark of the Old Ones. No doubt she had felt the eldritch light of photocopiers flood her mind and the damnable ecstasy of being faxed across the limitless reaches of black space.

The next day, before curfew, he had gone to the fifteenth floor, where Amelia slept at night, and he had jammed the lock on the fire exit door.

That night he had stolen to her room. And when she had opened the door, a protest on her lips, he had entered and wrestled her to the floor. Now as she struck at his face and chest, he felt no pain, just the jostling of vision, and he thought he probably hadn't felt pain then, either, being so full of larger fears.

He had prepared during the day. He placed his trussed lover in the mail cart he had commandeered, tossed the tarp over her, and said, I COULDN'T LEAVE WITHOUT YOU, AMELIA. LATER. LATER YOU'LL UNDERSTAND.

Don't bet on it.

He pushed the cart into the hall. Since last night, the building itself had altered. Did others see this? Perhaps they saw it with greater clarity, with eyes attuned to the Old Ones, or perhaps this sense of ruin and decay (strange bulges in the walls, dark burn marks on the carpets, damp, gray fungus on the ceilings) seemed only familiar, not new at all but some comfortable, amphibious memory unworthy of remark.

He would never get used to being a helpless observer in a younger self.

Don't get in the elevator! he screamed, but to no avail. He was a wraith, with no volition. What had happened had happened. It was ordained, because it was done.

So what exactly *had* happened? The memory was so damned clouded, so tumbled and twisted—

He got in the elevator, the doors shut, and the lights went out.

That's right.

He blinked at the darkness. What had he done? He had fumbled his hand over the buttons, banged the one for lobby, or what he thought was lobby, and descended slowly.

The doors opened on the basement; he saw the bulletin board and the cafeteria carts lined against the wall.

The light coming through the hall allowed him to see the buttons. He pressed the one for lobby. He watched the doors slide closed.

A black gloved hand reached out, caught the door and held it while the man swung into view.

Oh yes, I remember.

Hal Ketch, in full security regalia, smiled his long-toothed grin. His eyes flattened a little as the corners of his mouth made dark incisions in his cheeks. He was holding a small television under his left arm, nestled in the crook of his elbow, and a blurred black and white image was rolling across the screen.

He held the television up. "Would you look at this?" he said. "They'll show anything on cable."

Philip stared at the two figures rolling over the floor. Perhaps recognition would have been slower, but he had seen it before. He was wrestling with Amelia, there on the floor of her room, under the cold, bleak eye of the video.

"You can see right up her nightie. Look there." Ketch tapped the screen, tapped it with the gun's barrel.

"I'm going to have to ask you to step out, Mr.

Kenan. And just roll Ms. Price along too, would you? That's right."

Philip watched himself step into the hall, saw the mail cart in front of him, the tarp under which his true love lay.

Ketch pointed the revolver at Philip. "We will just park your lady friend here in the hall." He put the television down on the floor (Amelia was on her back now; Philip was tying her feet). Ketch grabbed the mail cart and shoved it down the hall. It came to rest against the wall.

"Come with me," Ketch said.

They were going down the stairs again, to the basement beneath the basement, and it was going to be very, very bad this time but he could not remember a thing about it. Not one thing. Why was that? The answer, he thought, was simplicity itself. His brain, his consciousness, refused to go to that dark place of recall. He was not so unlike Amelia, who had chosen to block it all out. Any consciousness with an interest in self-preservation might have done as much.

"Are you comfortable?" Lily asked. She sat in the chair opposite Philip. She was wearing a shirt advertising a new Austin rock group called Biff and the Bellyachers and their album *Buttload of Blues*. The T-shirt, and a tendency his therapist had of sucking in her lower lip and thrusting her chin forward in a manner that suggested senile addlement, did not inspire Philip's confidence.

"I just don't think this is a good time for this experiment," Philip said. "I'm in real trouble at MicroMeg. I thought that was over and done with, that at least that battle was over, but I suppose I had never really thought it through. If the Old Ones move as effortlessly through Time and Space as I think they do, then maybe they can hammer away at an event until they reshape it."

Lily nodded. Her gray hair was particularly unruly this morning, as though field voles had played a game of soccer in it. "All the more reason for getting you out for good," Lily said. "And hypnosis can't hurt. And Ann Beasley has given the go-ahead."

"Dr. Beasley is convinced you can do no wrong," Philip said.

Lily nodded brightly. "So show a little faith yourself." Lily reached over and turned the little portable tape recorder on. She adjusted the volume. *Lub dub Lub dub Lub dub.*

"Heartbeat," she said. "I want you to listen to this heartbeat, Philip. Close your eyes. We are going to go through a series of relaxation exercises and when you are ready, I'm going to put you into a trancelike state where you will be more susceptible to suggestion."

Philip nodded his head.

His therapist began to speak in measured tones, adopting a rhythmic cadence. "Let's see about those shoulders, first." She led him through some physical, muscle-stretching exercises, then breathing exercises, then imaging.

"The hill you are standing on is covered with the world's greenest grass, untroubled waves of grass under the bluest sky. Let's bring flowers to bloom. First dandelions, those hearty, yellow stars. Dandelions flashing into exultant life, dotting the hills. Now smaller, sprinklings of pink, let's say..."

Lub dub Lub dub Lub dub.

"Your heart sounds like the ocean, is in unison with the ocean. Sometimes this bigness scares us, this huge oneness, but there is nothing to fear because you can assert your individuality at any time. The great wheel of the world can contain you and hold you, but it cannot rob you of yourself."

Lub dub Lub dub Lub dub.

"You are safe."

Lub dub Lub dub Lub dub.

Huge, blue-black pistons rose and fell in Philip's field of vision.

They were in the basement of the basement at MicroMeg. And they were moving through a forest of machines, the huge trunks of oiled black cylinders rising and falling, the hiss of vented steam, and the hum of some monolithic generator.

They came to a door.

"Open it," Hal Ketch said. Philip could not see Ketch, but he assumed the security guard was behind him. He also had some memory of being prodded by the revolver, although now he felt nothing.

They entered the office.

I remember.

Desks, row upon row of desks, stretched out like mirrored reflections echoed into infinity. On each desk, an identical computer terminal rested. And seated at the desks were men and women, or what had once been men and women.

Ronald Bickwithers, Philip's supervisor, came briskly down an aisle.

"Philip, Philip," Bickwithers said, rubbing his hands together, "congratulations." Bickwithers smiled broadly and extended his hand. As usual, the man's suit appeared to have been slept in, and his shoe-polish-black wig had the unsavory sheen of a South American river leech.

Philip did not take the offered hand.

Bickwithers dropped his hand and nodded. "It's unsettling at first, I suppose. You have to see the big picture before you can truly appreciate what's happening here, what technology has wrought. And, of course, none of it would have come about without the transcendent help of the Old Ones."

Bickwithers shook his head. He extended an

arm. "Look, there's someone here you know. Follow me."

The floor of the room was strewn with junk: old screws and bolts and bits of wire. Philip's vision was troubled by that same silvering of the air that he had witnessed the previous evening at the ritual.

"Say hello to an old friend, Philip."

The thing at the terminal turned and grinned. A small, mossy stubble of hair (crew cut) grew on the single fragment of skull that sat like an island on the naked brain. The eyes were lidless and so robbed of much expression, or rather preserving an expression of constant surprise. A scaffolding of punched metal strips, like the toy girders in an erector set, held the features in place, but the naked musculature was plainly visible, and the way tendon cooperated with tendon when the creature grinned, sickened Philip.

"Welcome to the team," the man said. He sat upright in the chair and wore a white shirt, sleeves rolled up.

MERV? The voice was unrecognizable, but the inflection was familiar.

"We are golden on this," Merv said. "Golden."

I THOUGHT YOU WERE DEAD.

"Love to talk," Merv said, "but this deadline is stepping on my dick. Gotta roll." He leaned toward the screen.

"Death is so inefficient," Bickwithers said, throwing an arm around Philip. "We asked Merv if he would like to participate in this project. He was excited. He's a trooper, you know."

Philip saw that the computer had no keyboard, that wires sprouted from Merv's fingers feeding directly into the computer's back. Merv's hands trembled as the screen scrolled, a rolling sea of glowing green letters.

Philip read the words as they scrolled by, too fast for full comprehension. He recognized phrases, though.

Dear God.

THE NECRONOMICON.

"Ah," Bickwithers said. "You're familiar with Abdul's book. A masterpiece—and sadly corrupted by bad translations. Until now the only English version available has been Dr. Dee's immensely flawed one. We are correlating every translation, and using some other sources that seem relevant. It's quite a project, and when it is finished the book should be much more useful. I was hoping we could persuade you to pitch in. A terminal has come free, and we could really use you."

NO THANKS.

"Don't be like that, Philip. You haven't heard the whole package. I think a substantial salary increase would be in order, for one thing."

NO THANKS.

"Well it is not as simple as that, Philip. You are going to at least give it a try. You can do that for us."

Overhead the lights flickered and dimmed, then came back to full brightness. "Ah," Bickwithers said, looking up. "I hear there is quite a storm brewing overhead. Nothing to worry about here though. The computers have their own generators—which are quite impressive. Let me show you."

Philip walked behind Bickwithers and in front of Hal Ketch, trying not to look closely at the grisly crew that sat at the rows of desks and manned the computers. They were in various states of decay. Plastic tubes in a dozen bright colors (yellow, red, purple) pierced their peeled bodies. Webs of sheathed electrical wire wound in and out of flesh, terminating in dangling integrated circuits, knots of microchips, capacitors, resistors. One elderly woman, whose gold wire-rimmed glasses seemed firmly embedded in her cheekbones, rattled violently as they passed. Her hair went up in a whoosh of flame.

"Oh my goodness, oh my goodness," the old woman howled, rocking back and forth. Her voice was a raucous shriek, mindless, a parrot set on fire.

"Goddam," Bickwithers snapped. He whipped the radio from his belt and spoke into it.

"Overload at one nine two," he said. "This is Bickwithers. Overload. That's one nine two. Mrs. Lindsey has burnt out."

They moved quickly on, Bickwithers apologizing. "This sort of thing doesn't happen much anymore," he said. "And it is not the System that is to blame. We've fine-tuned the interview process, so we won't be getting any more folks like Mrs. Lindsey here. She was hired before we really had a good working model for an interview. We kept her on out of sentiment. I do believe a company has got to have a heart, but frankly I'll be glad when the last of these early hires is retired."

Bickwithers opened a door and Philip followed him into a harshly lighted arena. Bickwithers leaned over a circling iron railing. "Down there," he said.

WHAT IS IT?

"A Shoggoth," Bickwithers said. He chuckled genially. "I believe you're familiar with the term. Your file shows that you are something of an authority on such matters, in fact."

It's a Shoggoth. These were the monstrous, viscous creatures that the Old Ones had created to do their bidding. This one, black and massive and surging with strange, internal lights (like a huge amoeba that had fed on lava lamps) was, no doubt, the creature of his nightmares. He had tried to obliterate its memory, but its unholy image had burned itself into his subconscious and returned in dreams. Various wires and cables extruded from the body which was being used as a giant, living battery.

THE OLD ONES THEMSELVES ONCE LOST CONTROL OF THE SHOGGOTHS AND PAID A TERRIBLE PRICE. WHAT MAKES YOU THINK YOU CAN CONTROL THEM?

Bickwithers was unperturbed. He patted his shiny wig and preened. "The Old Ones assure us that these specimens are quite chastened. It is a shame, of course, that we have had to go back six hundred million years just to get good help. That says a thing or two about the sorry state of the world economy. It used to be that we could find cheap help just across the border. Well, don't get me started. Anyway, these Shoggoths are the first export from the Old Ones. We'll have the Old Ones themselves here in no time. Their transport is complicated; they are more sophisticated entities than Shoggoths, but I wouldn't be at all surprised if they arrived this very night. There is another Welcoming in progress as we speak, and no reason it shouldn't prove successful. Listen. Yes, I think you can hear the chanting. Hear it? Well, no matter. Soon we'll be rubbing elbows—or at least some sort of articulated appendage—with Tsathoggua, Cthulhu, Yog-Sothoth himself."

YOU WILL DESTROY HUMANITY!

"Any enterprise worth pursuing has some risk. The risk has to be measured against the potential gain. The gain here, for MicroMeg and its affiliates, is so immense that not acting, not seizing this opportunity, would be a sort of sin."

YOU CANNOT DO THIS. THEIR INTERESTS ARE NOT OURS.

Bickwithers looked at his watch. "I would like

to continue this discussion, but I have a meeting to attend. And, in any event, you have work of your own to do. We can't afford to pay you for your opinions. There's no market for opinions, Mr. Kenan."

Bickwithers suddenly began to shimmer. An aura of blue light surrounded him. The world lost focus. Philip remembered. Hal Ketch had just gripped his left arm and shoved the needle in. He was losing consciousness. He closed his eyes.

Darkness.

"Philip, can you hear me?"

"Yes," Philip said.

"I am counting backward from ten. Between six and two you will begin to awaken. On one you will be fully awake."

"Okay."

"Ten nine eight seven six..."

"I don't think I will be able to come."

"Five four three two..."

"Sorry."

"One. Philip. Philip. Wake up."

"I'm sorry. I was afraid of this."

❋

I was afraid of this. He came out of the darkness and blinked at the green cursor. The screen of his consciousness shifted. He saw his hands, resting over the keys.

"Ah, you are awake," a voice said. "Good."

He didn't turn his head. As he remembered, he couldn't.

A smiling, long-faced man in a lab coat leaned into Philip's field of vision. "Good to have you on board. We start new people out with a keyboard. It is much more efficient to direct feed, but we've found it is best to start folks out with input that is a little more familiar. We like to give you time to get used to the programs."

LET ME GO.

The man leaned forward, still smiling, and pressed a button on the keyboard. Instantly, the screen of Philip's vision shuddered. He was, he remembered, experiencing a profound pain, as though his entire nervous system were trails of gunpowder and someone had just ignited them with a match. The vibrating screen in front of him was, in fact, his own tormented and electronically bound body buzzing with agony.

"We have," the man continued, "really excellent motivators built into this program. I like to think that any employee who has worked here for more than three days is a team player. We would have one hell of a softball team here if these workers were ambulatory." The man touched the red button again and the screen ceased shivering.

"Let's start you out with something simple," the technician was saying. "We'll log you on to the Necronomicon routines. Just type NECRO. There. We'll probably have you doing some simple translation comparisons for the next couple of weeks. We'll—"

Voices welled suddenly in the distance. The air seemed to grow luminous. Philip's field of vision shifted, and he saw the ceiling bulge and something made of molten silver writhing above him.

"Excuse me," the man said. "I believe a historic moment is at hand. We'll continue this lesson in a bit. I just want to take a peek in the Welcoming room. Back in a jiffy—"

What happens next? Why couldn't he remember? Obviously, he had come through MicroMeg. How? There was a rending sound overhead. The voices continued to grow in volume, and it seemed that one voice, suddenly joining the others, was not human at all, was the strange, articulated speech of stone rubbing against stone. A scraping, scrabbling sound came from the ceiling, as though a plague army of rats were clawing their way through the plasterboard.

❈

"Philip?"

"What?"

"Philip, this is Lily. Wake up."

"I can't. They are coming through. I think..."

"Philip?"

"I think we lost this time."

"No, Philip. All you have to do is wake up."

"Well, I can't."

"I can help you. Tell me where you are?"

"I am beneath the basement of MicroMeg. I am electronically glued to a computer and the Old Ones are coming through."

"A computer."

"Yes."

"Perhaps—"

"Got to go."

The voices grew louder. *Amelia!* Amelia was in the hall, lying at the bottom of a mail cart and covered by a tarp. He remembered that, remembered how she had refused to let the incident go, how she had insisted that being bound and stuffed into a mail cart was symptomatic of a relationship on the skids. She had moved out—moved, indeed, all the way to Austin.

But the point was she had survived the incident. She had not been killed by Cthulhu or enslaved by Yog-Sothoth. Somehow, she had lived.

I rescued her, he thought. But how? And perhaps what happened then was not relevant to this returning. Perhaps this time the doom was final, and the black shroud of destruction would enfold the earth.

"Philip."

"Lily?"

"Philip, listen. MicroMeg was destroyed. You told me MicroMeg was destroyed."

"I can't remember."

"The kid in the mail room. He was going to destroy MicroMeg."

"And Hal Ketch blew his head off."

"How was he going to do it?"

"What?"

"How was he going to destroy MicroMeg?"

"Bombs. He had planted bombs throughout

the building. But they killed him and removed the bombs."

"Maybe they didn't get them all. Maybe they didn't get all the bombs."

Above Philip, the rumbling intensified. His vision shifted, and he saw his coworkers, saw that their eyes were fixed on the computer screens, their fingers jiggling. Business as usual during Armageddon.

He heard Lily's voice again, but it was far away, faint, and he could not make out what she was saying. Something about the computer.

Any computer in MicroMeg.

F.F. had said, "It's all linked through the mainframes. I can go to any computer in this joint, execute the command, and *Kablam!* the Philistines are dust again, and Jesus is hugging Himself for joy."

What if they hadn't gotten every single bomb? Flatulent Freddie had been busy, busy as a beaver. He had that smirky, something-up-the-sleeve look, a trickster, a clever crazy. What if they hadn't cleaned out his stash?

If that were the case, Philip could just execute the command, and... and *Kablam*!

And what was the command? F.F. had not volunteered that information. It would be hidden, of course. It wouldn't be brazenly sitting on any directory. It might move around, might—

I know what the command is. Was he remembering it or had he really figured it out? Well, if he was remembering it now, he had had to figure it out before, right? Again, reflections on the loop of time threatened to paralyze him. No time for that.

Voices roared. Silver shapes pressed against the ceiling. A large eye glared malevolently from a nest of bright, wirelike filaments.

"The Philistines are dust," Flatulent Freddie had said.

Samson. The command was *Samson.* And Philip was powerless to execute it. He was a ghost inside his own mind.

SAMSON!

"Philip, can you hear me?"

Not right now, Lily.

Philip screamed at his frozen hands. *Move!*
Dammit, move!

Nothing.

"Philip. Philip."

Not right now. Not— Wait.

"Lily. Take my hands. Hold my hands."

"Philip. Wake up."

"Lily. I need you to hold my hands. Squeeze
them as hard as you can."

"Philip—"

"Right now!"

Nothing. Wait. Philip saw the fingers of his
hands contract.

"Yes. That's right. Now Lily, you need to do
exactly as I tell you."

"All right, Philip."

"Take the ring finger of my left hand and push
it down, hard, don't worry about hurting me,
press it down h—"

The finger moved. On the screen a green "S"
appeared behind the glowing cursor.

Yes.

"Now the little finger of that same hand."

An "A" appeared. Philip continued to speak rapidly. Lily followed his instructions. The caps marched across the screen, bright warriors: "M. S. O. M."

Jesus. Not "M," "N." The backspace/delete key was up from the right hand, about two inches to the right.

"Lily. We hit the wrong key. Lift my right hand up and move it about two inches forward and to my right. Stop. Maybe a half inch more to the right. Okay. Press down the little finger. Okay! Great. Now back. I need an 'N' now. That's the first finger of the right hand down and a little to the left. All right. Now shift my right hand over. We need to execute the command. That's the little f—"

"Well, well. What are you up to, Philip?"

Ronald Bickwithers' smiling face loomed into view. His eyes were almost luminous with excitement.

"One of the techs paged me. Said we had some unauthorized movement. I really hated leaving the Welcoming, but I'm a manager, and

I have a manager's obligations. So I thought I'd take a look. I'm disappointed. This is not what we are paying you for, Philip."

Bickwithers reached toward the keyboard.

Philip watched his own finger press the "execute" key. Blip.

Bickwithers' hands stopped moving toward the keyboard.

PRAISE JESUS! PRAISE JESUS!
PRAISE JESUS! PRAISE JESUS!
PRAISE JESUS! PRAISE JESUS!
PRAISE JESUS! PRAISE JESUS!
PRAISE JESUS! PRAISE JESUS!
PRAISE JESUS! PRAISE JESUS!
PRAISE JESUS! PRAISE JESUS!
PRAISE JESUS! PRAISE JESUS!
PRAISE JESUS! PRAISE JESUS!
PRAISE JESUS! PRAISE JESUS!
PRAISE JESUS! PRAISE JESUS!
PRAISE JESUS! PRAISE JESUS!
PRAISE JESUS! PRAISE JESUS!
PRAISE JESUS! PRAISE JESUS!
PRAISE JESUS! PRAISE JESUS!

PRAISE JESUS! PRAISE JESUS!
PRAISE JESUS! PRAISE JESUS!
PRAISE JESUS! PRAISE JESUS!
PRAISE JESUS! PRAISE JESUS!
PRAISE JESUS! PRAISE JESUS!
PRAISE JESUS! PRAISE JESUS!
PRAISE JESUS! PRAISE JESUS!
PRAISE JESUS! PRAISE JESUS!
PRAISE JESUS! PRAISE JESUS!
PRAISE JESUS! PRAISE JESUS!
PRAISE JESUS! PRAISE JESUS!
PRAISE JESUS! PRAISE JESUS!
PRAISE JESUS! PRAISE JESUS!
PRAISE JESUS! PRAISE JESUS!
PRAISE JESUS! PRAISE JESUS!
PRAISE JESUS! PRAISE JESUS!
PRAISE JESUS! PRAISE JESUS!
PRAISE JESUS! PRAISE JESUS!
PRAISE JESUS! PRAISE JESUS!
PRAISE JESUS! PRAISE JESUS!
PRAISE JESUS! PRAISE JESUS!
PRAISE JESUS! PRAISE JESUS!
PRAISE JESUS! PRAISE JESUS!

PRAISE JESUS! PRAISE JESUS!
PRAISE JESUS! PRAISE JESUS!
PRAISE JESUS! PRAISE JESUS!
PRAISE JESUS! PRAISE JESUS!
PRAISE JESUS! PRAISE JESUS!
PRAISE JESUS! PRAISE JESUS!
PRAISE JESUS! PRAISE JESUS!
PRAISE JESUS! PRAISE JESUS!

The computer screen glowed with green rejoicing, filling completely and then beginning to scroll. Then it went blank.

Overhead, the ceiling was ballooning. Large, mercury-silver globules the size of basketballs detached and fell, slowly as though almost weightless. They hit the floor and exploded softly—*pock! pock! pock!*—and some living thing began to *reassemble* itself. As a work in progress, it was grotesque beyond description, and Philip knew somehow that the finished product would be yet more hideous.

He saw his hands in front of him, pushing the computer terminal over. It toppled with a crash. *The program had released him from his electronic thralldom.* Around him, other employees were tumbling or attempting to stand or clawing the air with their hands. One man was screaming as he staggered to his feet, his mouth spewing shattered teeth and blood.

A muffled thud sounded overhead. Then two sharp cracks. Yes. F.F. had managed to hide a few of them. But would it be enough?

Philip's vision lurched as Bickwithers enfolded him.

"You rotten malcontent!" Bickwithers screamed. "Slacker. Bum. Lazy welfare parasite scum!"

They rolled on the floor. Out of the corner of his eye, Philip could see a monster rebuilding itself. For the first time in his life, Philip prayed. *Sweet Jesus,* he prayed. *We need more bombs.*

And, perhaps because he had not overused prayer, had not used it for trivial petitions, an explosion answered his plea. The room turned into deafening noise and a welter of flying objects. The ceiling was snapped open. A scream of rage echoed across six hundred million years, and the thing on the floor vibrated and jerked like a snake in the jaws of an invisible bird of prey. It rose in the air, twisting, and disappeared in the roiling dust that poured down from the ruined ceiling.

Philip staggered to his feet. Bickwithers did not rise. He lay amid large shards of cinderblock, his bald head gushing blood. His wig lay just out of the reach of his outstretched hand, as though he had meant to retrieve it and so restore order.

Too late, Philip thought.

I QUIT.

Philip turned and fled. MicroMeg rained down. The vast pistons were stilled in the room of giant machinery.

The world was reduced to snapshots of falling concrete and plaster and dangling cables and hissing ducts.

He found the mail cart in the hall, tore the tarp away and felt his heart leap with thanksgiving. Amelia was alive, her eyes bright with that clear intelligence and fire that had so attracted him to begin with.

I'LL EXPLAIN EVERYTHING.

Whup. "Philip, thank God." Lily was looking down on him. Her features were a map of concern and compassion. Philip lay smiling up at her. He forgot, momentarily, that the use of his body was returned to him, so he did not respond or try to move until his therapist asked him if, in fact, he *could* move.

"Well yes, I think I can," Philip said, pushing himself into a sitting position.

"This hypnosis was not such a hot idea after all," Lily said, once she had helped him into a chair. She was shaking. He realized it had been an ordeal for her too.

"On the contrary," Philip said. "Hypnosis was a great idea. Without it I think the world as we know it would have ceased to exist."

Later that day when Philip went to Group, Olivia asked how he was doing.

"I think I have had a breakthrough," Philip

said. "I'm beginning to see Amelia's side of things."

"Amelia?"

"My ex-girlfriend. I'm beginning to understand why we broke up."

"Yes?"

"I think she wanted someone a little more solid. I mean, what kind of life can a woman have with a novelist?"

PART THREE

THE PERILS OF PELIDYNE

our months after the publication of the first volume of *The Despicable Quest* (entitled *The Blight*), Philip received his first fan letter, forwarded by his publisher without comment. The envelope was purple and the letter was handwritten on purple stationery in a large, exuberant script:

Dear Philip—

I stayed up all night reading this book, and all I can say is Wow! and Wow! again. It was sooooo good.

I can't wait to find out what happens next. Does Daphne escape from Bleakham? Don't tell me.

Dirk, my boyfriend, doesn't like you. He is jealous. Ha Ha. He wanted some action last night, and I said, "No thank you. Get that thing away from me. I am reading this great book, and I can't be bothered."

Naturally, we had a fight. When he passed out I took my picture out of his wallet.

I am sending you this picture to serve him right. I think you are a great writer, and I hope the next book comes out soon.

Love, Sissy Deal

PS I liked your picture, but I think you should get a new one made for the next book. You look too sad, I think. I also think the mustache should go. My guess is it was just an experiment, and maybe your friends have already voted and you have shaved it off. I can tell by your eyes that you

are a very sweet and caring person, so the
mustache doesn't fool me, but it is kind of shifty
and some people might find it a definite turn-off.

Philip studied Sissy's photo and rubbed his upper lip; the mustache had been a mistake, deleted soon after the book's publication, and he was impressed by this stranger's insight. He was equally impressed by the photo which showed a young woman wearing a Panama hat and nothing else. The photo was taken outside, next to a bright yellow plastic wading pool. She had obviously been persuaded to remove her bathing suit—the blue bikini top lay in the grass at her feet—and the whiteness of her breasts and hips indicated that she was not in the habit of going nude outdoors. She rested her hands on her hips, leaning slightly forward, her lithe body easily dispensing with any artistic cavils regarding composition and lighting. She was laughing, her red hair tumbling over her shoulders in a shining tangle. Philip couldn't see her eyes, which were lost in the shadow of the hat's brim, but he knew they were full of high-spirited mischief, and he suspected they were blue.

If he were only going to get one fan letter, Philip thought, this wasn't a bad one to get. He wrote her back—to an address in Tallahassee.

"Dear Sissy," he began, "Your letter arrived at a low point for me, professionally and personally, and I can't tell you how much I appreciate your kind words and the charming photo you enclosed. I fear I have bad news for the both of us. My publisher has just informed me that the dismal performance of my first book makes continuing the series untenable. I have also learned that my ex-girlfriend is getting married, which destroys my dream of a reconciliation."

When Philip had gotten out of the psychiatric hospital, he had hoped to persuade Amelia to come and live with him. "I'm a changed man," he told her. "I had some major revelations in treatment. I see your side of things, now. And I'm on very effective medication. No more Cthulhu. No more Yog-Sothoth."

Amelia had been skeptical, of course, but that was just to be expected. He hoped to win her back with patience and love.

But he made no progress toward the harbor of her heart. Although she agreed to see him for an occasional Saturday lunch date, she remained skittish, as though he might at any moment tie her up and deposit her in another mail cart.

Philip was worried about Amelia's employment at Pelidyne, and when he saw her, he was often dismayed by the extent to which the workplace ruled her conversation. He saw no signs of domination by malevolent creatures from outer space—this medication really *did* work— but her world seemed narrow and airless and unhealthy. She seemed paler than usual— although this might be a new cosmetic experiment—and her mouth had lost some of its lively delight in the words it formed.

He loved her. He was worried about her. He felt that she was moving away from him.

Philip secured the occasional word processing job through a temporary employment agency called On Time. These jobs would last a few days or a few weeks and then end. There was plenty of time for the writing of novels, but Philip found that the medication that kept the monsters at bay was equally effective in repelling the muse. During his off hours, he thought about Amelia.

He lay in his apartment on rainy nights listening to the water pour through the system of pipes that he had cleverly rigged to send the ceiling's waterfall directly to the sink in the bathroom. He drank beer, more than was, perhaps, prudent, and he thought about Amelia in her small garage apartment in Hyde Park where she had settled after she left her sister's house.

Philip missed her with a kind of stretched-tight yearning that was exhausting. If he could be with her, he would ask nothing more. He would be content to be invisible in her presence, a well-behaved ghost.

This thought (engendered, no doubt, by a fatal combination of psychotropic drugs and alcohol) evolved into a plan of action. It required a movie theater that was next to a hardware store. Once such a theater was discovered, Philip had to wait until a movie was showing that appealed to Amelia. Then he had to convince Amelia to go. She was disinclined to go, indeed she was growing more remote with every meeting or phone conversation, but Philip eventually prevailed. It was a Saturday afternoon. That too was critical, since the hardware store closed at five in the evenings and was not open Sundays.

Philip easily slipped Amelia's apartment key from her purse at the start of the movie, left Amelia in the darkened theater— "I've got to get popcorn," he told her—and took the key to the hardware store. The clerk made a duplicate, and he was back in the theater buying popcorn in less than fifteen minutes. "Long line," he whispered to Amelia. He dropped her own key back in her purse.

During the day, he would let himself into her apartment and lie on her bed. Sometimes he would drink a couple of beers while lying there. The effect was soothing, reassuring. Surrounded by Amelia's sweet clutter—she was not an orderly woman—Philip would sense a kind of karmic marshaling of powers. She never made her bed, and he would lie on top of the sprawl of pale yellow sheets and smell the dazzle of different perfumes she wore and imagine her there. He knew, of course, that he was invading her privacy, and that what he was doing was indefensible, but, as is the case with all lost souls, he reveled in his abject condition.

He would bring a small travel clock with him, setting it for four in the afternoon in case he dozed. He did not want Amelia to catch him sleeping in her bed. He expected that such a discovery would seriously impair his efforts to win her back.

He was right.

His heart recognized the sound of the key in the lock and all its implications before his clouded brain knew anything. He came out of sleep with his heart racing and blinked at Amelia's stunned features at she stared at him from the bedroom door. She had come home early. Without a word, without a scream, she dropped the briefcase and fled. Philip jumped up and ran into the living room. The door to the apartment was open.

He saw her climbing into her car.

"Amelia!" he shouted. She did not turn around.

He went back inside and gathered the beer cans and the travel clock and put them in a paper bag. He locked the door behind him and walked down the stairs. Amelia was sitting in her car at the curb. She glared at him as he approached. When he was ten feet from her, she leaned on her horn, and roared away.

Downcast, Philip got in his own car and drove back to his apartment.

There was a message on his answering phone.

"How could you?" Amelia sobbed. "How? Don't ever, ever talk to me again."

Philip was fairly certain that there was nothing he could do—at least immediately—that would improve the situation.

Philip was still seeing Lily Metcalf once a week. She told him, "You wobbled outside the bounds of acceptable social behavior, Philip. I suppose you can see that? I'm sure you have a better grasp on such things than poor Jay Martin, who, if you will recall, was not one of your favorite people in treatment and who urinated in the saltwater aquarium without giving it a second thought. I like to think that your understanding of society's little rules is sharper than Jay's."

Amelia had called Lily, who had persuaded the younger woman not to go to the police.

"I told her you weren't dangerous," Lily said, "although I confess my opinion there is intuitive and not exactly reinforced historically. She said you tied her up once and put her in a mail cart with a tarp over her."

"I saved her life," Philip said.

Lily nodded. "Uh huh. Well, I assured her that you would leave her alone."

"Maybe you could explain how I have been going through some hard times."

Lily shook her head slowly. "No. I don't think mitigating circumstances are what she wants right now. I think she wants a reassurance that you will leave her alone."

"The thing is—" Philip began.

"Philip!"

"Well, okay, sure. I understand how this is a major setback."

"Philip," Lily said, "Amelia is engaged to be married. You are not winning her back."

And the very next day, when Philip watched Amelia pull into evening traffic from the parking lot of Pelidyne, when he followed her—in a rental car; he was no fool—north on Lamar, he knew the truth of what Lily told him. He didn't have to have it spelled out. He didn't really need to see them embrace on the porch steps.

Amelia's fiancé was a tall, good-looking guy, obviously just off work himself, his tie loosened. He kissed her long and hard in the dappled sunlight. They were both wearing suits, and there was a certain androgynous aspect to their lovers' clinch until he slid a hand in her blouse and she laughed and pushed away, exposing a wanton glimpse of breast and bright red bra.

No, Philip felt that this scene was overdone. The Dark Gods must have thought he was particularly dense, that he had to have everything spelled out.

All right. All right. She's romantically involved.

It was fitting that a letter should arrive, the very next day, from his publisher saying that *The Despicable Quest* was terminated.

"**W**ow!" Sissy wrote back.

I went out to the mailbox and there was your letter, and I called up my friend Louise and said you sent me a letter and she said What did it say? and I said I don't know cause I haven't opened it and she said You goof and we both had a good laugh and when I hung up I read the letter and it was so sad I cried so that Dirk asked me what was the matter and I told him and we got in another fight and I crashed his car, which is a long story. He blames you for crashing his car. Can you believe it?

Anyway, I think it is awful about your book and I hope your publisher eats poison snails in some geeky New York French restaurant and dies, and excuse me but your old girlfriend doesn't sound like your type anyway, and I think you are well off without her.

You need a woman who is also a big fan. I guess that is not a hint, but you could take it that way and I wouldn't mind.

The letter was eight pages long and narrated the events in Sissy's life and the lives of her numerous siblings and relatives. The family seemed to be a contentious one, and they were presently fighting over the custody of a child with the unlikely name of Gator, the offspring of someone named Skeet who had disappeared and was rumored to be living in Alaska.

A week after receiving this second letter from

Sissy, Philip found himself at a party thrown by his therapist.

"It is not kosher to fraternize with clients," Lily told him, "but I met Al through you, so it is fitting you should come. Besides, I'm retired. Who's gonna fuss?"

Midway through the party, Al Bingham climbed up on a chair and announced that he was going to marry Lily Metcalf.

Everyone applauded as the loving couple embraced and kissed.

As the party wore on, Philip found himself experiencing the usual sense of disorientation and loss. He didn't know anyone at the party except Lily and Bingham, and he was standing amid several college professors.

A fat man with a close-cropped gray beard studied his coffee cup. "This china is rather like the china they had when I visited Yale to deliver my paper on cognitive responses to sexual imagery in male adolescent peer groups."

A shrill young woman leaned forward, "I can't tell you the amount of coffee I drank while studying under York who has gone on to win a Nobel, you know, and who said I was probably the best student he ever had."

A very thin man nodded his head. "Feldstein always spoke highly of York. I had come down to UT to deliver a lecture which Dean Markson later said was the highlight of the semester, and Feldstein came up to congratulate me on the Morrison grant and..."

Philip drifted away from the group and was on his way out the door when Bingham caught him.

"Leaving so soon?" the old printer asked.

"I've got to get up early tomorrow," Philip said. "The temp agency called with a job."

"Ralph was asking about you yesterday," Al said. "Said he missed you."

"I bet."

"Yeah. Well, you know Ralph."

Philip and Bingham walked outside and stood on the lawn.

"I'm pretty excited about marrying Lily," Bingham said.

"I think it's great. Congratulations."

"Thanks. Hey—" Bingham grew suddenly awkward, fishing a cigarette pack from his pocket and tapping one out on his sleeve. "Since you brought us together, I was wondering if you would be best man."

"It would be an honor," Philip said. "When is the wedding?"

"Next week. Saturday."

"That soon?"

"Gotta move fast," Bingham chuckled, at ease again, clutching Philip's shoulder. Bingham winked lasciviously. "Wouldn't want her to get knocked up out of wedlock."

For the wedding, Philip wore a rented tux, brown and shiny. When he tried on a smile in the mirror, he thought he resembled some sort of aquatic mammal, an insincere seal corrupted by long association with a carnival, perhaps.

The wedding ceremony itself was brief. Both Lily and Bingham were as excited as children at a costume party.

Some people, Philip thought, *never* lose their enthusiasm.

Driving home from the wedding, Philip squinted into the descending sun and reflected on how very flat and unappealing his own life had become. Life had occasionally seemed hopeless when vast, malignant creatures were manipulating humanity for their own inscrutable purposes, but the monsters now seemed trumped by the unbearable weight of daily existence. Reality's bored visage... this was more dreadful than the star-shaped face of Cthulhu himself. Philip resolved to stop taking his medication.

On Sunday, Philip read the help-wanted ads and circled several. He was sick of temp jobs, folding envelopes or wrestling with unfamiliar computer software.

Over the course of his life, he had learned to interpret the language of want ads. "Entry level" meant a dismal minimum wage job that never evolved into anything else since even the toughest and most desperate of employees only lasted a month before quitting. "Go-getters" were solicited for sales positions hawking products like life insurance and shared vacation time. "Must love people" was a clear warning that the customers were difficult, perhaps psychotic. "Industrious" people were requested to apply for work at sweatshops filled with dispirited, bitter employees. Ads offering work in the "entertainment" industry were invariably seeking clerks for video stores.

On Monday, Philip called a company that was seeking a full-time word processor, and he went to their downtown offices and filled out an application. He was called that same afternoon and scheduled for an interview on Wednesday.

The interview was conducted by a pale, multi-chinned man whose dark hair was firmly slicked down. He rattled Philip's résumé and leaned forward.

"Says here you've written and published a novel," the man said.

"Yes," Philip said. He had debated adding this information to his résumé, but the help-wanted ad had asked for someone with writing skills. The published novel, Philip reasoned, might be a credential for such a job.

"This position we are offering is not glamorous like writing novels," the man said. "I don't know that you would be happy typing up letters and reports after writing novels."

Philip assured the man that he would be happy with steady work.

"I'll be candid with you," the man said, displaying yellow teeth, "we have got seventy-two people applying for this job. I can't hire but one. Should I take someone who has been laying back making up stories, sleeping till noon, living off big checks from New York and maybe taking enough drugs and booze to kill a rhinoceros?" He raised a pink hand to stop Philip from interrupting. "I know, I know, you are gonna tell me you aren't anything like that, but I'm saying I got seventy-two people hungry for this job, and some of them have been steady, solid word processors for years now. They are sharp with a lot of software packages, and they wouldn't *read* a novel much less write one. They are reliable, matter-of-fact people. What am I gonna do?"

Philip realized the interview was at an end, thanked the man and left.

He kept his novel on his résumé for three more interviews, then deleted it. The final decision to do so came when Philip was interviewed by a thin, nervous man who had, himself, written three novels, none of which had been published, because New York publishing was now ruled by faggots and militant feminist lesbians. The man maintained that anyone who could get a novel published was a pervert or a pussy-whipped lackey.

In his dentist's office that weekend, Philip read a magazine article, a survey of various jobs rated according to prestige. Being a writer was in the top five percent.

On Monday Philip's temp agency, On Time, sent him on a new job. He found himself entering data on a computer lodged in a small office that was being used as a temporary storage space for moldy boxes of old paperwork and large coils of electrical wire. Somewhere above him his beloved Amelia chatted with coworkers, stopped for a drink at the water fountain, spoke on the phone, conferred with her boss. Philip was at Pelidyne.

His first day at Pelidyne seemed excruciatingly long. He was convinced that Amelia would think he was spying on her if she saw him. An explanation was on his tongue all day long, ready to be blurted.

But he did not encounter her.

When he drove home from work, exhausted, a woman jumped up from the curb in front of his apartment and shouted his name.

She ran up to him. "I'm Sissy Deal," she said, snatching her sunglasses off and smiling. She winked. "Recognize me with clothes?"

ctually, she did look slightly different with clothes. She was wearing a dress—which is not what Philip would have expected—and it was a sort of old-fashioned, matronly dress, dark blue with small white dots. The dress didn't seem to fit properly. Later, Philip came to realize that Sissy was one of those beautiful women who did not wear clothes well, thus giving men an aesthetic as well as a sexual motive for urging her out of them.

"I should have called or something," she said. "But I got in a fight with Dirk. I was gonna go down to St. Petersburg and stay with Leda, but I got to the bus station and asked How much for Austin and it was reasonable, so I said Sold!"

"Come on inside," Philip said. He picked up her suitcase and she followed him up the wooden stairs to his apartment.

In the room, there was only the chair and the bed, so he sat her in the chair and went and made tea.

"You look a hundred percent better without that mustache," Sissy said.

"Well, thanks. You were right about the mustache. It was a bad idea."

"Sometimes a beard is good if a man has a weak chin. But mustaches are sort of pointless and kind of, no offense, vain."

Philip nodded. "You're right. You're right."

Sissy got up and came into the kitchen to watch Philip pour the hot water into cups.

"I know I should have called or something," she said.

"No, that's fine," Philip said. "Really fine."

"I didn't think it through."

"I'm impulsive myself," Philip said, handing her a steaming cup.

"On the bus I sat next to this red-faced guy in a suit, and we started talking, I don't know, about the weather and stuff and how his wife hated him and wouldn't give him a blow job. I tried to change the subject, so I told him about your book and showed him it—I brought it along for you to autograph—and he said—can you believe it?—that he didn't go for books that had monsters or fantastic things in them. He liked books that were just like life. Why would anyone like books that were just like life? So he told me about this book he had read that he thought was great about this businessman on a bus who meets this redheaded woman and they do all kinds of sexual stuff, right on the bus, very explicit, cock-this, pussy-that, you know." Sissy paused, lowered her tea cup from her lips. "I bet there isn't any such book. What do you bet?"

"Maybe not," Philip said.

Sissy stayed at Philip's apartment that night. Philip offered her the bed, but she insisted on sleeping in the ancient sleeping bag he hauled out of the closet.

"I don't want to inconvenience you," she said.

"Not at all," Philip said. "I'm glad you came. I've had a rough day, actually. The temp agency I'm signed up with sent me to the place where my ex-girlfriend works."

"Gosh. Did you see her?"

"No. But I felt pretty weird."

"Sure."

Philip hadn't had a sympathetic ear in a long time. Well, there was Lily, of course, who helped him sort through things and who certainly had his best interests at heart—but that was still a client/counselor relationship. Lily was not apt to say something like, "Amelia doesn't understand you. She is a cold-hearted bitch, and you are better off without her."

Sissy and Philip went out and ate at a cafeteria-style restaurant, Dan's Texas Bar-B-Que, and Sissy had to explain to the cashier about change. The cashier was a dark, hairy man in an apron, and when he handed Sissy her change, a dime fell to the floor and Sissy had to retrieve it. She stood up and leaned across the counter, past the cash register, and caught the man's arm.

"It's not your fault," she said. "A lot of people do it that way. Just because no one told them otherwise. They slap the bills down, and then they pour the change on top, so that it naturally slides right off. They do it over and over again without a clue. They must think they have a lot of clumsy customers, is all. Look, open your hand. Okay. I put the change in first. Then the bills. Not very complicated."

The man blinked at her, holding the money.

She smiled, nodded.

"Change first," she said, presenting her palm.

The man poured the change into her hand and then the bills. He smiled.

"That was easy, wasn't it?"

He laughed. "Sure, lady. I think I could master it with practice."

After they ate their meal, the cashier, who was also the owner and was, in fact, named Dan, came around and offered Sissy a job. He offered it jokingly, but Philip could see that he was also serious.

"I'm just visiting Austin," she said. "I'm on vacation."

That first night, Philip pretended to read a detective novel, but he kept peeking over the top of the book to study Sissy. He could not keep his eyes away from her. Propped up by pillows and wearing a blue nightgown, she was reading.

Philip kept the air conditioning on high. He knew this was an energy-wasting, environmentally unsound practice, and he felt guilty about it but was unable to resist doing so. Sissy was, consequently, snuggled deep in her sleeping bag, and there was nothing about her form, a shapeless, muffled lump, to inspire prurient thoughts. Oh, the circumstances themselves might have inspired such thoughts...

a pretty girl in a nightgown; a man pining for a lost lover, celibate for far too long. But it was not sexual yearning that kept Philip darting glances in her direction. He studied her face, the brightness of her eyes, the way her lips formed an almost spoken word. He studied her with breathless intensity.

And if she had suddenly turned, caught him staring, thrown down the loose pages, leapt up and hurled herself into his arms, he would have been hurt. She was reading his manuscript, the rest of *The Despicable Quest*, and reading it avidly—fascinated beyond passion's reach.

True readers were rarer than lovers.

He fell asleep, and in the morning, when he woke, she was still reading. He brought her a cup of coffee and asked if she wanted breakfast.

"Nah. I'll get something out of the fridge later."

Philip hovered over her.

"Do you like it?" he asked. She didn't respond. She clutched a hefty section of the typewritten manuscript, leaning forward. Her expression was that of a tourist peering into the Grand Canyon. A critical thumbs up, Philip decided.

"I've got to go to Pelidyne," he said. "I hope you can stay. I hope I'll see you this evening."

Sissy looked up. "See you," she said.

Philip's first day at Pelidyne had been uneventful except for the anxiety produced by his proximity to Amelia. His second day was, to describe it succinctly and literally, dreadful.

As on the previous day, a small woman whose gray-black hair resembled an imperfectly sculpted shrub accompanied Philip to the basement, booted his computer up, and showed him the reams of paper, the results of a questionnaire on some new software package and its ease of use.

Since Philip had already mastered the art of transferring the X's and O's to the computer templates, he was spared the previous day's instructions. The woman left him, closing the door after delivering yesterday's injunction, "And please, Mr. Kenan, no smoking." As on the previous day, Philip assured her that he did not smoke, and she smiled and nodded with the air of someone too polite to dispute a bald-faced lie.

Alone, Philip began inputting data. The computer, of course, would log the number of papers entered, so there was no goofing off. On the other hand, it made no sense to move too fast in the morning. The day was long and you had to pace yourself.

At lunch, Philip went down the hall to the snack room and got a meatball sandwich out of the vending machine. He microwaved it into steaming glop. Not bad. He washed it down with a Coke, ate a bag of Fritos to ensure the proper amount of roughage in his diet, and went back to his office.

He had just settled down in the chair when the overhead lights flickered and the screen shivered. *Shit.*

The screen returned to normal, blanked, and began to flash the all-caps message: EXPERIENCING POWER FLUCTUATION/ FAILURE PROBLEMS. ALL OPERATORS ARE ADVISED TO SAVE FILES IMMEDIATELY.

The lights went out, plunging the windowless room into darkness. Philip stood up and stuck his arms out in front of him and groped his way to the door. He found the doorknob and opened the door. Lights were out in the hall, but the darkness wasn't absolute; some of the day's light was seeping in through narrow slits high in the wall at the end of the corridor.

"Hello," Philip shouted. "Hello."

Philip was used to power failures, and he was disinclined to look for a stairway and seek out someone who might direct him to some other busywork that did not require the empowerment of electricity. If his services were really needed, they knew where to find him.

He made his way back to the chair in his office. As soon as he entered the room, the darkness folded around him again. He turned back to the door and propped it open with a heavy cardboard box, allowing the feeble light from the hall to enter. The room was still dark, and if he looked away from the door, toward the back of the room, he studied a wall of night.

He stared at this darkness, waiting to see if eventually it would lighten, if his pupils could dilate more or those light-gathering rods critical to night vision could muster up new enthusiasm for perception. As a long-term temp and employee at many menial jobs, Philip's mind was adept at discovering games and methods for making a stationary, near-vegetable existence more endurable.

He may have fallen asleep briefly. Or he may have simply been taking a breather from thinking. In any event, a scraping noise commanded his attention, and he discerned, simultaneously, a slow, white blur in the darkness.

He was staring at the back wall where the vaguest sort of half-light had folded itself around several metal cabinets and a collection of wall shelves.

Something over one of the metal cabinets was moving, a rectangle, like a piece of typing paper shifting from the horizontal to the vertical. The scraping noise accompanied the motion.

At first Philip could make no sense of this

pale moving square and then, through powers of deduction more than observation, he realized that he was looking at some sort of air vent grill or grate. And it was being moved, pried open, by something on the other side.

He would have left then. MicroMeg—not to mention Ralph's One-Day Résumés—had exhausted his store of curiosity. But he could not move. The paralysis that overtook him was, it seemed, produced by a strange odor, something between dead fish rotting on a beach and cloying, lavender perfume. This stench seemed to strike at his volition, so that his arms and legs were divorced from his will.

Surely this was some sort of dark, unpleasant dream that had ambushed him when his senses were not fully employed.

And in the next instant, he knew it was not a dream, because his subconscious was not capable of conjuring what he saw.

A bald, grotesque head appeared, accompanied by a single knobby, bare shoulder. Like some insect crawling from its larval shell, the creature flexed and emerged, tumbling onto the top of the metal cabinet with an unholy, leathery thump.

Philip stared at the creature, which was, in fact, a pale old man, simian-featured, shrunken and misshapen, but undoubtedly human. His flesh was faintly luminous, and when he grinned, his teeth showed pink and pointed in a round, lipless mouth.

He had seen Philip, for he nodded in Philip's direction and stretched a hand toward him. It contained some flickering square of paper, a white moth in the gloom.

The man was bare-chested, the bones of his rib cage like the legs of giant spiders or crabs. He wore dirty gray trousers and black, pointed shoes that were surprisingly shiny, like polished coal.

He spoke, leaning forward suddenly, expelling the word like a cat coughing up a dead lizard. "Team," he rasped. "Team." Then, more chilling yet, he said, "Dagon."

A single dirty piece of cloth was knotted

around his thin neck, and Philip recognized it for the remnants of a tie.

The man turned and began to climb down the metal cabinet.

Philip's consciousness tried desperately to rally his arms and legs, but those appendages had abandoned him. The bone-penetrating reek had bound him to his chair.

The small man, his hunched and knobby back facing Philip, made shrill, wheezing noises as he clambered slowly down the cabinet.

He reached the floor and turned.

He came quickly, with a crablike scuttle, to Philip's side.

At this point, Philip thought he might have blacked out, a final evasive action on the part of his reason. But if he blacked out, the respite was brief. He woke, felt the creature rummaging through his pockets, and watched as it extracted a pencil.

"Ah," it sighed, turning the pencil in front of its round, delighted eyes.

As Philip watched, the ghoul thrust the pencil through one of its cheeks and out the other. It laughed then, and Philip could see the yellow shaft of the pencil above a greenish tongue. "Huh huh," the creature wheezed.

It waved a piece of paper in front of Philip, reached out, and tucked it into the pocket of Philip's shirt. A flat, rubbery hand patted Philip's chest. "Team," the creature said again.

Light flickered overhead. A generator made a sound, a *whunk*, and Philip felt as though a metal drawer were suddenly slammed shut within his chest.

"Eeee," the thing shrieked, cowering away from the burst of overhead light. The room dove into darkness again.

One burst of light had been enough to rob Philip of his hard-won night vision. All was darkness now, as Philip listened to the scrambling and animal coughs, a final scraping sound, and then silence.

Ten minutes later, before Philip's eyes had rekindled any images, the overhead lights went on. Philip found that he could stand. The odor had abated. Overhead, the grate was back in place.

The computer screen, blinking green, was uttering the codes of its rebooting routines. Philip went to it and turned it off.

He left the room and walked quickly down the hall.

"Mr. Kenan," the woman said, intercepting him at the end of the corridor, "are you leaving?"

"I'm afraid so," he said. "I'm not feeling well."

Outside the cause of the power failure was evident. Another rainstorm shook the city, sheets of rain jiggling the disabled stoplights. Rainstorms had not done well by Philip in Austin, and he drove slowly, tensed for disaster. But nothing untoward occurred, and aside from getting drenched in his dash up the wooden steps, he reached his door unscathed. Sissy opened the door as he was about to insert his key into the lock and—having completely forgotten about her—Philip screamed.

"Rough day?" Sissy asked.

Philip had recovered himself and was lying on the bed, his tie loosened, a pillow propped up behind his head. He didn't trust himself to talk; he nodded grimly.

"It is a crime that you should have to work at a stupid office anyway," Sissy said. "You are a genius. You should be spending all your time writing. *The Despicable Quest* is the greatest book in the world."

"Thank you," Philip said, grateful for the praise.

"Sure." Sissy brought Philip a beer and sat on the bed next to him. "Some of it is pretty scary though. Like when Daphne goes into Blackwater Mountain during the Festival of the Blood Leech. I had to close my eyes during parts of that. Does it scare you too? I mean, when you write it, does it scare you?"

Philip drank the beer. "Yes. It scares me sometimes."

He frowned as a thought surfaced, one that looked like truth as he spoke it although he had never fashioned it before. "But I thought if I wrote them inside a story, they would stay there. The world would be safe."

"Didn't work, huh?"

Philip sighed. "Amelia thinks it just made it worse. She thinks I made up a lot of monsters. So does my therapist."

"It's cold in here," Sissy said. "You really like to crank the air conditioning up, don't you?"

"I guess I do. Texas is pretty hot, you know."

"It's not hot in here; it's cold. We should get under these covers."

They lay under the covers, staring at the ceiling with its assortment of pipes. Sissy apparently found nothing remarkable about this solution to the leaks.

"This was called bundling in colonial times," Philip said. "People would lie under the covers in bed, fully-clothed, perfect strangers."

"I feel like I've known you forever," Sissy said.

"Today, at work, the power went off and while it was dark, this creature crawled out of an air vent, this horrible little ghoullike old man. I couldn't move. I was paralyzed by some sort of nerve gas coming from the vent. I was terrified."

Sissy was silent.

"Well?" Philip asked. "What do you think?"

"Lying in bed with all your clothes on is kind of sexy, you know. Stupid, but sexy."

"Do you think I'm crazy? Do you think I was suffering from some sort of hallucination?"

Sissy pushed her face across the pillow so that it was an inch from Philip's. She had freckles on her nose and on her cheeks, small orange constellations that could, with study and time, be given names and legends. She smiled wickedly and said, "Do you ever screw your therapist?"

"No. Of course not," Philip said, hearing a certain huffiness in his voice.

"I didn't think you did."

Philip smiled, a polite but baffled smile.

"Well I'm not your therapist. I wouldn't want you to mistake me for your therapist."

Sissy reached out and tapped Philip's nose with a silver-dollar-sized foil-wrapped package. "I'm a modern girl," she said. "And this is modern bundling."

Sissy made love wordlessly and athletically. Her body was generous and warm and more finely modeled than her midday Polaroid declared. She slid amid the sheets with happy, dolphin grace and got up occasionally to change a CD on Philip's player. She was very particular about lovemaking music and found Philip's collection lacking ("Bob Dylan and Lou Reed may be great artists and everything but they are cold water on naked romance. Oh hey, you've got k.d. lang. Now that's more like it".)

In the morning, Philip woke early and lay on his side studying the sweet, eloquent and beautifully wanton curve of Sissy's body. She lay curled on her side, facing away from him, revealing the golden arc of her hip, her glorious, confident bottom, and her bright, declarative thighs that flowed into youthful calves and on into feet that were exclamations of delight... the poet in Philip soared, then caught its fleshy feet on a glimpse of the red tuft of hair that flared between her thighs. He snuggled next to her, stiff now, a blind, all-business cock pressing a pliant buttock. He snatched another condom from the end table; rolled it on with clumsy haste, finding something wildly erotic in this under-the-sheets furtiveness.

"Hmmmmm," Sissy murmured, as Philip's hand traveled the warm country road of her spine. She thrust back against him. He entered her.

She laughed softly, still full of sensual sleep. Her hand turned backward and brushed his cheek. "Love," she muttered. "Lovecraft."

When Philip came back from the bathroom, he found the piece of paper lying on the floor where it had fallen out of his shirt pocket the night before.

He knew it instantly, intuitively, for the paper that the ghostly little man had left him the day before.

He unfolded it and read a crude, photocopied flyer entitled HAPY TEEMS NEWSLEDDER.

It was hand-lettered, and began, DONT EATS YOUR PARDNER. EVERBODY GETS PLENTY HAPY IF THEY WORK TOGEDDER LIK TEEMS. DONT KIL PEOPLES. LIV TOGEDDER. BEST POLICY. KIS AND MAKEUP. DONT BITES WRONG PEOPLES BUT SAY SORY YOU ARE WRONGS AND DONT KILL THAM ANY. DONT STEEL NOTHN BUT ASK PLEEEZ. ALWAYS DO WHUT YOR BOSSES SAY WITHOUT GROWLS OR SLOBBER. DONT—. A sinking sensation, as though he were being lowered into his grave, accosted Philip. He knew instantly what he was reading.

He showed it to Lily when he went to his session. She put her glasses on and studied it.

She looked up at him over the tops of her reading glasses. "What did you say this was?"

"It's a motivational tract," Philip explained. "Like the ones I got at Ralph's One-Day Résumés. The author is urging his fellow office workers to live in harmony and be part of a team."

"Doesn't make much sense to me," Lily said.

"I think," Philip said, "that there is a degenerate subculture living within Pelidyne, an atrophied race of office workers. I think they have regressed through inbreeding and through their alliance with..." Philip hesitated. He didn't want to talk about this, but he saw no alternative. He had to warn Amelia, and Lily seemed his best hope. He paused, exhaled. "I distinctly heard the creature say 'Dagon.' I think we are talking ancient entities here. I think we are talking malign, distorting forces."

Lily sighed. She lit a cigarette. "Are you taking your medication?" she asked.

"I don't think I can afford to take any drug that might impair my reflexes. It would be different if I could just walk away from the whole thing. But I can't. I think that's clear."

"What does your new girlfriend, this Sissy, think about all this?"

"She says she isn't my therapist."

"Well, she has a point there, but she must have some opinion on your monsters."

"She says all artists have their demons."

Al Bingham came into the house. He had been out back, painting the tool shed green. He wore shorts and a baseball cap, splattered with green paint. His face was sunburned and full of domesticated joy.

"Hey Philip," he said. "How are you doing? That wife of mine shrinking you down to sane size?"

"I guess so," Philip said.

But Philip knew Lily was worried. She even spoke of his returning to the hospital. She said she wanted him to talk to Dr. Beasley again. And

Lily had made no firm commitment to warn Amelia of the dangers lurking within Pelidyne.

Philip had driven back to his apartment, tormented by a sense of urgency, of conflicting emotions. He found, to his surprise, that Sissy had redefined Amelia. Amelia was his old love, strangely distant, her face and features now remembered with affection—and without yearning or any sense of loss. She was getting married; he wished her well.

A strident, moral voice spoke: *Does this mean you are just going to leave her to her fate?*

I'm not well, he told his conscience. *There aren't any monsters. I'm mistaken about all that.*

Hah! his conscience snorted.

Back at his apartment, Sissy wrapped him in her arms. "I got a job," she whispered in his ear. She had walked down to Dan's Texas Bar-B-Que and taken the owner up on his offer.

In the weeks that followed, a kind of moral

lassitude came over Philip. Circumstances conspired to lull him into denial. He was in love; the world was benign. His temp agency did not return him to Pelidyne. His life altered. He was now part of a partnership, a dialogue of mind and body, and only occasionally would he be startled to discover how utterly he had adapted to the concept of twoness, the shared toothpaste and alien clutter and additional opinions to be sorted and considered.

One day, when a temporary job placed him downtown near Pelidyne, he thought he might stop by and speak to Amelia. But the job was abruptly terminated two days before its scheduled end, and Philip found himself working on the other side of the city. There was something fateful in this near miss, so he called Amelia. He got her answering phone. Amelia and her now live-in boyfriend had created a joint message. Amelia would speak a line, then her boyfriend. The effect reminded Philip of something school children might present at a parent/teacher gathering.

Amelia: *Hello, this is Amelia Price.*

Boyfriend: *And this is Mike Lawson.*

Both: *We are not in right now, but we would love to hear from you.*

Amelia: *Please leave a message at the tone.*

Boyfriend: *We will get back to you as soon as we can.*

Both: *Thank you for calling.*

The message was so unrelievedly cheerful that Philip winced when he heard his own worried, querulous voice pouring onto the tape. "Amelia, this is Philip," he said. "I was worried about you and thought I'd call and say hi. I worked over at Pelidyne for a couple of days some time ago, and it was a disturbing experience, and I just wanted to see how you were doing. Give me a call sometime."

He knew she would not return his call.

I tried, he told his conscience.

Hah! his conscience said. *And Reagan and Bush tried to help the poor.*

Then On Time sent him to Pelidyne again.

e was assigned a different office, but the same woman, whose sculpted hair might have represented a thick-bodied bird defending its nest, showed him to his new workspace.

She was in an expansive mood and told him her name, Gladys Fenninger. She could not resist showing him her picture in Pelidyne's office newsletter, *Personality Bytes*. The photo showed

Gladys, sporting a toothy grin that wreathed her face in wrinkles and holding a plaque, thrusting it forward for the camera's scrutiny. The caption under this photo read: EMPLOYEE OF THE MONTH.

"Well, congratulations," Philip said.

Gladys giggled. "There's some don't think I should get it," she said with real glee, looking behind her quickly to see if anyone was in the corridor. "There's some think they worked harder, but I say"—here she wobbled her head from side to side while declaiming, harking back to some childhood recitation no doubt— *"There's some must win, there's some must lose. Don't play the game if you can't stand the bruise.* You don't get this award just for being a drone. You need brains to carry the day in this kind of competition. I suggested the sorted paper clip bins, didn't I? I suggested the double-stick recall slips, didn't I?"

Philip smiled, sure that she had. Gladys, in the best of spirits, booted Philip's new computer and showed him how to log the X's and O's this time around.

She patted the computer. She winked. "You might think of a career with Pelidyne," she said. "This place recognizes merit, Philip."

He said he would think about it.

Later that day, he thought about working full-time at Pelidyne. The thought made his bones feel like rusty pipes wrapped in tar paper.

Day after day, On Time kept sending Philip to Pelidyne. The job lasted a week, then two, then three. It was inevitable that he should encounter Amelia.

"Philip?"

He turned and there she was, behind him in the cafeteria line. She wore purple lipstick and her eyelids were light blue. In other respects, she was a model of conservative style, wearing a light blue blouse and a gray suit.

"It's okay," he said. "I've got a legitimate reason for being here. I'm a temp."

"I know," Amelia said. "It's okay."

They ate lunch together. Amelia said that after his phone message, she had called Lily.

Amelia had been worried. "You didn't sound so hot.

"Lily told me you did some temp work here," Amelia said. "So when I saw you, I figured that was the case again."

Philip nodded. "Yep. I'm in the glamorous world of data entry."

They discussed their lives. Amelia was greatly relieved to learn that Philip had a new girlfriend, excessively so, actually.

"That's very romantic," Amelia said. "I mean, her coming all the way from Florida because she read your book."

"Where did you meet your fiancé?" Philip asked, to change the subject. He wasn't really interested, and Amelia's reply went by him. He was annoyed by Amelia's undisguised delight in discovering that his interest now lay elsewhere. True, he had been a difficult lover. There was the mail cart incident, his housebreaking, and even at the best of times he had his obsessions, quirks that would have tried anyone's patience. But she didn't have to be so unseemly in her relief. A light, slightly rueful pat on the hand accompanied by a quiet, "I'm so happy for you" would have sufficed.

If he hadn't been miffed, he might have spoken with more care. Who knows? When Amelia began talking about her job at Pelidyne—she was a coordinator of publications—any fool could have seen that she was excited. Her immediate supervisor was leaving, and it looked like the position would go to Amelia. Anyone could tell that what was wanted here was a hearty congratulations ("terrific," "way to go," "good luck," et cetera).

Instead, he listened to Amelia talk enthusiastically about Pelidyne, its benefits package, its prestige, it wealth, its employee incentives, and then—perhaps he even interrupted—he said, "I have reason to believe that not all employees are upwardly mobile. I have reason to believe that there is a subterranean network of decayed, atrophied workers living in the walls and in derelict parts of the building. I suspect they are cannibalistic and that they are in thrall to Dagon, which is, of course, just another name for the Old Ones."

Almost anyone could have told him that this was not the politic thing to say. He needed her trust if he was going to help her. This confrontational approach was doomed.

Amelia narrowed her eyes and stiffened, straightening her back. She glared at Philip. "Still seeing monsters," she said. "Still not in the pink of mental health, are we?"

They argued. It was a longer argument than Amelia usually indulged in. Apparently she had thought more than a little about Philip since last seeing him. "Monsters!" she screamed. "I'll tell you about your monsters. Your monsters are cowardice and laziness and self-pity and arrogance and anything that gives you an excuse to run away. Look at you, Philip. You are forty-five years old and you are working as a temp, sitting in some stupid cubicle doing data entry. Why?" Amelia stood up. "Monsters. That's right. Because monsters are always sabotaging your chances. Hairy house-sized spiders from outer space. Yep. Old Philip could have amounted to something but a space octopus from Yuggoth stole his dreams."

Amelia was on a roll. She listed Philip's monsters, getting most of the names right, and described the specific ways in which they had interfered with his life. Philip was impressed. He had not realized that she had been so attentive to the details.

The irony, of course, was that her litany about MicroMeg and its horrors was ransacked from her own subconscious—Philip had never even tried to tell her the grisly specifics—and what she spoke of mockingly was dreadful fact, buried deep in her memory beneath layers of denial.

Oblivious to this truth, she railed on. "You don't have to be a shrink to see what you're up to. It's a responsibility dodge, that's all. You want to be the eternal child. Wait till your new girlfriend figures that out. And unless she is a moron, she *will* figure it out. She may like your book, but I don't think she is going to be delighted when she learns it is also your life."

Amelia stalked off before he could respond, and Philip was left to finish his ham sandwich (chilly, leatherlike fare) with only his thoughts (equally indigestible) for company.

As he chewed, his resolve solidified. The easy course now would be to wash his hands of her, to shrug and get on with his life. He would not do that. He would rescue her in spite of herself.

And to do that, of course, he had to learn the exact nature and extent of the threat. He shivered. The thought of hunting down the lair of that little, misshapen and degenerate man sent a cold, bleak wind blowing through him.

He could not afford to contemplate what lay ahead. His nerve would fail if he stood too long at the gate. And so, after lunch, he dialed Dan's Texas Bar-B-Que and asked to speak to Sissy.

"I've got to work late tonight," he told her. "Don't wait up." He was tempted to add, "If I don't come back at all, don't come looking for me. Don't alert the authorities. Forget you ever heard of Pelidyne. Go back to Florida. Marry. Raise children. Live a good life. The Old Ones don't know you. We are of no interest to them unless we directly interfere with their purposes. You are safe in their shadow." Instead, he said, simply, "I love you."

"Hey, are you okay?" Sissy asked.

Philip could hear the lunch crowd din behind her. Someone shouting from the restaurant's kitchen, a cash register ringing, a door banging open.

"Sure," Philip said. "I've just got a deadline here, and I've got to put in some extra hours. I didn't want you to worry." He hung up.

He knew the drill. He waited until the evening rush was at its height, the lobby filled with milling office workers frantic to get home. He signed out, turned, uttered a theatrical "Damn it!" and imitated, for anyone watching, a man who has just remembered something left behind in the office. He turned and darted back to the elevators, got in one that was just dispelling its clot of workers, and punched the button for the basement.

He got a turkey sandwich from a vending machine, found an office full of broken chairs and dusty filing cabinets, and crawled behind a desk to wait.

e leaned his back against a wall and closed his eyes, waiting for the building to clear. He had no plan.

He woke suddenly when something yanked his feet, jerking him forward. The back of his head thumped the carpet.

Ooph!

He tried to rise, but the speed with which he was dragged forward kept him off balance. His legs were numb, wrapped in steel bands. He tried to lift his head, to see his attacker, but he could not. He was being dragged rapidly across the darkened room. He thought he heard a voice, or voices, but he could distinguish no single word.

The ceiling rolled by overhead, panels of darkened fluorescent lights passing like black, rectangular clouds. He was in the hall then, speeding along the carpet on his back.

Wham! A door was sprung open. Stairs. Great. The back of his head counted stairs. Thump, thump, thump, thump. He lost count.

He regained consciousness in a dank, chill room where the reek of oil and burnt rubber mingled with the familiar, frightening stench of long-dead fish. *Paralyzed!* he thought—and scrambled to his feet in wild, arm-flapping panic. No. He was all right. He was—

He was staring at row upon row of cylindrical, glass containers, each one perhaps eight feet tall, each containing an upright human body. The naked bodies floated in a bright green liquid and large, viscous air bubbles crawled over white flesh like sentient, translucent slugs.

Philip sensed that he was far from Pelidyne, that he had not merely descended steps into some subterranean chamber but that he had crossed a boundary of rational, physical law and now inhabited another dimension.

"Drone," a voice said. It was a hollow, mechanical voice that had no specific location but seemed to come from above.

"Identify yourself," the voice boomed.

Philip shouted his name at the ceiling.

"I will consult my data. I have consulted my data. You are a transient contract drone on a time-limited assignment. Time log would indicate that you have left the premises. Either you are lying about your identity or, rightly identified, have practiced deceit in declaring your exit."

"Well, actually—" Philip began.

The voice interrupted. "I am proceeding with physical identification."

Blinding lights burst on overhead. From

between dark pillars, crablike robots scuttled forth. They were the size of large dogs and moved with unnerving speed. One came from behind Philip. It announced its presence with a high whine, and Philip turned as it enfolded him in bands of steel. Something whirred near his ear, and his shirtsleeve fell away, cut by a thin beam of red light. Spidery fingers encircled his elbow. Something stung his arm, and Philip stared at a translucent bubble that floated in front of his eyes. The bubble turned red, filling—he was certain—with his blood.

It disappeared, and another machine, this one tall and made of what looked like black, shiny plastic, leaned forward and pressed some filmy, rubberlike material against Philip's face. He screamed, certain he was being suffocated.

As he screamed, the thin membrane spun away, and Philip saw it, in the shape of his own howling face, spin toward the illuminated ceiling, dwindling like a kite whipped into autumn skies.

The machines backed away, leaving Philip on his knees, sick with terror.

"Your identity has been verified," the voice said. "You are, however, unauthorized. I am only a second generation servant of Yog-Sothoth. I will summon your own kind."

A siren began to wail.

A man in a uniform immediately burst through a door.

"What's going on here?" he shouted.

Philip found himself staring into the cold eyes of Hal Ketch, MicroMeg's security guard.

Ketch nodded his head slowly. "It's like the Disney dolls say." He flashed a cold grin and drew his pistol. "It's a small fucking world."

Ketch led Philip from the room at gunpoint. As they passed the green, bubbling tanks, Philip recognized Gladys Fenninger. Her hair miraculously retained its bird-winged shape even while immersed in green fluid.

Philip was surprised to discover that Gladys had a pretty good body: firm breasts, perky nipples, a flat, trim tummy and soft, rounded hips.

"Move it," Ketch snapped. "Don't gawk at the prizes."

"That's Gladys Fenninger," Philip said. "She's my supervisor."

"Not anymore. She won a ticket to Yuggoth. Employee of the Month. E.O.M.'s automatically go. She's history at Pelidyne."

"Jesus."

Ketch turned. "That's sharp, Kenan. Matter of fact, Jesus was taken to Yuggoth, although the Elder Ones are embarrassed about the whole thing. He got away from them briefly. You want to see an Elder One oscillate and turn purple, just mention Jesus."

The door in front of Philip swung open and he entered a dark corridor.

"Don't try to run," Ketch said. "I'll shoot out your spine, and you'll spend the next couple of millennia as a smart switch in a temporal gate."

"Huh?"

"Trust me, you wouldn't like it."

The corridor was dank, the fishy smell

powerful—although not, Philip noted, incapacitating—and the walls were covered with gray fungi that writhed unpleasantly, that seemed, indeed, to sense the passing of Ketch and Philip and stretch to touch them.

"You don't want to brush against these walls," Ketch said, as though reading Philip's thought.

Ketch indicated a corridor to the left, and Philip ascended three stone steps and entered a darker passageway. They came to a rusty, metal door. Philip pushed it open at Ketch's urging, and a din of voices and machinery poured out.

They entered a vast, cold room and proceeded quickly along a raised catwalk. Philip clung to the shaky metal railing and peered down into what he later came to identify in his mind as Office Hell.

Here was where the little man had come from. The floor of the room was filled with desks and computers and laboring ghoul-workers. Some wore shreds of old office clothing; some were naked. All had dead-white, leprous flesh. The floor of the room was strewn with paper, printouts, and bones. Philip saw a pile of skulls next to a broken water cooler. Screams, cries, shouts, and hideous laughter filled Philip's head. A thin, tinny radio played, something with violins and flutes, yes, *Yesterday*. As Philip watched, a fight broke out between two men. One of them, thin and stooped, wore nothing but a hat. The other wore a ragged coat. The hat man pushed the other against a desk, and a computer monitor toppled off, smashing with an explosive sound that ignited a chorus of human whoops. A fat woman in a red dress rushed to the defense of the pushed man and other workers quickly joined the fray.

Ketch and Philip came to the end of the catwalk, and Philip pushed another metal door open, and when it closed behind them silence immediately descended.

This hall was carpeted and lighted and elegantly wallpapered. As they moved down the hall Philip heard the sound of girlish laughter, a phone ringing with a discreet, lilting note, and soft music, strings: *Yesterday*.

The outer office was decorated in muted blues and greens, and a large section of one wall consisted of an aquarium in which brightly colored fish moved sedately. Two secretaries, both of them dressed as though for a fashion shoot, looked up as Philip and Ketch entered the room.

The secretary who had been perched on the edge of the desk jumped down, adjusted her short orange skirt and smiled at Philip.

"Hey," she said.

"Is Mr. Melrose in?" Ketch asked.

The secretary behind the desk, who had high cheekbones and unfriendly gray eyes, studied Ketch. "Maybe he is, maybe he isn't."

Ketch shot her through the forehead. The other secretary screamed and fled the room.

"This is a security matter, sister," Ketch said, frowning at the empty chair (she had tumbled down behind the desk, disappearing instantly, and Philip questioned the reality of the wild, startled eyes and the black hole between them).

Ketch reached down and pushed a button on

the phone and spoke into the speaker. "Mr. Melrose?"

"Yes."

"This is Hal Ketch. We've had a security breach. A temp. I know this guy. He blew up MicroMeg right before the Big Leap. He doesn't look like much, but he's trouble. Could be he's with the Mi-Go or a Renegade faction. I thought you might want to talk to him."

"Good work, Hal. Come on in."

Philip heard the electronic locks unbolt. Ketch motioned him to push the door open, and they entered.

r. Melrose, wearing a brown suit and a dark blue tie, sat behind a large silver desk. He was a broad-shouldered man with a worn, prizefighter's face.

He regarded Philip with cold, black eyes. "What they paying you?" he asked.

"Seven-fifty," Philip said.

"Seven hundred and fifty thousand?"

"No, seven dollars and fifty cents an hour," Philip said.

"Don't jerk me around."

Ketch hit Philip in the stomach and Philip sank to his knees, pain radiating from a center of nausea.

Melrose waved Ketch away. "Okay. Wait outside, Hal. I want to have a conversation with this guy without you gut punching him every other sentence."

"Mr. Melrose," Ketch said. "This guy is dangerous."

Melrose's eyes narrowed. "I know that, Hal. I appreciate your concern. Wait in the other room please."

Ketch left.

"Have a seat." Melrose pointed to a large gray armchair.

Philip sat.

Philip looked around the room in an effort to collect his thoughts. The room was decorated sedately in metallic silver and gray, enlivened by large green plants in blue vases. A large, multipaned window showed a grid of blue sky. Cumulus clouds moved slowly over a landscape of rolling hills and green trees. It would have been an idyllic scene were it not for several winged creatures that disported amid the clouds, creatures somewhat like barn-sized lizards but with something suggesting a marine existence, perhaps the satiny, black sheen of their skins or the hundred-yard strands of ribbonlike flesh that trailed behind them through the air and filled Philip with the instant conviction that these fleshy kite-tails were lined with stinging nettles, and that they were trolling the air and land for living organisms. How he knew this he could not say, but he seemed to have seen the creatures before, perhaps in a dream that was not a dream at all but a momentary disruption in the space/ time continuum. With an effort, he looked away from the window.

"Well mister—What's your name?"

Philip told him.

"Okay. Kenan. K-E-N-A-N?"

"Yes."

Melrose leaned back in his chair. "You aren't with a Renegade. You ain't the Mi-Go either." Melrose laughed. "You are a fucking temp!" He laughed, slapped his hands on the desk-top. Spittle flew from his mouth, his face turned red. He stopped abruptly. "That's right, isn't it?"

"Yes," Philip said.

Melrose looked down, opened a drawer. "I should have just stuck with my old man's grocery store. He wanted me to have it. But I wanted to be a hotshot, went into big business so I could fuck secretaries, eat lunch on someone else's dime, the whole deal. Shit." He took a wallet-sized object from the drawer and slapped it in front of him. He looked up at Philip. "I got ulcers on top of my ulcers. You're working for that asshole Baker, aren't you? He wants to make me look bad, wants to fuck me over. Baker, right?"

"No."

Melrose chuckled. "You got that wimpy temp look down, Kenan. I mean, you are some kind of professional. You got plausibility. That's worth a fortune in a mercenary. So maybe you are working for Malzberg. He couldn't find his ass in the dark, but he thinks I stole his promotion. Okay, Malzberg?"

"I'm a temp," Philip said.

Melrose shook his head, laughed. He opened the checkbook, picked a pen off the desk. "Right. And you are making seven-fifty an hour." Melrose began to write. "Okay. I'll give you ten to do your temping somewhere else. I could have Ketch shoot your head off. He wants to. I know my boy, and he has a hard-on for you, Kenan. Or I could feed you to some lawyers that regressed, got a taste for human flesh, would scarf you down in the blink of a billable hour. It's just I'm a businessman. I know a good employee when I see one. You got talent, I can see. You got plausibility. I'm asking you to give your old employer notice, Kenan. You send me his head in a box, FedEx it, and I write you another one of these suckers."

Melrose tore the check out and handed it to

Philip. Philip stared at the one followed by six zeroes.

"A million dollars," Philip said.

"And another million when you send me your boss' head." Melrose scowled. "But don't try to squeeze an extra penny from me. Don't get greedy."

Philip just blinked at the check.

Melrose got up from behind the desk and came around to Philip. He put an arm around Philip's shoulder. "I got a soft spot for guys like you. Just doing a job, just trying to get by. I'm a foot soldier myself. I'm not running the show. I'm just an advance man for the carnival. Come on, let me show you something. We'll go out the back way here, let Hal cool off in the waiting room."

Philip followed Melrose through the door, into a dimly lit corridor. The dank, suffocating fishy smell asserted itself and the temperature fell, the air suddenly chill.

They descended a flight of metal stairs, their

footsteps booming. The wheeze of pistoning machines rose up from beneath them.

"Here." Melrose pushed open a door.

❀

"I think it was Azathoth himself," Philip told Lily. "Melrose called it The Committee."

Philip was back in the hospital. He was lying in bed. Lily looked at her notes. She read, "A sort of blue octopus the size of a football field with human heads on the ends of its tentacles. Parts of the creature appeared to be semi-liquid, like blue Jell-O, and human sexual organs, a stew of vaginas and penises, floated in the liquid—like rats." Lily looked up, raised a quizzical eyebrow. "Rats?" Lily stared blankly at her notebook and the words she had committed to it. "You don't want to go near a Freudian interpretation of this," she muttered, as much to herself as to Philip.

Philip sat propped up in the bed, his hands

folded in his lap. He didn't say anything. He hadn't expected this session to go well.

"Well," Lily continued. "It's all a blur to you. This creature dragged you down and enfolded you in its frigid embrace. Dreadful, once-human voices spoke to you of hideous rituals that took place on the shores of alien seas on worlds mankind was never meant to visit."

Lily had captured Philip's rhetoric. Philip had to admit that it did sound a little overblown and melodramatic. But any bald statement of the facts was going to seem outlandish. The truth was too loathsome and ghastly to rest sedately in the limited, cloistered realm of human reason.

"I blacked out," Philip said. "It's the mind's defense mechanism."

"Hmmmmm," Lily said. She closed her notebook. "What Mr. Melrose at Pelidyne tells me is that you were in an employee orientation meeting, and you suddenly began screaming and speaking incoherently. Speaking 'in tongues' is how he put it. When they tried to calm you, you bit the man giving the presentation and tried to break the television monitor used for the video. Security was called, and you were restrained until the police arrived. Dr. Beasley was notified when they found her card in your wallet."

Philip was surprised at how calm he remained while listening to this fabrication. "Did you ask Mr. Melrose if it is customary at Pelidyne to have employee orientation classes in the dead of the night?"

"Well no. The police were called at eight-thirty in the morning."

Philip knew there would be no convincing Lily. He spoke to collect his own thoughts, to clarify the horror. "I think Melrose just wanted me to have a look at his boss," Philip said. "Melrose didn't anticipate Azathoth's snatching me up and dragging me into the pit. Naturally I blacked out, and when Azathoth tossed me back, my derangement presented a problem. I'm surprised they didn't just kill me or send me to Yuggoth for parts." Philip paused, puzzled, groping for some clue to Melrose's motivation.

"Maybe he thought I could still be helpful. He was confused about just who I was. Maybe—"

"I don't think," Lily said, "that you want to trouble yourself overly about any of this, Philip. I'm going to send a nurse in and she is going to give you a shot. It's just something to calm you. I want you to sleep for awhile. We'll sort this out later, all right?"

Philip did feel tired.

"Okay."

After the prick of the needle, his body filled with golden honey. Just before he slept, he thought he saw Sissy leaning toward him. But perhaps it was a dream, for this was a solemn and bleary-eyed Sissy, not at all like his smiling companion and ardent fan.

When he woke again, Sissy was in the room, so she was not a dream. She did look tired and her smile, when she saw he was awake, didn't erase the worry lines in the corners of her eyes.

"Philip, are you okay?"

"I'm fine," Philip said. "Wow." He touched his forehead where the pain crackled like cellophane. "I dreamed I was in this orientation class," Philip said. "I dreamed that Pelidyne was going to hire me full-time, and I had to go to this miserable, boring orientation."

"You did," Sissy said. "And you had an epileptic fit or something."

Philip was silent. The dream was very realistic. But if they thought that it would mask the truth—or even confuse him—they were wrong. No doubt the golden honey drug had contained the lie. The opposite of a truth serum: a *falsehood* serum.

They were powerful. They had substituted this drug without Lily's knowledge, certainly. They had gotten to the nurse or a doctor. They had sent him this phony memory, detailed and reasonably convincing. But did they honestly think it would fool him? Probably not. Certainly not. They just wanted to flaunt their power, their dreadful ubiquity.

Sissy said she couldn't stay long; she had to go to work at Dan's. Philip reassured her that he was fine now and would call her at work later.

After she left, Philip conjured up the spurious memory of orientation at Pelidyne.

The potential new employees—there were five of them besides Philip, three men and two women—were ushered into a conference room with a long, mahogany table and a television and video tape player at one end. Mr. Melrose was there to greet them, smiling and blander than the man Philip remembered.

Melrose's assistant, an extremely round, extremely bald man who ducked his head, smiled even more relentlessly, and reminded Philip of a dog that has been beaten into fawning servility, passed out a variety of forms that required filling out. Everyone bent to this task with stoic energy.

Philip logged his tax status and employment history and education. He puzzled over what sort of benefits package he would prefer. Did he want an HMO or Blue Shield? Did he wish to apply to the credit union? In the event of death on the job, who was his beneficiary? Was he willing to have his urine searched for mind-altering substances?

Melrose's assistant, Bob, explained each form and fielded questions. Philip's mind drifted, as it always did when confronted with a form, and he came back to an awareness of his surroundings just as one of the women was asking what would happen if she got pregnant.

The question hung in the air. Philip reflected that women were forever asking this question and that Bob looked as uncomfortable as most men do on hearing it. Philip hoped that Bob would say the right thing, would say that he would marry her, but the question actually concerned health insurance and maternity leave and Bob answered it appropriately.

When the forms were filled out and gathered by Bob, Melrose took over again, saying how delighted he was to have everyone on board.

He told them that Pelidyne was not some overgrown corporate giant, shackled by its size and history, that it was a dynamic, ever-changing corporation that wanted to hear from each and every employee. Melrose asked Bob to dim the lights. Melrose turned on the monitor and started the video.

The video was an overview of Pelidyne, beginning with an airplane soaring over blue lakes. The video had been played for countless orientation classes, and its soundtrack (which Philip identified as generic TV newscaster intro music) wobbled some and the image fuzzed at the edges.

The scene changed. A man behind a desk began to talk.

Behind the man a paneled window showed bright skies and cumulus clouds. No monsters patrolled the blue skies, but Philip was certain it was the same gray and silver office where he had first met Melrose.

Melrose was not behind the desk however. A kindly, gray-haired man wearing a blue suit smiled at the camera and spoke as though addressing an old friend. He talked about Pelidyne's vision of the world as a better place.

As he talked, Pelidyne's diversity was illustrated. People were shown working in labs. People of a more blue-collared aspect were shown welding convoluted metal structures. Pelidyne's investment and insurance holdings were illustrated with shots of a bustling office filled with smiling people who exchanged paper documents or pointed at computer screens with delight. The women were all elegantly dressed, tottering on high heels. The men wore conservative suits.

The message of the video was simple: The sooner America was entirely owned by Pelidyne and its subsidiaries, the better, since Pelidyne was everything good and noble about the American way. At the end of the video, two of the men and one of the women applauded.

In what Philip saw as a particularly shameless bit of toadying, one of the men stood up and shouted, "Bravo! Bravo!"

The next video was an instructional piece, designed to show new employees the proper way to relate to their fellow office workers and supervisors. There was something amateurish about this production. The actors delivered their lines in self-conscious, awkward bursts surrounded by dead air.

Philip did not give the video his complete attention. Each skit boiled down to a simple injunction: Do not gossip. Do not argue with your supervisor. Do not loaf. Do not dress outrageously. Do not waste electricity. Do not steal office supplies.

Philip doodled a cartoon dog on the legal pad he had brought with him. The dog's head was tilted back, its mouth open.

"Ooooooooooooooooooh," Philip wrote inside the cartoon balloon erupting from the canine's mouth.

Philip looked up when he heard Amelia's voice.

Amelia was in the video!

Philip leaned forward. He hoped he hadn't missed much.

Apparently he hadn't. The narrator's voice-over was saying, "There are times when any job will make additional demands on its employees. Deadlines have to be met, and it is an unfortunate fact of life that sometimes several projects will come due at the same time. At such times, you may be required to make an extra effort."

Amelia was shown holding the phone's receiver to her mouth. "Paul," she said, "I'm just leaving. I'll be at your house in a half hour, and we can go to dinner and that show. I'm really looking forward to it."

At this moment, the actor who played everyone's supervisor came on stage.

"Ms. Smith," he said. "The Brodkey project has to be on a plane at eight tomorrow morning. Can you work on it this evening?"

"I'm sorry Mr. Johnson," Amelia said. "I have a date for this evening."

Good for you, Philip thought—but of course this was the bad scenario, the one demonstrating a poisonous lack of company pride and team spirit.

The makers of this video foresaw the

possibility that morons might view it and fail to understand that what was being portrayed was not being condoned. To demonstrate that these first scenes were examples of bad attitude and unacceptable behavior, a frame was frozen and the universal symbol of a circle with a slash was imposed over the still.

Philip was staring at Amelia's face. The narrator's voice-over continued, but Philip could not hear the words.

He was suddenly terrified for Amelia. The stark symbol of negation that overlay her features seemed blatantly threatening, a sort of totalitarian curse, a mark of doom.

"Amelia!" Philip shouted, and he stood up, moving toward the screen.

The figures on the screen were animate again, unwinding in a positive example of workplace solidarity and loyalty.

Philip placed his palms flat on the screen, preparing to topple it over, already anticipating the satisfying explosion of the picture tube. The confusion around him was considerable: shouts, a chair tumbling over, the blur of bodies in motion.

His chest was encircled by unforgiving, powerful bonds. A deathly cold enclosed his heart. He was yanked backward.

Out of the corner of his eye, he saw the creature slide from beneath the conference table. It seemed to move in several directions at once, and yet Philip was certain it was a single entity, its chaos possessing logic in a different dimension.

A fleshy hand slapped at his face, slid to cover his mouth and silence his screams. Philip bit down on the flesh between thumb and forefinger and was rewarded with the cause-and-effect of a scream that had a train-going-into-a-tunnel quality as the room darkened and came to an abrupt, black standstill.

When Philip awoke it was night outside. He went to the window and looked out at the parking lot.

Here I am again.

He would tell Sissy to go home, go back to

Florida. He would elicit Lily's help in sending her away.

"I'm afraid Philip is not getting better," Lily could tell Sissy. "I'm afraid he's out there on the open sea, about as far as you can get from solid land."

Philip hoped, of course, that Sissy would protest. "Philip is an artist," she would say. "He is coming to terms with his art."

Lily would be eloquent, though: "The terms are insanity, honey. Philip is bug-house, cock-waving, sheer-slobbering Insane. Not to put it too bluntly."

Philip found his clothes and put them on. He walked out into the rec room and turned the television on. He was beginning to feel at home here, a frequent flyer in his hometown airport. He watched an old Charlie Chan movie, seeking some clue to his plight in the broken-English wisdom of the Chinese detective. Nothing profound came to him, and he drifted back to his room and lay on the bed.

Something crackled in his pocket, and he

reached in and pulled out the check, unfolded it and stared at the line of zeroes.

Well.

In the morning he filled out one of the two crumpled deposit slips he kept in his wallet, bummed an envelope and a stamp from a nurse, addressed the envelope to his bank, and asked the ward clerk if she would mail it on her lunch break.

She assured him she would. He ate breakfast and went to group.

R outine is a drug, Philip thought, filling the mind with lethargy, turning the extraordinary events of life into so many telephone poles whipping by as you drive down a flat west Texas highway.

Routine kicked in quicker than the psychotropic drugs. Every morning there was group. A fat teenager complained about how his teachers hated him (which, Philip expected, was true), and an elderly man talked about how he had suddenly become frightened by his penis, and a woman named Martha kept trying to get everyone to pray. She was tireless in this endeavor, keeping after the group the way a teenage boy will hammer away at his girlfriend's sexual reservations. "We could get down on our knees. Just for a minute. Jesus don't need no long drawed out story. We could just say hello to Jesus and…"

Philip said he was recovering from another attack by ancient monsters from out of space and time. No one commented on this, although a gloomy, dark-skinned man nodded his head sadly.

In the afternoons, Philip would talk to Dr. Beasley or Lily. Al Bingham would sometimes visit. Sissy came every day.

Bingham came in one day at around six in the evening just as Sissy was leaving. He watched her go.

"That's a fine-looking woman," he said.

Philip sat in the bed, his lap filled with mail she had brought from the apartment.

"That's Sissy," Philip said.

"A redheaded woman is good luck," Bingham said. He sat in a chair and lit a cigarette.

"I don't think you are supposed to smoke in these rooms," Philip said.

Bingham closed his eyes and let the smoke snake through his nostrils and mouth. "Probably not. Probably not supposed to jerk off either." Bingham chuckled. "How long you been here now?"

"I don't know."

"Well I know. Three weeks yesterday. Lily says they want to keep you long-term this time. Like six months, a year."

"Yes."

"What do you think about that?"

"Well, I don't know. They are the professionals. I guess I am pretty sick."

"What does that redheaded woman think about all of it?"

"I don't know."

Bingham stood up and crossed the room to

stare out the window. "You are in a state of high ignorance, aren't you, Philip?"

Philip felt a blaze of anger beneath the apathy. "I am trying to do what people tell me. My behavior does suggest that I should not follow my own impulses."

Bingham turned around and went back to the chair. He sat down and leaned forward. "I love my wife," he said. "But she is dead wrong if she thinks you should hunker down in this drool factory till Judgment comes. How long do you think that redheaded woman is going to wait for you to get upright again?"

"Sissy," Philip said, feeling the anger jump now. "Her name is Sissy."

Bingham nodded cheerily. "Sissy. A fine-looking woman. But redheads ain't noted for patience, Philip. They can tolerate a certain amount of moaning, pissing, and flat-on-your-back self-pity from their men—a lot of them are Irish after all—but when they get a craw full they take action. They leave. They don't look back."

The anger went out of Philip, and he felt himself flattening on the bed as the self-righteousness evaporated. "I guess she will leave. I guess it is for the best."

Bingham made a disgusted noise. "Noble Philip." He stood up. "I'm going myself. I got to get to work. I'll see you later."

After Bingham left, Philip lay on the bed feeling exhausted. Everyone wanted something from him. Doing the right thing was not easy when your mind was untrustworthy.

Philip looked at the mail on his lap. Several of the envelopes clearly contained bills. The other stuff was junk mail, advertisements. Not a personal letter in the batch. Philip felt self-pity rising up in his chest like methane gas in a swamp.

Watch it.

He shuffled the advertisements for life insurance, carpet cleaning, cheap pizza. He stopped. This wasn't an ad. He plucked the staple from the folded, clay-coated paper and opened up the newsletter, *Personality Bytes*. Pelidyne had put his address in their computer. They had sent him their newsletter.

Don't look at it. Drop it on the floor.

He looked at it, of course, and it was harmless enough. There were the usual fuzzy halftones of suited men and women giving and accepting plaques. There was a photo of a new computer to be launched by one of Pelidyne's subsidiaries. Opening the newsletter, there was a photo of Pelidyne's softball team and a photo of an aging woman in horn-rimmed glasses who was retiring. This woman was quoted at interminable length in an interview of almost supernatural tedium. Philip felt gratefully drowsy at the end of the article and thought he might sleep some. Absently, he closed the newsletter.

Amelia's photo was on the back. She looked even more mimelike than usual, staring point-blank into the camera, her shadow stark behind her, her glasses headlighted by the flash.

EMPLOYEE OF THE MONTH the

caption read. Twelve point, Times bold. Dear God.

Philip went to the phone in the hall. He dialed Amelia's number. A male voice answered.

"Is Amelia there?" Philip asked.

"No, she is out of town for a few days. Who's calling?"

"Out of town?"

"Yes. A spur-of-the-moment business trip. She called from the office, didn't even have time to come home. Are you a friend of hers?"

"Look, when she called did she sound different? Did her voice sound, well, mechanical in any way? Did it have... did it have an insect-like quality?"

Silence.

"Hello?" Philip shouted.

"Who is this?" The man's voice was wary now. "Is this Philip Kenan?"

"Yes it is. I'm trying to get ahold of Amelia."

"She doesn't want to talk to you, Kenan. I think you know that."

"Yes, I know that. That's unimportant. That's—"

"You may think it is unimportant," the man interrupted, "since you seem to have no interest in anyone else's feelings, but I think it is important, and I will do everything in my power to see to it that you don't cause her any more suffering than you already have."

Obviously Amelia had vented her feelings to her fiancé.

"I don't blame you for feeling that way," Philip said. "But—"

The man hung up. Philip started to redial the number and then stopped. Amelia's fiancé was not going to be an ally in the present situation; the possibility of convincing the man that his girlfriend was being shipped to Yuggoth was slim.

Philip dialed his house. Sissy answered.

"I need your help," he said.

He had to escape. There was very little time.

Possibly it was already too late. But that thought had no utility; he let it go.

He slipped past the nurse and down the hall. There was a small laundry room next to the rec room. White uniforms were spinning like dancing ghosts in the industrial-size dryer. Philip opened the door and fished through the clothing until he found an orderly's shirt. It was a little too large and still damp, but it would have to do. He donned it and stepped back into the hall.

If he kept his head down as he walked toward the double doors perhaps they would not recognize him. If he made it through the doors, he would hit the lawn running. He had told Sissy to pick him up at the Seven-Eleven on the corner.

"Hey Philip," the ward clerk said, waving. "How's it going?"

"Okay," Philip said as he walked through the doors and out into the night air.

He remembered now that they didn't lock the doors until nine, and that he was free to go outside until then. They didn't expect him to run; he wasn't on the high security floor.

He felt a momentary sense of anticlimax accompanied by a gust of depression, but he shook the mood off. The real trials lay ahead. All his cunning and courage would be required soon enough.

Sissy was the only woman Philip had ever met who did not ask him to explain his actions. He loved her for this and found it especially gratifying on this night, when an explanation would have been complicated and time-consuming.

Sissy kissed him passionately, and he returned the kiss. He pulled away from her, and she shook her red hair and smiled.

"We've got to rescue Amelia," Philip said.

Her smiled faltered.

Philip spoke quickly. "It's okay. I'm not in love with Amelia. I'm in love with you. But I can't let Amelia become the pawn of the Old Ones simply because my affections lie elsewhere. I've got to do what I can to save her, common humanity demands it. And tomorrow we are leaving Texas, Sissy. We might visit your folks, if you'd like."

Sissy's smile returned. "All right!" she shouted.

He gave her directions to Ralph's One-Day Résumés and leaned back in the car's passenger seat, closing his eyes.

When they got to Ralph's, it was ten in the evening. Philip would have preferred to wait until two in the morning, when the last of the printers would be gone, but he had a long night ahead of him. He still had to go to Pelidyne.

Don't think about it. One step at a time.

"I'll walk from here," Philip said. They had parked at the far end of the parking lot near the exit. "Keep the motor running. If I'm not back in half an hour, leave."

Sissy stared at Philip. "I'm not leaving, so I guess you better come back."

Philip kissed her and got out of the car. He walked across the darkened, empty parking lot. The absence of cars meant nothing. The remaining employees would be parked in back, behind the building.

Philip tried the door. It was locked.

He had anticipated that. He was prepared to break a window if the lock had been changed. It hadn't. The key on his key ring fit, and the bolt slid back.

The reception area was dark. The hallway exhaled feeble light that outlined the long counter. Philip stood in the darkness, listening. Barely audible music reached his ears: violins and horns. He leaned forward on the balls of his feet, straining for a trace of human industry beneath the radio's hum. Nothing. He recognized the tune: *Yesterday.*

He moved slowly across the lobby and down

the hall. To his right the corridor led to Ralph's office, Philip's ultimate destination. For now, he needed to reconnoiter. He needed to see who was in this part of the building. The printers, lodged in their ear-splitting, backroom ghetto, were not likely to come up front.

He moved quickly now, vulnerable in the corridor. Anyone coming out of typesetting or graphics would see him. No hiding here.

Bright light fell from the door to typesetting, and Philip flattened against the wall and eased his head around the door frame.

Monica.

She was hunched over her computer, typing rapidly, her shoulders rocking as though to lively music—not the case, though; *Yesterday* still played. She was wearing a shaggy shawl of some green material, and her hair stuck out in curious tufts, as though she had been pulling on it.

Next to her, a large, thickset woman leaned over a drafting table.

Who?

The woman turned to thrust a piece of paper

through the waxer, and Philip recognized the flat, stolid countenance. Helga. Sworn enemies laboring side by side.

Philip felt cold, muddy dread. Helga and Monica, working in tandem, seemed to herald Armageddon. How had Ralph accomplished this? The answer came to Philip immediately: Zombies harbor no grudges.

Philip backed away from the door. He turned and ran back down the hall and around the corner toward Ralph Pederson's office. Fear had overthrown caution, and he was no longer interested in discovering just who was in the building. Philip paused at the closed door to Ralph's office. Was Ralph inside? Philip leaned his ear against the door and listened. He heard nothing. He pushed the door open. The room was dark. He breathed a sigh of relief and fumbled for the light switch.

The stark fluorescent light bathed Philip in a moment of bright terror. Irrationally, he expected to see shattered window glass on the carpet, and, looking toward the ceiling, encounter the sanity-searing visage of Yog-Sothoth.

But there were no signs of that day's violence. The carpet, indeed, appeared to be new, a thick gray pelt.

Philip moved across the room and behind the desk. He tugged open drawers. One was locked.

He found scissors on the desk and pried at the wood. The lip of the drawer splintered, but the drawer remained locked.

Philip was frantic. This wasn't any high security safe. This was just a goddam wooden desk, a flimsy, cheaply constructed, mahogany-veneered desk with a locked drawer that any secretary worth her steno pad could open with a hairpin.

The room was having an effect on Philip. The horror that had hurled him back to MicroMeg had come through this very ceiling, and he couldn't shake the notion that it lay, flattened like a truck-sized scorpion, in the overhead crawlspace.

Panic seized him. He squatted on his heels,

clutched the base of the desk with both hands and heaved.

The desk rose up and crashed forward and Philip stood and kicked violently at the exposed underbelly of the locked drawer. The slats splintered and he reached down and jerked them away, a sharp fragment of wood sliding brightly into his thumb. The large, dark, ancient book fell halfway out and he grasped a corner and hauled it the rest of the way, dropping it on the carpet when its icy chill surprised his touch and the dead-flesh feel of its leather binding conjured loathsome images.

Philip stared at the *Necronomicon* as it lay on the carpet. This unholy map of black space and time, mad Alhazred's accursed book of spells and portents, appeared to pulse, as though breathing. Philip looked wildly around the room. Had anyone heard the desk overturn? He had to get out of here. He couldn't bring himself to touch the book. He would have to, soon enough, but not now, not in this room with its violent assault on his memory.

A printer's apron hung on the coat rack, and Philip grabbed it, tossing it over the book. He reached down then, and clutched the hefty volume through the apron. It seemed to expand and contract, a hideous sensation, but at least no vile vision of other worlds leapt to his mind.

Philip hugged the swaddled book to his chest and turned to the door.

Ralph Pederson stood in the doorway. He held a revolver in his hand.

"Philip," Ralph said. "This will all come out of your pay, you know."

"I don't work for you anymore," Philip said.

Ralph shook his head sadly. "You've never had an ounce of loyalty," Ralph said. "Things get a little rough, you don't get a raise every six months, and you are out the door. And always complaining. You don't know what hard work is. Your whole generation doesn't know spit about hard work. It is all you can do to wipe your own ass. When I was fourteen years old, I was holding down three jobs. And ask me how many hours a day I work now."

"I don't—"

The revolver exploded. The desk shook.

Jesus.

"Ask!" Ralph roared.

Philip heard his voice, small and shaky. "How many hours a day do you work?"

"Twenty," Ralph said. "I work twenty hours a day." Ralph's head dropped forward and he was silent, staring at the carpet, his eyes sullen and stupid, his lips pooched out in a drunken pout. His arm dropped to his side, the revolver's barrel pointing at the floor.

Philip stepped forward.

Ralph came alive with a start. His arm jerked up, the gun pointed directly at Philip.

Jesus. Ralph was going to pull the trigger. Philip could see it in the crazy, red-rimmed eyes.

"Don't shoot," Philip said. "I'm no good to you dead."

Ralph grinned.

Well, that was a stupid thing to say, Philip thought. Dead, he would become a paragon of industry—like Monica.

The corners of Ralph's mouth inched toward his ears as he slowly squeezed the trigger. Philip saw someone move behind Ralph. It was Bingham.

The gun exploded as Ralph lurched forward, Al Bingham's hands around his throat. Philip fell to his knees, dropping the shrouded *Necronomicon*.

In front of Philip, the two men wrestled. Bingham, his bald head gleaming under the lights, clutched Ralph's gun hand and banged it against the wall. Ralph rolled from under the older man and kicked out. Bingham half rose, banging against the wall and bouncing back into Ralph. They rolled on the floor. The gun went off again.

"Al!" Philip shouted.

Philip watched as Ralph Pederson, muttering darkly, rose and stood shakily over Bingham who moaned as he tried to push himself up from the floor. Bingham's left hand was bright with blood.

"You goddam can't get decent help," Ralph muttered and he stood up very straight, straightening his shoulders, and then tottered and fell stiffly backward, hitting the carpet with a *whump*. He had fallen back out the door, so that his legs and polished shoes were all that entered the room.

Bingham was staggering to his feet. He held his left hand with his right. "Fucker shot off the top of my little finger," he said. "Goddam cheap low-rent sonofabitch."

Philip and Bingham walked to the door. Ralph lay on his back with his eyes open. He looked angry and preoccupied at the same time. The front of his shirt was saturated with dark blood.

"Shot his own lights out, too," Bingham said, with an air of faint disgust. He squeezed his injured hand. "This hurts like a sonofabitch. Hand me old Ralph's tie."

Philip undid the dead man's tie, sliding it through the collar, and offered it to Bingham, who frowned and continued to clutch his wounded hand. "I'm gonna need your help here."

Once the tourniquet was applied, Bingham looked around the room.

"What a mess," he said. "I suppose you have an explanation for all of this."

Philip said he did, but that it was long and he wasn't sure if time permitted its telling. Bingham suggested Philip just hit the high points.

"...so I came here to get the *Necronomicon*. There are incantations in it, rituals that are effective against the Old Ones..."

"And I suppose you know just where to find them," Bingham said.

Philip felt extremely tired. "No. I guess I'll need all the luck and inspiration I can find."

Bingham shook his head. "Wonderful. What a plan." Bingham gave the room one more disgusted look. "Well, first things first. Let's tote old Ralph out to the trunk of my car. I'll dump him in the old quarry later."

Dead, Ralph remained a difficult man. His corpse was unwieldy and heavier than it looked. They lugged him down the corridor toward the side exit in the back. They had to pass the lighted door of typesetting, and Philip, who was in the lead, paused and peered in the door.

Monica and Helga were dancing to the radio. The tinny tune fell unrecognized on Philip's ears, and it was only as he came out into the night air that he identified it: an easy listening version of *All You Need Is Love*.

They tumbled Ralph into the trunk of Bingham's car and went back inside. Philip could not resist another peek at Monica and Helga as he crept by the door.

Helga appeared to be leading, moving with slow, sliding steps, her feet never leaving the floor. She was wearing a small black beret and a black dress with small white dots. Monica, her hands on Helga's shoulders, was singing loudly, shouting each word as though urging on a rowing crew.

Back in Ralph's office, Philip gingerly gathered the *Necronomicon* from the floor, bundling it again in the apron.

"Wait," Bingham said, moving to Philip's side.

He reached for the book.

"You don't want to touch it," Philip said.

"I guess I know that," Bingham said. "Although I doubt it affects me the way it does you."

Bingham took the book, opened it, and gingerly turned the pages with an index finger.

Philip looked on in wonder.

Bingham nodded his head as he flicked pages. "Tax evasive rituals," Bingham muttered, "lawyer conjuring, inner child exorcisms, women (attracting, warding), travel (dimensional, linear, time), demon entreating... here: demon repelling, binding, contracts."

Bingham flipped another page, nodded his head, and closed the book. He folded the apron over the book and handed it back to Philip.

"*Na'ghimgor thdid lym,*" Bingham said. "That's where you want to start."

Philip's eyes were wide. "How do you know all this?"

"I been around," Bingham said. "I was hauling bricks before you were an argument in the backseat of a car. I'm a union man. I guess I've seen a few monsters."

"You've known all along that they were *real!*" Philip said, no accusation in his tone, simply bafflement.

"Let's get out of here," Bingham said, taking Philip's shoulder.

They walked through the lobby and out the front door. As they crossed the parking lot, Sissy came out of the car, running, and hugged Philip.

Philip introduced her to Bingham.

"Pleased to meet you," he said.

Sissy got back in the car, started the engine.

"I gotta go clean up Ralph's office," Bingham said. "Then I gotta dispose of Ralph. I guess I'm out of a job."

"I'm sorry," Philip said.

The old man shrugged. "I was getting too old for the work, anyway."

Philip had to ask. "Why didn't you tell me you knew about the monsters?"

"Hell," Bingham said, "everyone knows about the monsters. Some people just catch a slither out of the corner of their eye and some people just get an afterimage when they turn on the lights at two in the morning. Most folks make their accommodations quicker than you have. Most people make a deal so quick, they don't even know they've made it. I saw them Old Ones for awhile, but I don't see them anymore. I got no time and patience for them now. What truck do I have with big, steamrolling forces? I got my bowels to worry about, and the weather, and my wife, and the rent. I got no time for your Yog-Sothoth."

"Don't worry about losing your job," Philip said. "I'm going to send you and Lily some money; I've got more than enough."

Bingham smiled sadly.

"It's true," Philip said. "I've got a lot of money."

Bingham patted Philip's shoulder. "That's all right, Philip. Better get going, now. That Sissy is a fine woman; hang on to her. I told you: a redheaded woman is good luck. I'll say hi to Lily for you."

As they drove away, Philip looked back. Bingham was already turned around and headed toward the building, stoop-shouldered, his bald head gleaming faintly in the darkness. He didn't look like a man with enough stamina left to straighten a room and dispose of a corpse, and Philip felt a pang of guilt.

Then he remembered Amelia, the lateness of the hour, and the perils ahead. He turned and stared grimly toward the future. Sissy pulled out onto the empty roadway.

"Turn left here," Philip said. "We'll want to get on Mopac and head south, downtown."

As they took the on ramp, the first large raindrops smacked the windshield.

Philip had Sissy park three blocks down
from Pelidyne.

"I'll walk from here," Philip said.

"Let me come with you," Sissy said.

"No. If I thought you could help, I'd ask you
to come. But I'm the only one who can do this—
and only if I do it alone."

Sissy didn't argue. Perhaps she understood,
from reading *The Despicable Quest*, that her first

look on the abyss, on the shifting visage of Azathoth, would render her useless.

Philip had been through the fire of unreason, and his patched-together sanity was cauterized, sealed against the dark miasma of the Old Ones and their lurid blandishments of madness.

Or so he hoped.

He walked slowly down the sidewalk, cradling the apron-swaddled *Necronomicon* in his arms. Austin's late night was cool and damp, the street deserted. He had formed no plan, trusting to the inspiration of need. There was still something of the romantic in Philip, and he felt that a just cause and a good will might serve as a talisman against evil. He had, of course, no reason for such faith.

Pelidyne towered over him, its dark, gleaming lines thrusting skyward with malevolent illogic. Philip's resolve faltered. Amelia was already dismembered, no doubt, the patterns of her personality transferred to throbbing nets of alien tissue or gleaming, dispassionate machines.

Run.

Philip stopped and stood very still. His heart beat rapidly.

Run as fast and as hard as you can and be grateful that your blind, puny existence has been spared.

A chill wind blew up the street, throwing a handful of stinging grit in his face. The stench of long dead fish filled his nostrils. His eyes watered.

"Amelia," Philip said, and then he shouted her name, "Amelia!" His heart slowed a little, and the bleak voice lay silent.

He stepped forward. One foot in front of the other. Hate helped him on. *You dirty stinking space spiders. You rot-bred intergalactic ticks. It's over. Kiss your hairy abdomens goodbye.*

The doors to Pelidyne would be locked. The lobby's security guard would be on duty. Perhaps Hal Ketch himself would be patrolling the halls.

The thought of Ketch, shark-mouthed and vigilant, made Philip's heart roar again, as though a reckless child had twisted the volume control.

A man came out of a door, bursting onto the sidewalk like a blackbird that's been trapped in a chimney. Philip jumped back, and the man, bundled in a heavy overcoat, swayed quickly past. Philip turned and watched the man move swiftly down the sidewalk. Something in the way he walked caught Philip's attention, a kind of sliding, leaping gait that suggested ignorance of earth's gravity. The back of the man's coat seemed to squirm oddly.

That's nothing human, Philip thought, as the figure turned a corner.

The building the man had abruptly exited was a low, dirty brick structure that leaned against Pelidyne, as an alley cat might lean against the tailored trouser leg of an elegantly attired businessman. Philip walked to the door and read the blue neon sign: JOE'S FANTASYLAND ADULT VIDEO EMPORIUM. Beneath these glowing words, black and white print strongly urged that anyone entering the door have two IDs indicating an age of eighteen years or older.

It was also suggested that a potential patron not be offended by explicit photographs of sexual acts.

Philip pushed the door open and entered, plunging immediately into a brightly lit, heavily perfumed space whose walls were plastered with magazines and video boxes depicting men and women copulating garishly.

A fat man with a goatee perched on a stool. His arms were laced with tattoos of dragons and serpents. These intertwining reptiles were, Philip felt certain, etched over older tattoos, faded images that were still evident by reason of their ghastly subject matter. The blazing head of Cthulhu was unmistakably present behind the scaled visage of a fire-breathing lizard.

The fat man nodded slowly and Philip nodded back, passed through a small gate, and entered the room. Two men, both of whom appeared to be human, studied the walls with identical expressions of boredom.

Philip adopted this expression and drifted

slowly around the room. It was a long, narrow room and the racks of video boxes and magazines displayed the variety—and sameness—of the human sexual impulse. Some of the videos were imaginatively titled: STIFF COMPETITION, PORN ON THE 4TH OF JULY, DRIVING MISS DAISY CRAZY, YUPPIES IN HEAT, SATURDAY NIGHT BEAVER. Other videos were rather matter-of-factly packaged: INTERRACIAL ORAL SEX #9, CLIT-O-RAMA, SUZIE'S SUCKFEST, TRACI'S HOTTEST THREE-WAYS.

Philip blinked at a video located in a section entitled, simply, "Breasts." A woman with breasts considerably larger than her head leaned forward grimly under a red-lettered title that troubled Philip. The title, BUTT-NAKED BREASTS, bothered Philip, who was something of a prude when it came to logical sentence construction. Breasts did not have buttocks and could not, therefore, bare them. As usual when encountering such constructions, he felt an almost irresistible urge to point this out to someone in authority, but he realized he had a mission to accomplish. He moved on.

He came to a dark-curtained room and entered.

He moved quickly past rows of bondage magazines and videos for yet more specialized tastes. This room was a little darker, the lighting in keeping with the impulses pandered to. Indeed, as the corridor narrowed, the darkness seemed to increase.

He hurried past rows of foreign pornography, the titles no longer in English.

He paused, stricken, in front of what, of course, he had been seeking.

The video box displayed a spiderlike thing, wrapped in the naked embrace of something resembling a giant sea anemone. On other boxes, lurid organs caressed unspeakable appendages.

Alien porn. Here the Old Ones came to satisfy their fibrillating libidos, to clatter their chitinous mandibles, to drool acid and undulate in the promise of secret, forbidden pleasures.

And, of course, the corporate bigshots would have discreet access to this room. They wouldn't—like that poor scuttling bug he had passed on the street—have to march through the front door. There was, Philip was certain, a passage leading directly to Pelidyne.

It took him ten minutes to find it, harrowing minutes when the certainty of the proprietor's hand on his shoulder made him tremble.

The lever was concealed—purloined-letter-like—as the third silver dildo in a gleaming display of eight. Pulled forward, the lever activated a section of magazines which rolled back to reveal a dark, musty-smelling concrete stairway leading upward. Philip entered and found a switch that set the door clattering back to its prior position.

I'm in it now, he thought, and he ascended the stairs.

 e came out in a janitor's closet filled with cleaning supplies, mops, an ancient floor waxer, and 50-gallon drums of disinfectant. The hall was empty.

He remembered that Amelia's offices were on the fifth floor. That seemed the logical place to begin, although he didn't expect to find her there. If he found her desk, her computer, he might (bloodhoundlike) sniff through her papers and pick up her trail.

He stood in front of the elevator and pushed the "UP" button. As he waited, he glanced at the ubiquitous bulletin board. Amelia's photo jumped out at him again, the same photo he had recently seen in *Personality Bytes*. Again, *EMPLOYEE OF THE MONTH* was the caption.

Philip scanned the copy, "Let's all congratulate Amelia Price on a job well done. Amelia will be receiving a commemorative plaque recognizing her achievement and she will be officially entered into the Employee Merit Hall of Fame at a short ceremony that will take place..."

Tomorrow.

Philip felt the first real surge of hope. If Amelia was accepting an award tomorrow, then she was still alive and still on earth.

The elevator arrived and its doors opened with a hiss. Philip jumped inside and punched the lighted "5."

The fifth floor was as silent as the third.

Usually, a corporation like Pelidyne had at least a dozen workers on any floor no matter how late the hour. This stillness was ominous, as though a sudden eruption of terrible industry were brewing.

Philip ran down the hall. He stopped abruptly in front of the door marked GRAPHICS SUPPORT. He pushed it open and peered inside.

All the lights were on in the room. Amelia sat stiffly in front of her computer, her back to Philip.

"Amelia," Philip said.

He ran to her. She did not turn until he touched her shoulder and then she swiveled in her chair.

Her eyes were blank, emotionless.

Some sort of hypnotic trance, Philip thought.

Her mouth opened suddenly, the action accompanied by a whirring sound, and she spoke. "Whag... on... wah... bah," she said, her voice low, as though recorded speech were played on a sluggish, dying tape recorder. Then, with a whoop, the pitch rose and quite distinctly,

Amelia said, "I can't tell you how delighted I am to accept this honor. Working at Pelidyne has been a wonderful experience and..."

Philip knew then. Knew he was too late.

"You are too late, my friend."

"I know," Philip said.

He turned, not at all surprised to see Hal Ketch, welcoming the man's familiar, uncomplicated evil. Ketch was wearing his uniform, his cap pushed forward over his eyes.

Amelia droned on: "When I first came here, I had no idea I would come to love it so much, that I would..."

Ketch was slouched against the door frame and now he shrugged himself upright and sauntered toward Philip.

There isn't going to be a better time, Philip thought, and he lunged toward his enemy.

Ketch saw him coming and drew his revolver. He didn't have time to fire it before Philip was on him and they both tumbled to the ground, banging against a light table that crashed to the floor instantly, like a prizefighter taking a dive.

They fought amid broken glass. They rolled across the carpet, collided with Amelia's chair which fell on its side, sending her sprawling. She continued to speak, "Being part of a team, having a real sense of belonging, is something I've always..."

Philip was no match for the security guard.

Ketch pushed the gun barrel against Philip's cheek.

"So long, mutherfucker," Ketch said.

"It's a great honor," Amelia was saying. "I couldn't have done it without..."

"Shit," Ketch said, his weight lifting from Philip's chest.

Philip, surprised to be alive, blinked at the running form of Hal Ketch.

Amelia was marching stolidly toward the wide plate glass window.

"Stop!" Ketch shouted, leaping toward her.

"I accept this award for my colleagues as much as for myself. I understand—" Arms outstretched, Amelia crashed through the window and into the night.

Ketch grabbed for her legs and hauled her back inside. Amelia was floundering oddly, arms pinwheeling. She fell back into the room and opened her mouth and coughed a glittering mass of capacitors, resistors, ICs.

The light in her eyes flickered and died. "Without the help of my.... without the help of my... without the help of my..."

"Shit," Hal Ketch was grumbling, rising on his knees, the revolver inches from his hand. He found it as he began to turn.

Philip rushed forward, hitting the man hard and low, hoping to bring him down.

He failed in this too. Ketch hit him in the face with the gun and Philip screamed.

Amelia was on her feet, arms still flaying the air, locked in an epileptic seizure of circuits. A large rent in the side of her neck revealed metal tubes and bright, colored wires.

"So long, sucker," Ketch said, crouching for the kill.

Amelia's arm caught him on the chin and lifted him.

Ketch made a noise, not a grunt or scream but something closer to an articulated word, as though he had spoken a comic-book balloon: "Gaagh."

Ketch rose up and out, the night sky and the gleaming stars behind him. He rose effortlessly, as though levitated, his chin balanced precisely on robot-Amelia's arm, and then the delicate balance was broken, that moment of suspense suddenly only a memory, and he fell, crying out, arms clawing indifferent air.

He was gone, embarked on five stories of falling, his scream modulated by wind and distance and velocity, his death ruled by mathematics.

Robot-Amelia spun and toppled to its side and could not right itself again but flipped on the floor, whirring and clicking.

Philip crawled away from the facsimile of his ex-lover. He spied the *Necronomicon* where it lay on the floor, the printer's apron spread out under it like a drop-cloth. The fiendishly conceived volume seemed to glow, gaining strength, no doubt, by close proximity to its ancient progenitors.

He rewrapped the book, lifted it, and lurched back into the hall.

He took the elevator to the basement. He seemed, now, prescient in his awareness, and there was no question of his destination.

Although he had been dragged there while unconscious he could have found that dreadful room had it been hidden amid a hundred million worlds in a million galaxies.

It is the obvious that we find unbelievable, he thought, as he crawled over ruined computers, rusting file cabinets, coils of copper wire, broken ergonomic chairs.

How many times had he watched an awards ceremony, muttered, "God, what a lot of robots," and so missed the truth by speaking it?

He came to Yuggoth's waiting room.

He found Amelia almost instantly, before the crablike robots were alerted, and he did not hesitate (indecisiveness was behind him) but smashed the glass container with the fire extinguisher he'd grabbed from the wall.

The emerald liquid poured out, oozing over the polished floor, enveloping Philip in its rotted fish reek. He held his breath, knelt down, lifted Amelia's nude body in his arms. She coughed violently, her lungs contracting to disgorge the stagnant seas of Yuggoth.

She'll be all right, Philip thought, knowing he was right in this too.

Alarms were ringing now. But lights did not flare overhead, and the implacable alien voice did not boom from the rafters.

Pelidyne's resources were elsewhere engaged.

Luck?

Why not? Philip thought. *I'm due.*

A single, crablike robot clattered across the floor. Philip turned, lay Amelia on the floor beside the *Necronomicon*, and stood up. He was not frightened. He felt oddly invulnerable.

Perhaps it was just such a feeling that would get him killed.

The robot swayed slowly on thin, articulated legs, as though engaged in the alien equivalent of some martial arts discipline.

"Go away," Philip said. "I don't want any trouble here. I'm leaving. I quit."

The robot scuttled forward.

Philip swung the fire extinguisher over his head. He spun it in a warning circle. "Scram!" he shouted. "Get!"

The robot skittered three feet closer.

Philip released the extinguisher, and it flew through the air. Effortlessly, with the laconic skill of an outfielder snatching a lazy fly ball, the robot snagged the red cylinder with three whiplike appendages.

Philip turned, tossed the wrapped *Necronomicon* on Amelia's stomach, and lifted her in the air, cradling her in his arms.

"Hang onto that book, Amelia," he whispered. "We are going to need it before this is over."

Philip turned and hurried toward the door. He looked back to see if the robot was following.

It was not. It was turning the bright cylinder over, tumbling it from tentacle to tentacle as its ocular units extended and retreated. It made a whirring noise, perhaps the machine equivalent of a man's vocal accompaniment to thought: Hmmmmmmmm.

Philip had almost reached the door when the fire extinguisher erupted, a spray of foam hissing into the air. This violent, accidental detonation seemed to cause some reflexive locking mechanism to occur within the robot. Rather than release the trigger, it stiffened. Philip was reminded of a wasp, stilled instantly by a poisonous burst of insecticide.

Philip moved on toward the door, looking back one last time to see the immobile robot, transformed into a vision of some skeletal sculpture in the aftermath of a snowstorm. Foam continued to spew into the air, cotton-candy clots scudding across the smooth floor.

Philip kicked the door open with his foot and entered the hall.

This hallway was unfamiliar. It was cold and

poorly lit with walls of dirty cinderblock. When he came to the first doorway on the right, he opened it.

He was in some sort of laboratory, with long sinks and white counters and banks of equipment and glinting glass. One long table was occupied by a pale white corpse, male, nude. Philip lay Amelia on the floor. He spied a lab coat hanging from a rack and grabbed it. He bent over her.

"Amelia," he whispered. "Can you hear me?"

She opened her eyes. "Philip," she said. "What are you—"

She became aware of her nakedness, sitting up abruptly.

"Where are my clothes?" she screamed, scrambling away from him.

"I don't know," Philip said. "Here." He extended his hand with the lab coat. She grabbed it from him and donned it instantly.

"You'll go to jail for this!" she screamed.

"I didn't take your clothes off," Philip shouted back. "What kind of person do you take me for?"

"A crazy person," Amelia said. "The kind of

person who would break into my apartment when I'm at work and lie on my bed. And drink beer! I always wondered why the place smelled like beer. The kind of person who would drug a woman and take advantage of her while she was unconscious, like some sick pervert, like, like a psychiatrist, like that psychiatrist they wrote a book about. The kind of person who should be locked up for life."

Philip spoke slowly, trying to calm her. He was hurt by these accusations, only some of which were true.

"I saved your life, actually," Philip said. "Well, I hope to save your life. We aren't in the clear yet, and I don't think we can afford to stand here discussing this at length right now."

"Where are we?" Amelia asked, looking around her with a wary eye.

"Pelidyne," Philip said. "Or a parallel Pelidyne. Think. Maybe you can remember. They switched you with a robot and brought you down here. They were going to send you to Yuggoth. That's what they do to all the Employees of the

Month. My guess is they like to weed out any humans who are a little too innovative, too intelligent. They don't want them in the workplace. So..."

Amelia turned and began to walk away.

"Where are you going?" Philip shouted after her.

"Anywhere away from you."

"Wait. You don't even know where you are. This is not—"

Amelia began to run, her bare feet slapping on the tiled floor.

Philip snatched up the *Necronomicon* and raced after her.

She banged through a white door.

And fell, pitched into the abyss.

Philip paused, swaying on the edge of the dark, fetid pit. He clung to the doorway, hearing Amelia's scream, already dreadfully distant.

Dear God!

He opened the *Necronomicon*. A dark wind from the depths whipped the apron violently and Philip almost lost his grip. He clutched the book fiercely as the apron swam out over the black void, like some flat, bottom-dwelling fish.

He held the book tighter, despite the grim images it engendered, despite the rotted-flesh feel of its binding.

He found the page, the page Al Bingham had marked. He spoke loudly, his words ringing out over the pit.

"*Na'ghimgor thdid lym,*" Philip screamed. "*Myn th'x barsoom lu'gndar.*"

He did not know the meaning of the words, but he felt the power of their shapes, and sensed that these vocals were more than words, were conjured entities.

From the dark pit sounds began to rise. And light.

Philip read on. "*In'path gix mth'nabor. In'path nox vel'dekk.*"

Suddenly, with a shriek of wind and a noxious odor that was palpable and vile, the monster surfaced. It came from the other side of space, perhaps, shedding electric sparks. The eye could not hold it all; no human eye would wish to.

Amelia, her white lab coat flapping, screamed as the mad god Azathoth waved her as though she were a handkerchief in a knot of giant worms.

Philip stopped reading. "Let her go!" he screamed into the rising wind.

Abruptly, Amelia rose high in the air, then down—a softball pitcher's windup—and flew through the open doorway and past Philip. She rolled as she hit the floor, coming to rest against the white sink counter. Philip ran to where she lay.

"Amelia?"

Her eyes were closed. She was alive though. She breathed.

Philip turned and quailed before huge, staring eyes that crowded the doorframe.

Philip felt words thunder in his mind.

"Drone. You deign to harness an Overlord?"

Philip felt his soul shrivel. Something was being pulled from him, extracted, some life essence.

He looked down at the throbbing book. His hands were bleeding. The page in front of him was unreadable, the alien words blurred beyond recognition by the pain in his head.

He read them anyway.

"*Yig sudeth M'cylorim. M'xxlit kraddath Soggoth im'betnk.*" The evil thunder in him abated some. But still it shook him.

There were no words, but the sense of it was this: "Drone, I will paper the universes with tiny pieces of your pathetic sentience."

Philip read on. And as he read, he began to understand what he spoke. The sense of it was this: "You will leave this spot, which spot denies the logic of your coming and going, and you will take, in the Name of the Nameless One, all your minions and their devices with you. And even the uttering of your name will be lost to this world until Time has eaten its Own Head."

The waves of Azathoth's hate still beat within him. There was a ritual, a gesture yet to make, some switch to turn.

Philip glanced up from the book, seeking a weapon.

The monster sensed this momentary release,

and it shot a single cold tentacle across the distance and wrapped Philip's ankle in scaled, burning muscle. Philip screamed, and the pain darted like cockroaches up his spine.

Dear Jesus.

He turned, dropping the *Necronomicon*. He clutched at a desk as he fell, trapped by the burning, viselike grip on his ankle.

A drawer fell out, clattering next to him (pencils, pens, a pocket calculator, a book of crossword puzzles, rubber bands, a condom, a broken cigarette, paper clips).

Paper clips. The glue of bureaucracy. The heart-sinking, tedious, menial egg cases of the lumbering, soul-breaking business world. Paper clips. The drawer-crouching, bright, cheery, phony, truant darlings of time-servers and despairing clerks.

Philip scrabbled to snare a paper clip between thumb and forefinger. As usual the small, silvery bug eluded him. The pain ran briskly up his neck and squatted at the bottom of his brain.

He grabbed the clip, slapped his palm down

on a rubber band, and screamed again as the monster continued to drag him toward the abyss where—this vision was too precise not to be an image from the creature itself—his skin would be sucked from him by a thousand rasping mouths.

He bent the clip against his palm, slipped the rubber band between thumb and forefinger, and lurched upright on the edge of the precipice.

"You stinking space slug!" he screamed, and he fired a paper clip into the great, blank eye of implacable evil.

He could not say what happened next.

Something appeared to scream inside his head. *"Nog s'dath blexmed!"* he shouted, releasing the entities of sealing, those words that closed the way back.

He flew through the air. Perhaps he lost consciousness. Certainly time was fragmented, although that might have been the result of other forces. In any event, he found himself lying on top of Amelia. The doorway was empty, with curious lights shivering and flashing in the darkness. The building itself was rumbling and shaking. Above him, plasterboard crumpled like cellophane. He gathered the inert Amelia in his arms and fled.

Somehow, through falling plaster and dust and the unholy shifting of hallways, he found his way to the surface. He walked through an empty lobby whose floor leapt and buckled as though huge steel pistons pummeled it from below. The glass doors were locked, but he smashed them with a chair and carried Amelia through.

It was raining, and he walked through the rain carrying Amelia. He walked out into the parking lot. He stumbled and fell. He did not think he could get up again, and so he sat in the rain, cradling Amelia, gazing upon the quivering, black tower. Lightning harried the sky, affording brief glimpses of shape-shifting Pelidyne. As he watched, it suddenly shivered, a vile, orgasmic tremor that ran its length beginning at its base and echoing upward. This shiver was accompanied by a rending, splitting sound that dwarfed the thunder.

And then the black walls themselves peeled

back, like burning cardboard, and something dark and convoluted, something beyond description, broke free of the walls and rose in the air, some noxious insect shedding its larval case.

Philip looked away, sickened by wonder and loathing. And when he looked back, Pelidyne had shrunk somehow. It still towered above the other buildings, and the general population, inured to sleek architecture and unobservant at the best of times, might notice nothing different. But it was small now, insignificant, mundane. The whole block was black, not a light to be seen.

"No power," Philip muttered.

Amelia stirred in his arms. She would come awake with complaints and accusations. She was consistent in that regard.

A car was racing toward him. It braked, screeching on the wet pavement, and Sissy jumped out.

Running through the rain, her red hair darkening, she looked as beautiful and full of salvation as any angel, although less serene. She looked concerned, a little scared perhaps.

Philip smiled and waved.

EPILOGUE

egan was two, and she ran everywhere. She was running across the lawn, herded slightly by her older brother Michael. Michael was five and full of sad wisdom and resignation acquired, Philip assumed, in a previous incarnation.

"Megan doesn't trust walking," Philip explained. "Running has the law of inertia going for it: A body upright and moving fast tends to remain upright and on the move."

"Daaaaaaaaaa," Megan said, colliding with Philip's leg and presenting her father with a crushed daisy that had lost most of its petals.

Philip thanked her and fluffed her fiery hair.

Al Bingham reached down and lifted Megan in the air. She giggled.

Sissy and Lily came down across the lawn. Sissy was carrying a tray of iced drinks.

It was a year since Lily and Bingham had last visited, and Philip had been initially troubled by Lily's new fragility. She had lost weight, turned gossamer and insubstantial.

Perhaps some metaphysical law of energy conservation was at work here, for when she spoke it was clear that she was grumpier than ever, more opinionated and peremptory, as though her soul had put on weight.

"Philip is just naturally secretive," Lily was telling Sissy. "It's pathological. Has to do with control, power. It's a male thing, the little-boy, clubhouse mentality. Secret rituals, codes, passwords. He ever tell *you* where he got all that money?"

"Sure," Sissy said. "He said he earned it working as a temp."

Lily snorted her disgust. "It's women like you that keep men from growing up."

They all sat in lawn chairs and looked out at the North Carolina ocean, which, excited by news of an approaching storm, raced and tumbled over the sand.

Megan walked over to a blanket and dropped into sleep instantly, her thumb in her mouth.

Michael, relieved of his sister watch, climbed solemnly into his father's lap.

"I open up that envelope," Bingham said, perhaps for the five hundredth time, "and there is a check for one hundred thousand dollars and I'm shaking my head and thinking it's a sorry shame that Philip has gone so far round the bend, and Lily, she snatches that check and says, 'We'll just deposit it and see.'" Bingham laughed. "Guess she knew something I didn't."

"Philip's a wild card," Lily said. "I knew that."

They sat in the lawn chairs enjoying the last warm rays of the sun and the way the salt wind licked their faces. After an hour, they got up and went inside, Bingham carrying the conked-out Megan.

After dinner, they sat in the living room and talked about old times. Lily remembered the first time she met Philip. "I wasn't sure I could help him," she said.

At around ten that evening, the phone rang. Philip went into the bedroom to answer it. It was Azathoth. The connection was bad; the Old One was somewhere out beyond Andromeda. He asked about the kids.

Strange how old adversaries can gain respect for each other, learn that what locks them in combat is a common interest, a shared obsession.

"The Amelia one," Azathoth asked, "what of her?"

He had never asked before.

"I hear she is still married," Philip said. "And

glad to be shed of me. She has a new job, working for a company called Findel Limited."

Azathoth made a noise that was difficult to interpret.

"You've heard of them?"

"A rival," Azathoth said.

"You sound tired," Philip said.

"I am thinking your Wordsworth poet was right," Azathoth said.

"How's that?"

"It is of rats and their race," Azathoth said. "You know. I utter the quote: 'Getting and spending we lay waste our powers.'"

"Well, that's true," Philip said.

"It has its kind of truth, yes." Silence. The electric crackling of light years. "I must go now. Meteors eat the Mind Gates. Goodbye."

"Who was that?" Sissy asked when Philip came back into the living room.

"Arnie."

"Your friend from Virginia?"

"Yes."

"How is he doing?"

Philip shrugged, flopped down in the ancient armchair. "Oh, I don't know. He's confused. Midlife crisis, I suppose."

"How about you?" Sissy said. She came over and sat on his lap, leaned forward, kissed him on the cheek. Lily and Bingham had retired. The children were asleep.

"I love you," Philip said. "I am the world's most fortunate man. I have a beautiful, loving wife, model children, good friends—and two weeks ago I resold *The Despicable Quest* and it will be published as a single, massive hardback."

"Lily's not entirely happy about that development, you know." Sissy ran her fingers through Philip's thinning hair. "She still thinks the book might, well, *aggravate* your condition."

"That was long ago. Things have changed."

"How?"

For answer, Philip lifted Sissy in his arms and carried her into the bedroom.

"I've made peace with my demons," Philip whispered in her ear. "My Enemy has become my Muse."

Sissy put her arms around her husband. "I love it when you talk literature."

"Kafka, Vonnegut, Poe, Peake, Barth." Wet kisses, a deluge. Small, bright lightning of tongues. "Brautigan, Matheson, Dickens, Defoe."

"Lovecraft."

"Lovecraft."

"Love."

illiam Browning Spencer was born in Washington, D.C. He has held a variety of dismal, dead-end jobs (excellent research for *Résumé with Monsters*). Like Philip Kenan, the novel's protagonist, Spencer has often worked as a typesetter or graphic artist (he illustrated and designed the covers for his first two books). *Résumé with Monsters* is his most surrealistic novel but also, he maintains, his most autobiographical. Joe Lansdale, writing in the Austin American Statesman, has compared this novel to the work of Philip K. Dick, asserting that Spencer possesses that same ability to "warp reality to such an extent you find yourself looking over your shoulder to see if the world is being dismantled behind you."

BEREAVEMENTS

Richard Lortz
Paperback

ISBN 1-56504-937-3
$5.99US/$7.99CAN

"A talented writer...a kinky, bizarre, macabre story."
—— Publishers Weekly

"This myth of resurrection and death is a literate horror story."
—— Library Journal

"Mother Who Lost Son Seeks Son Who Has Lost Mother," pleads the advertisement in The Village Voice. For Mrs. Harrington-Smith Evans, her wealth allows her to indulge in all the declarations of bereavement that money can buy, including a surrogate son who might ease her grief, forestalling her encroaching madness.

Richard Lortz combines the ancient terror of death with a frightening lightness of tone that will make you laugh and feel guilty all at once.